THE CLEARING

THE CLEARING

A NOVEL

SIMON TOYNE

WILLIAM MORROW

An Imprint of HarperCollinsPublishers

HarperCollins books may be purchased for educational, business, or sales promotional use. For information, please email the Special Markets Department at SPsales@harpercollins.com.

FIRST EDITION

Photgraphs by Ryan DeBerardinis and houchi/Shutterstock, Inc.

Library of Congress Cataloging-in-Publication Data

Names: Toyne, Simon, author.
Title: The clearing : a novel / Simon Toyne.
Description: First edition. | New York, NY : William Morrow, an imprint of Harper-Collins Publishers, [2023] | Series: Laughton Rees ; book 2 |
Summary: "In this gripping suspense novel from the bestselling author of the Sanctus trilogy, a series of disappearances in a small town near the Forest of Dean lead forensic expert Laughton Rees to uncover a dark plot, decades in the making"— Provided by publisher.
Identifiers: LCCN 2023012582 (print) | LCCN 2023012583 (ebook) | ISBN 9780062329820 (hardcover) | ISBN 9780062329844 | ISBN 9780062329837 (ebook)
Subjects: LCGFT: Thrillers (Fiction) | Novels.
Classification: LCC PR6120.O98 C54 2023 (print) | LCC PR6120.O98 (ebook) | DDC 823/.92—dc23/eng/20230317
LC record available at https://lccn.loc.gov/2023012582
LC ebook record available at https://lccn.loc.gov/2023012583

ISBN 978-0-06-232982-0

23 24 25 26 27 LBC 5 4 3 2 1

THIS IS DEDICATED TO ALL THE READERS,
BOOKSELLERS, LIBRARIANS, REVIEWERS, AND
BLOGGERS WHO HAVE READ AND RECOMMENDED
MY BOOKS OVER THE PAST TEN YEARS. A BOOK
WITHOUT A READER IS ONLY A HALF-FORMED THING.
SO THANKS TO ALL OF YOU FOR HELPING TO MAKE
MY STORIES WHOLE.

The charcoal burner has tales to tell.
He lives in the forest, alone in the forest,
He sits in the forest, alone in the forest.

A. A. MILNE

Even on the brightest day,
the forest is filled with shadows.

TRADITIONAL SAYING—ANON.

THE CLEARING

PROLOGUE

GREEN-DAPPLED SUNLIGHT AND ANCIENT SMELLS. Earth. Moss. Rot.

He breathes it in, all of it, filling himself with the warm forest air and the faint smell of woodsmoke that clings to his clothes.

The whine of tiny insect wings rises by his right ear, but he does not move to brush it away. He stands in the shadows, hidden by leaves, matching the stillness of the green that surrounds and swallows him.

He learned the art of stillness from the forest just as he learned many things, ancient secrets whispered by the wind through high-reaching branches and murmured in the gentle flow of water in the brooks and streams that feed the roots beneath. The forest's secrets are his now, and his are theirs. He is the forest, and the forest is him. He knows what nourishes, what poisons, what gives life—and what brings death.

He looks up, his attention caught by a new noise, the soft sound of movement from something scuffing closer over dusty ground and dry leaves. He turns his head slightly, his ears fixing on the soft sound like a bat tracking a fluttering moth, until he sees it.

The rabbit is young and small, its lithe body moving steadily through slashes of sunlight that dapple the narrow path, which winds its way through the forest and past the shadowy spot where he stands so silent and still.

The rabbit stops and looks around as if sensing something. It's a doe, a juvenile on the cusp of adulthood, still timid and uncertain. It looks back, sniffing the air, eyes wide and alert as she scans the pathway, tilting her head slightly to reveal a mark on her neck then looks forward again, almost directly at him, though he knows she cannot see or smell him. He is standing downwind of her, veiled with leaves, the forest keeping him hidden like one of its many secrets.

The rabbit listens for a moment longer before moving again, hurrying up the path, drawing closer to where he stands waiting. He follows her with his eyes, raising the pipe to his lips, so slowly that the movement is lost in the constant, restless shifting of the forest. He takes a breath, fills his lungs, and holds it, his eyes unblinking as the rabbit draws nearer. She passes by so close he can hear her rapid breathing and see the mark clearly on her neck, a star outlined in fading blue ink. He follows her with the end of the pipe as she starts to move away, then pushes the air from his lungs in a sharp and concentrated breath.

The rabbit does not react to the sting of the dart immediately. She hurries on for a moment or two before starting to weave, staggering a little and then a lot until she stumbles, falls, then lies perfectly still, half on and half off the path.

He emerges from the shadowy leaves and stands for a moment, listening to the soft creaks and whispers of the forest and watching the breath from her pink, open mouth lifting tiny puffs of dust from the path's surface.

A new sound pierces the woodland whispers, harsh and unnatural and accompanied by a low buzzing noise. His hand tightens around the pipe and the noise comes again. He takes another step closer to the rabbit and sees the source of it, lying on the ground by the rabbit's paw, the rectangular screen glowing in the gloom of the forest floor with the single word "MUM" displayed on it.

He raises his boot and brings it down hard, silencing the rabbit's phone with a swift crunch then kicks it away into the thick bracken. He grabs the rabbit under her arms and drags her off the path, her dark hair falling over the tattooed star on her neck as she disappears into the shadowy green of the forest.

PART 1
DAY ONE

JUNE 25

THE MORNING AFTER
MIDSUMMER'S EVE

1

MADDIE!

Adele violently shakes out another black bin-liner.

Where the hell was Maddie?!!

She scans the campsite, looking for her sister through the bone-colored bell tents and artfully rusted camper vans, staggering closer wearing last night's clothes and a blank expression. But all she sees are a few casualties from the Midsummer's Eve revelries lying on the ground where they'd passed out the night before, smoke from dying fires drifting across them like gunsmoke from a lost battle.

It's a mess, it was always going to be a mess, and it all needs cleaning up before eleven, when the council refuse lorry arrives. That's why she'd asked her older and supposedly wiser sister to help this morning, why she'd allowed her to crash on her floor in exchange for a promise that she would help with the post–Midsummer's Eve clear-up. And yet here she very much was not.

Adele wrenches the lid off one of the bins, her long brown hair scraped back and already sticking to her skin with the rising heat of the day, her thin, wiry body nut-brown from having to work outside all summer. She recoils at the stench that billows out along with a squadron of angry flies then violently twists the top of the bag into a knot, imagining it's Maddie's neck.

I'll be there—Maddie had said. *I won't stay out long but I promised to meet someone.*

Adele lifts the heavy, stinking bag out of the bin and dumps it on the ground to be picked up by the honey-wagon, an old, repurposed electric milk float Maddie should be driving but obviously isn't because she's not here. She fits a new liner into the bin and lets the lid fall with a loud bang.

Movement catches her eye in a dark pool of shadow beneath a syca-more tree as a man wearing a Cinderman costume of charcoal-blackened sacking lifts his head, roused by the sound of the banging bin.

"Morning!" Adele calls to him, loud and bright.

He winces as if the word is made of sharp metal, then looks up, eyes screwed tight against the brightness, trying to remember how he ended up under this tree. He looks so wretched with bits of twig and leaves in the greasy tangle of his hair that Adele pulls the bottle of water from her belt and tosses it over.

"Drink!" she commands.

He reaches to pick it up, spots a puddle of puke on the grass nearby with flies lined up along the edge of it, and turns away, blowing his cheeks out as if he's about to add to it. He unscrews the cap and takes a tiny sip of water before lying slowly back down on the ground, hugging the bottle to his chest.

Adele yanks another bin liner from her belt and marches past him, heading to the next overflowing bin that needs emptying, scanning the campsite for Maddie again as she works the phone from her pocket.

No missed calls.

No texts.

She taps the screen to unlock it but it won't respond to her fingers in-side the rubber glove, so she shakes her hand violently until the glove flies off, finds the last number she dialed, and calls it again, her fingers leaving steamy fingerprints on the screen. She holds the phone to her ear and screws her nose up against the foul smell of rubber and rotting garbage coming from her hand.

Hey, leave me a message and I'll call you back.

Maddie's smiling, childish-sounding voice cuts in without it ringing, which shows that her phone is still switched off.

Adele disconnects without leaving a message because she's left several already and instead scrolls through her contacts, looking for the names of people who might have been with Maddie last night, or might still be with her, or might at least know where she got to. She spots a contact for Ronan, one of Maddie's ex-boyfriends, and taps the contact to call him. Again, voicemail cuts in without it even ringing, because of course, all of Maddie's loser friends will still be sleeping off their hangovers this morning.

Yo, this is me, do the thing after the thing.

Adele clenches her jaw, waits for the tone, then forces her voice to be light.

"Hey, this is Adele, Maddie's sister. If you're with her, could you get her to give me a call, please? Thanks. Tell her I'm not mad, I'm just checking in."

She *is* mad of course and getting madder with every stinking bag she has to deal with, but inflicting her mood on Maddie's friends isn't going to accomplish anything. She scrolls through her contacts looking for more friends, ex-boyfriends, possible current boyfriends, though Maddie stays pretty tight-lipped about her love life. She says Adele is too judgy, which is true, because who wouldn't be judgy about the guys Maddie tends to go for? Laid-back, amiable losers are still losers.

She calls a couple more numbers, leaves a couple more messages, then snatches the glove back up off the ground, works her hand back into it and scans the campsite one last time.

"Where the fuck are you, Maddie!?"

2

SHE WAKES TO DARK BEYOND blackness and the heavy smell of earth.

She is on her back, arms by her sides, legs stretched out, staring straight up at—nothing. She studies the black, blinking slowly a few times to check that her eyes are actually open, but it looks the same either way.

She raises her hand in front of her face, moves it a little, touches her palm to her nose to prove it is there, then reaches up slowly and carefully into the blackness, both wanting and not wanting to touch something. She stretches up until she can reach no further then moves her arm in a slow and widening circle, feeling the faint chill rinse of cold air across her skin but touching nothing but darkness.

She lets her arm fall back down to her side, feeling in her pocket for her phone so she might use its light to see with, but the pocket is empty.

She takes deep breaths, flooding her lungs with damp-smelling air, and tries to remember where she is. She remembers walking through the forest but then nothing. She was there and now she is here, wherever "here" is.

She spreads her fingers and starts feeling around at her sides for her missing phone then widens her search, her palms skimming across the cold ground, reaching further and further until something brushes across the back of her right hand and she yanks it away. The sound of her gasp pushes back the dead silence and makes her realize that there are no other sounds here: no scratch of animals, no rustle of leaves, nothing.

She listens hard, studying the thundering quiet, listening out for the dry click of legs, or the patter of dislodged earth that might suggest that whatever her hand touched is alive and crawling closer.

She hears the thud of her own heartbeat and the whisper of blood in her ears but nothing more, so carefully, slowly, she reaches out again, feeling ahead with her fingers for whatever is there, tensing against the moment of its rediscovery.

She finds it again and freezes but forces herself to keep her hand where it is, stretched out in the dark with the unseen thing touching the back of it. She keeps as still as she can, ready to snatch it away at the first sign the thing is alive, but whatever it is, it remains perfectly still.

She takes a deep breath then slowly turns her hand, trembling slightly with the effort of reaching out until her fingers close around something cold and thin and fibrous. She tests it, squeezing it lightly and rubbing it between her fingertips. There are small hairs growing out of it and she almost drops it in revulsion but then a thought surfaces and she takes a firmer hold instead and gives it a hard, sharp tug. She feels it tighten in her hand and dirt patters down from where the thing is anchored in the earth.

She feels her away further up and along it, her fingers mapping the twisting fibers growing steadily thicker the higher she goes. The hairs grow thicker too, branching out from the main tendril and tickling the back of her hand until the whole gnarly thing disappears abruptly into a wall of crumbling earth and she knows in an instant what it is, and where she is, and fear takes flight in her chest.

The thing she is holding in her hand is a root. A growing root, the root of something big.

She was walking through the forest and she's still there.

But she is no longer in the forest.

She is under it.

3

—

ADELE HEARS THE LOW ROAR of the municipal refuse lorry before she sees it, like a prehistoric animal rumbling closer through the forest telling her she's out of time. She floors the "go" pedal on the honey-wagon but the ancient electric engine just carries on at its standard four miles an hour. The repurposed milk float is part of the eco-friendly credentials of the campsite, a nice idea in principle but a total pain in practice. Even totally empty it barely manages to go faster than walking pace and it has a habit of running out of power unexpectedly, meaning it has to be towed back to the charging station by a 4x4, which totally cancels out its eco benefits. She creeps onto the paved loading area behind the splintery storage shed the owner Bill insists on calling the "Sanitation Station," yanks up the handbrake, and pulls her phone from her pocket.

11:16.

No new messages. No missed calls.

The lorry is running late but even so she has only managed to empty about two-thirds of the bins dotted around the campsite. An hour earlier she was furious at Maddie for leaving her to do all the work; now she just feels worried and a little sick in her stomach. The phone buzzes suddenly in her hand and she stabs the answer button when she sees who it is.

"Hey, Ronan."

"Yo!" The voice sounds dry and creaky, like it's worn out from a heavy night and badly needs oiling. "What's up?"

"Nothing much, I just . . . is Maddie with you?"

"Huh?"

"Maddie. Have you seen her at all?"

"Nah, man, she bailed."

"Bailed from what?"

"She was supposed to meet us at the beacon fire after the Cinderfield Parade but never showed."

"Which beacon fire?"

"The big one over at The Clearing."

Adele feels the blood drain from her face at the mention of the place and her eyes automatically flick over to the shadowy edge of the forest.

"Are you sure it was the one at The Clearing?"

"Yeah, man. I bumped into her at the parade and she said she was gonna meet us there, said she might bring some dude with her, but I guess she musta changed her mind."

Adele's eyes find the darkest shadows and she quickly looks away, staring down at the brightest piece of sun-scorched ground instead.

"Did this dude have a name?"

"Yeah, sure."

She waits for a beat then remembers this is a hungover Ronan she's speaking to.

"Do you know what his name is?" she prompts.

"Nah, man, Maddie never said, but he gots to have a name, right? Everybody got a name."

Adele shakes her head. Maddie actually went out with this clown for about three months, and he wasn't even the densest of her boyfriends, not by a long way. A low IQ seemed to be like catnip to her sister.

"Listen," she says, fighting to keep the frustration out of her voice, "if you see Maddie or she calls you, tell her I need to speak to her, OK?"

"You got it."

Adele hangs up and stares at her phone.

The Clearing.

Maddie had never said anything about going to The Clearing. Then again, if she had, they would have got into an argument about it and Adele would have told her not to go, which is probably why Maddie hadn't told her.

The bin lorry arrives in a cloud of dust and stench, lets out a loud hydraulic hiss, and shudders to a halt. Three large men wearing yellow high-vis jackets, orange trousers, and not much else step out of the cab. The largest of the three jabs a gloved thumb at the metal bins lined up behind the shed. "Them bags are supposed to be in the skips, love," he says, "not on the back of your noddy car."

"Sorry." Adele unspools the charging cable that connects the electric vehicle to the solar panels on the roof and plugs it in. "I'm on my own this morning so I'm struggling a bit."

"Don't worry, darlin'" —he throws her a wink—"we'll give you a hand."

He starts plucking the bags off the back of the honey-wagon and dumping them on the ground by the business end of the lorry where the other two bears begin feeding them into the truck.

Adele glances back at the trees, her eyes drawn to the shadows shifting between fingers of sunlight. The Clearing is deep in the forest, a place neither she nor Maddie ever go, not anymore; they had promised each other. The shadows continue to shift, transforming into figures that watch her as if waiting for her to return.

She looks away, shivering despite the heat, and scrolls through her contacts looking for an old entry:

Grizz—The Clearing

Her thumb moves to the call symbol and hovers above it for a few long seconds before she changes her mind. That door has stayed closed for a long time now and she won't risk opening it again until she absolutely has to.

She stuffs her phone back in her pocket, her anger at Maddie entirely gone now and transformed into something else, something more like worry. Maddie had gone into the forest to meet someone at The Clearing. And now she is missing.

She looks out across the campsite, willing Maddie to emerge from the forest, shoes in hand, doing the walk of shame. It's getting busier now, tent fronts unzipped and tied open, knots of people huddled around gas cookers and rekindled fires, frying up breakfasts and hangover cures. Everyone looks pretty chill. No one looks like they'd give two shits if she didn't end up finishing her jobs that morning. She turns to the man in the high-vis vest. "Where you off to next?"

"Got one more stop at Wendell's Dairy then we're back to the dump to offload."

Adele nods. The municipal tip was on the far side of Cinderfield, about a half a mile down the road. Cinderfield was also where the nearest police station was. She could call but she knew from experience that her call would be diverted to some generic call center where someone on minimum wage would read from a crib sheet, give her a crime number, then fob her off with no way of following any of it up. It was harder to ignore someone who was standing right in front of you, especially when that someone was her.

"You couldn't give me a lift into town, could you?"

The man in the high-vis vest peers at her like he's not sure he heard right. "You want a lift? With us? On the wagon?"

"Yeah, if that's OK."

He shakes his head and sucks air through tobacco-stained teeth. "Well, technically only authorized council personnel are allowed to ride on the wagon."

"Oh, come on," Adele says, giving him the full beam of her smile. "I smell like a bin bag, so if anyone asks, tell them you chucked me on the wagon by mistake."

4

SHE TAKES DEEP BREATHS THAT taste of earth, eyes wide and staring at the darkness, and tries to stay calm, tries not to panic, tries to remember. She was walking through the forest, and then she was here. That's it. That's all she can recall.

She starts feeling her way along the wall of earth with the roots growing out of it, building a map of the space in her mind as her hands move along it, dirt pattering to the ground at the touch of her fingertips.

Every few steps she stops and listens, turning her head as her ears search the darkness for something, anything, to grip onto: the distant sound of birdsong, a whisper of breeze, anything that might hint at a way out.

Once, when she and her sister had been at The Clearing for maybe a year, Grizz had led a bunch of them into the woods after a huge rainstorm. She'd taken them to a distant part of the forest where a huge oak had been swallowed whole by the ground. Only the crown was still visible, a green, leafy dome arching over the mud and storm-shredded leaves on the forest floor.

Grizz told them that there had once been coal and iron ore mines all over the forest and that many of the old tunnels did not appear on any maps, their locations taken to the grave by the black-market miners who'd dug them in secret to steal a living from the land. The floodwater from the storm must have run through one of these old tunnels, she explained, wearing away the old wooden supports until the weight of the tree and the earth above had caused it to collapse, dragging the great tree down.

Maybe she is in one of those tunnels now, somehow had fallen into a forgotten mine dug by long-dead hands. Maybe she had stepped on a mat of loose leaf mulch covering a sinkhole that had been opened up by the drying earth. She could easily have banged her head on the way down, knocking her unconscious and fogging her memory.

She looks up and studies the darkness again, searching for any hint of light. But the darkness is total, and her fear starts to rise again, and she still feels woozy, so she closes her eyes and breathes through her mouth. At least with her eyes closed the darkness feels more normal, and if she can't smell the earth either, she can almost pretend she's not here at all.

5

MALLORY STOKER HAWTHORN KINGSTON, EIGHTEENTH Earl of Dean, paces in the dusty privacy of his study, red-eyed and sleep deprived, trying to remember how to act normal. He looks out across the green lawns of Cinderfield Abbey stretching away beyond the large, mullioned window to where a huge marquee is being erected between the Heritage Center and the forest. The Earl hates weddings, finds them vulgar and awful, but as weddings are about the only thing keeping the whole ship from sinking at the moment, he has no option but to put up with them.

He looks past the marquee to where the foresters' huts sit amidst smoking piles of blackened turf. They will have to douse them if the wind doesn't shift. Can't risk a bit of smoke getting in the nostrils of the wedding guests. Can't risk the angry emails, bad reviews online, and requests for refunds that would follow. He watches the groundsmen tidying the lawn around the big tent, pruning in the orchard, and tending to the charcoal burns, wetting down the sacks that cover them. There are only three groundsmen now, where once there was an army.

His eyes settle on a cracked pane of Tudor glass, one of many in the medieval window that he can't afford to fix. Little repairs like these confront him wherever he goes in the Abbey, tiny reminders of the steady decay that is only getting worse.

He turns away and collapses into the chair behind his desk in a cloud of antique dust and surveys the paperwork littering the desktop. It's bills mainly. He had started to sort them into piles of lessening urgency to try to give himself something to focus on, but as they all seemed to be final demands, it had ended up making him feel even more anxious, so he'd given up. He spots his phone in among the unpaid bills, picks it up, and checks his email.

There are six new messages in his inbox, mostly spam from catering and hospitality companies trying to sell him things, also an inquiry for another bloody wedding in two summers' time. Hopefully by next year he can tell them all to piss off, either that or the whole thing will have imploded and tacky weddings with awful guests and hideous brides will be the least of his worries. He finds a number in his contacts and dials it, taking deep breaths and blowing them out as he waits for it to connect.

"Hello?" The voice sounds guarded.

"Hi, it's Mal. Sorry to call you out of the blue like this but, something happened last night, something . . ." His voice trails off as he searches for the right words.

"What kind of something?"

"Something bad. It's . . . I don't know where to begin really. I . . ."

"Don't say anything else." The voice is suddenly all business. "Not on the phone. Let's meet somewhere."

"Right. OK. Why don't you come over to the Abbey?"

"No. Somewhere neutral and out of the way."

"OK, how about . . . the well? St. Anthony's Well."

"That'll probably be a bit busy today, although . . . actually, that might work. We can mingle with out-of-towners, hide in plain sight. Meet me there in half an hour, and don't say anything to anyone until you've spoken to me."

"OK, fine. I'll see you at the we . . ."

A click tells the Earl that he's already gone.

He checks the time and finds his son Sebastian's number and pauses for a second, then dials it. Talking to his son will be OK. He already knows everything anyway.

The phone connects and a flat male voice answers. "Hello?"

The Earl clears his throat. "Hey, Seb, it's me—how you holding up?"

"I'm . . . fine."

"Good, good. That's good. Are you back in London?"

"Yes."

The Earl nods. His son was always fairly monosyllabic and hard to read, which makes it hard to gauge his current emotional state. His mother, Aurora, had been the same. Mallory never had the slightest idea how she was feeling from the first moment their parents thrust them together in their teens to the day she swallowed a fatal overdose of sleeping tablets, soon after Sebastian's birth. The doctors said it was postnatal depression, but he had always wondered if, like him, she had been worn down by the burden of her own ancestral expectation and simply checked out in grateful relief the moment she had done her duty and provided him with an heir.

"You still there, Seb?"

"Yes."

"You know . . . what happened last night, it was—well, it was . . . unfortunate, but no one's blaming you. You were not to know. I mean, nobody knew, so . . . it was just . . ." An image flashes into his head of Aurora's lifeless body, fully dressed and neatly laid out on the bed, the note in her thin, porcelain-white hand containing just two words—Sorry Mallory.

"Listen, Seb. I just wanted to say that if you need to talk to anyone about . . . well, anything that's bothering you, you can always talk to me."

"I'm fine."

"Good. That's good. I'm just saying, we've all been through a bit of a . . . well, something pretty unusual, so please don't feel you need to keep anything bottled up. Our family has been on some pretty sticky wickets before, but we've always come through it by staying together and looking after each other. Family first, eh?"

"Right."

The Earl leans forward and pushes the letters and bills aside to reveal the map beneath, a detailed land survey showing the whole of the Cinderfield Abbey estate.

"Once we put this thing behind us, we can get back on track with everything. We just need to stay calm and act normal, and if we all keep our heads we can move on from this in no time, all right? In the meantime, if you do need to let off steam or talk about anything, you can always talk to me. Remember that, Seb. I'm always here for a chat."

"OK. I need to go now."

"Right, you go, there's a good lad."

The phone clicks and he's gone.

The Earl stares down at the map, the outline of the Abbey in the center and all the land surrounding it—forest, fields, the stone quarry, the lakes. It has been in his family since Henry VIII stole it from the Cistercian monks who founded it and gave it to Mallory's ancestor, the first Earl of Dean, almost five hundred years ago. That's a lot of history and noble tradition to look after. People who are not born into a title never understand the pressure that comes with it. To them it's all stately homes, plummy accents, and *Downton Abbey*. In truth, a title of ancient nobility is as much a burden as it is a gift. You never really own all the things that come with it—the title, the houses—you just become custodian of them until you can one day hand the burden on to your son for him to carry forward. All of that takes an enormous toll, both financially and personally. His father had only been sixty-two when he keeled over from the endless worry of it all, leaving Mallory with the roof crumbling, dry rot in the ballroom, and cracked panes of Tudor glass in almost every one of over three hundred windows.

That is another thing ordinary people don't understand. People who live in normal houses can simply pop down to the DIY shop, buy a new piece of glass for a few quid, and have a broken window fixed in no time. In order to mend one of his windows, Mallory first needs to get permission from some anonymous jobsworth in English Heritage, then find some forest-dwelling hobbit with a glass kiln who will charge him a hundred quid for a single piece of brittle, hand-blown cylinder glass made the same way they did it in Tudor times.

He grabs his cap from the desk, jams it onto his head and looks up at the portrait of his father, the seventeenth Earl, hanging over the fireplace and glowering down at him with what was probably intended to be a stern but noble demeanor, but feels more like a deep and permanent disapproval.

"Don't look at me like that, you bloody hypocrite," the eighteenth Earl murmurs as he heads for the door. "It's your fault we're in this mess in the first place, you and your bloody son."

6

CINDERFIELD TOWN CENTER LOOKS AS if a hurricane has ripped through it. Paper streamers droop from lampposts and trees, and wrap like bandages around the statue of the unknown soldier standing bayonet ready atop the war memorial in the Triangle. Adele picks her way through piles of cracked plastic pint glasses, greasy food wrappers, and empty pizza boxes, her phone clamped to her ear as it plays some annoying jazzy holding tune. She got two new text messages from friends of Maddie on her journey over in the bin lorry, both saying they'd arranged to meet Maddie at the beacon party at The Clearing, both saying they never saw her there. Neither knows where she is now. Adele called them both back but they'd gone straight to voicemail, so she's now pursuing other, potentially darker avenues to try to locate her sister.

The jazz music burbles on in her ear as she scans the litter-strewn street looking for anyone she knows. On any normal day she would recognize at least half the people here, Cinderfield not being that big and, until recently, not quite pretty enough to be overrun by second homers from London, though that was changing. The days around Midsummer had never been normal, though.

Every year more and more people poured into the town, increasingly alerted by social media to the summer fair with its roots stretching back to pagan prehistory. Most of the visitors were harmless tourists looking for a bit of summer entertainment or wanting to connect with something ancient and authentic. Many of them made a real effort, dressing in the traditional garb of Green Men, or Cindermen with their ash-smeared sackcloth smocks, who had once burned charcoal all over the forest and now lit the beacon fires that would burn through the short night and carry the light from dusk to dawn. Others were drawn by the witchiness of the summer solstice and the idea that it might produce extra spooky goings-on in the famously mysterious woods.

Whatever the reason people came, the Midsummer revels swelled the town with thousands of strangers and unfamiliar faces, and Adele, craving order and preferring everything to be in its proper place, did not like it one bit. Especially today.

The jazzy hold music cuts out and a faint voice answers on an even fainter line.

"Dilke Memorial Hospital."

"Yes, hi." Adele clamps her spare hand over her ear to block out as much of the ambient street noise as she can. "I'm looking for my sister and wondered if maybe she'd had an accident and might have been . . ."

"Can I have a name?"

"Yes, it's Maddie, er, Madeleine Friar."

Adele can just about hear the clack of keys on a keyboard.

"No, there's no one of that name here, I can check last night's admissions for the entire district if you like."

"Yes, please, that would be . . ."

"Just a moment."

The jazz returns and Adele continues up the road, scanning for familiar faces among the strangers but finding none. Her eyes settle on a gothic-looking, redstone building on the opposite side of the road, and a solid sick feeling forms like a knot in her stomach. She has bad memories of this building and what went on inside it, looming adults with stern faces, questions, and paperwork, the constant sick feeling of being in trouble, sharp-edged fragments from her childhood, like pieces of a broken plate. The jazz cuts out and Adele presses her phone to her ear again to hear the faint voice of the receptionist.

"I have no record of a Madeleine Friar admitted to A and E anywhere in Gloucestershire last night."

"OK, thanks."

"You're welcome."

Adele hangs up, a mix of relief and disappointment rushing through her. If Maddie had gotten drunk and ended up in casualty Adele would at least know where she was now. She stops in front of the red stone building and looks up at the words written above the door, thin blue letters on a flaking cream background spelling out POLICE STATION. The station building is old and built from blocks of the red sandstone the locals call "forest stone." The midday sun makes it glow a deep, metallic red, like the whole building has been soaked in blood.

Adele glances at her phone one last time, just in case Maddie or one of her friends has sent her a message that she somehow missed. But no one has called, and even Maddie's friends will be up and about by now, so she slips her phone back into her pocket, takes a deep breath, and steps into the shadow of the building.

7

ADELE STOPS INSIDE THE DOORWAY. The place hasn't changed at all; same dark wooden paneling, same dog-eared Crimestoppers posters, same cracked lino on the floor with the grime of decades ground into it by pacing civilians wanting information, or action, or just to get the hell out of here. The vague smell of disinfectant hangs in the air like an unpleasant memory, mingling with the smell of burnt coffee and body odor. Somewhere in the building an old-style phone is ringing, the bell sounding sharp and insistent. No one picks it up.

A beefy desk sergeant stands behind a wooden counter frowning down through greasy reading glasses at some paperwork on the countertop, his many chins spilling over his shirt collar. He does not look up.

"Can I help?" he says, scribbling something on the top sheet of paper.

"Yes, erm—yes." Adele's voice dies away in the wooden deadness of the reception area. She clears her throat. "It's about my sister."

"Mmmm-hmmm?" The desk sergeant's attention remains on the paperwork.

"She's not answering her phone. She was supposed to meet some people at a party last night, a beacon party, but she never made it. I haven't heard from her since yesterday evening."

"Have you called her friends? Boyfriend? Girlfriend?"

"Yes. No one has seen or heard from her."

"Have you tried the hospital? Sometimes people have accidents and . . ."

"Yes. She's not there. She's missing." This comes out with enough force to make him finally stop writing and look up.

She watches him take her in and sees herself through his eyes—sweaty, crazy hair, smears of grime on her face and arms. He can probably smell the bins on her too. His eyes slide back up to her face and she clocks the exact moment he dismisses her and feels an instant rush of blood.

"I came here straight from work," she says, her voice rising as she moves toward him. "I didn't stop to take a shower or change my clothes because my sister's missing and I figured it was probably more important to try to find her than make sure I looked nice."

"All right, love, calm down." The sergeant slides the keyboard of his desktop computer across the counter. "What's your sister's name?"

"Madeleine." Adele takes another step closer. "Madeleine Friar, though everyone calls her Maddie."

"Maddie." He pecks out her name on the keyboard using two fingers. "Date of birth?"

"March fifteenth, nineteen ninety-eight."

He taps this in too. "Physical description."

His eyes slide off the screen and over to her and Adele automatically looks away and starts scrolling through the photo album on her phone, looking for a picture of her sister.

"She's got light-brown hair, brown eyes, five foot three, skinny . . ." She continues to scroll and can feel his eyes on her, heavy and unwanted. She finally spots Maddie's face smiling out from a tightly wrapped bundle of scarf, hat, and winter coat. She looks at the date and feels a pang of guilt as she realizes that her most recent picture is over seven months old.

"This is Maddie." She holds the phone up so the sergeant can see it.

He peers at it then nods appreciatively. "Pretty." He looks at her over his glasses and smiles. "Looks exactly like you, though I think you're probably a tiny bit prettier."

Hot blood rushes to Adele's face and she glares at him, her mouth opening and closing as her mind tumbles with all the things she wants to say. But his eyes are back on the screen now, moving behind the greasy lenses of his glasses as he reads what is displayed there. He frowns. "Are you absolutely sure your sister is missing?"

Adele stares at him, still fuming at his behavior and attitude.

"Yes, she's . . . of course . . . she was supposed to come home last night, or this morning at least, and she . . . I don't understand the question."

He nods at the screen. "Well, she has quite the colorful history, your sister—three charges of being drunk and disorderly in a public place, some minor drug possession offenses, a restraining order from an ex-boyfriend."

Adele feels anger boil inside her. She wants to tell him to mind his own business, to just do his job and fill in whatever forms need to be filled in to officially record that her sister is missing so that someone can actually start looking for her. But she doesn't say anything because she's been in these situations before, standing in front of someone with a bit of power and some forms to fill in. Shouting and screaming never does any good. Losing it is called "losing it" for a reason. So she takes a deep breath and forces a smile, because this sweaty bucket of lard in the shape of a man is currently standing between her and finding her sister.

"Look," she says, keeping her voice low and steady, "I know my sister has got some history, but she's not some big-time criminal, she's just young and stupid. She's also not the type to take off with no warning. Last night she arranged to meet some friends at the big beacon party at The Clearing and she never showed up, no one I've spoken to knows what happened to her, or where she went, and she hasn't been seen or heard from since, so I would really like to file a missing persons report, please."

The sergeant stares at her. Doesn't move. "You know the chances are she just met some people and went off to a different party, right? I mean, it was Midsummer's Eve last night, it was carnage out there. I've got a couple of idiots asleep in the cells now who were caught wrapping toilet paper around the war memorial at three o'clock this morning, off their heads on Christ knows what. I bet your sister's sleeping off a hangover somewhere and will turn up in a few hours doing the walk of shame and wondering what all the fuss is about. You don't need to be wasting everybody's time filling in forms." He looks down at the paperwork spread over the counter in front of him. "I've got way too many on my plate as it is. Tell you what I'll do, if your sister's still missing in a couple of hours after I've cleared this lot away then we can . . . hey, what are you doing?"

He holds his hand up to block the bright light now shining in his face.

"I'm filming you." Adele moves her phone to the side to light up his face again.

"Why?" He moves his hand across to block the phone.

"You're refusing to help me find my missing sister, so I'm recording evidence for the official complaint I'm going to make. Could you state your name, please?"

"What? No, I'm not giving you my name. Put your phone down and stop filming me."

"So now you're also refusing to give me your name. Doesn't matter, I'm sure someone will recognize you when I post this online." She keeps moving to make sure she catches enough of his face to be identifiable. "This police officer is refusing to file a missing persons report. My sister is called Maddie Friar, she's twenty-four years old and has been missing since Midsummer's Eve. She's not answering her phone, I haven't heard from her, nor have any of her friends, I just told this police officer all of that and he is refusing to file a missing persons report."

"I never said that. I never said I wasn't going to file a report. Stop filming. I said I was going to fill in the form after I'd . . . look, I'll fill in the form now, OK? Put the phone down and I'll fill in the bloody form."

Adele lowers her phone but keeps it pointing at him. She doesn't stop filming until he's filled in the form and filed it.

8

ST. ANTHONY'S WELL LIES AT the bottom of a woodland hollow beneath ancient trees. A low wall of rough stone blocks surrounds the rectangular pool of pure, clear springwater which bubbles up from the ground, carrying the deep chill of the earth and the reputed ability to cure rheumatism, skin complaints, and even—according to one report from the early 1880s—leprosy. This reputation, coupled with its pretty setting, makes it a magnet for tourists, though it is oddly quiet this Midsummer morning. The only visitors currently are two men, one solid figure in nondescript hiking clothes with a trim, reddish beard fringing a ruddy face, and the Earl of Dean, who sits slumped on the wall surrounding the miraculous waters, his head in his hands as he talks, and talks, and talks.

The standing man is Russell Beech, one of the Earl's oldest associates, and someone who, partly through the Earl's patronage, has risen to the position of Chief Constable of the Gloucestershire Constabulary. He listens now, his pink face stern and serious as he stares down into the well. Eventually the Earl stops talking, leaving just the sound of birdsong and the trickle of water. Beech takes a long deep breath, blows it out slowly, then speaks in a low voice, barely audible above the sounds of the forest.

"Tell me what you know about the girl."

The Earl rubs his hands over his face and stares at the ground. "Sebastian met her in a pub."

"Name?"

"I think it was the Charcoal Burners."

Beech closes his eyes and shakes his head. "The name of the girl, not the pub."

"Oh, er . . . Maddie, but that's not her real name."

"Do you know her real name?"

"Yes, Helen. Helen Bailey."

"And do you know what name she is going by now?"

The Earl looks up at him with a look of confusion on his face. "I already told you, it's Maddie."

Beech's lips compress into a tight line. In all his years of dealing with the Earl and his family he has never failed to be surprised at how thick they all are, despite their noble breeding and expensive educations.

"I mean, do you know what surname she is using now?"

"Oh right, yes, I see. No, I don't know her full name."

The Earl looks back down at the forest floor and shakes his head, the strain of the morning etched on his face. "I didn't mean for any of this to happen. I didn't know Seb had invited this girl along or who she would turn out to be. I thought all that . . . unfortunate business was in the past."

Beech looks down at him, a look of disgust on his face.

Unfortunate—such a genteel word for such a sordid thing.

"Where's your son now?"

"Gone back to London. I thought it best to get him away from here. I mean, it's not his fault. He doesn't deserve to get in trouble for any of this."

Beech closes his eyes, astounded by the blind entitlement of these people. As long as they were all right, they never really gave a shit about anyone else, they just withdrew into their mansions and their titles and pulled up the drawbridge, leaving other people to tidy up their messes. Other people like him.

"Listen," he says, "people disappear round here all the time. It's not that unusual. People come, people go. From what you've told me it sounds like this Maddie was a pretty nomadic character anyway. It'll probably be a day or two before anyone even notices she's missing. Maybe no one will say anything."

"But what about the sister?"

"What about her? She could be anywhere. Could be in Australia for all we know, or dead. I'll do some digging, see if I can find out what happened to her. What was her name before she changed it?"

"Donna. Donna Bailey."

"OK. I'll look back through the records and see if I can pick up her trail. In the meantime, go back home, do whatever you normally do, act as if nothing has happened, because as far as everyone is concerned nothing has happened. We need to stay calm, keep our heads and figure out the best thing to do, for all of us, because there's too much at stake here. We can't afford any kind of scandal or scrutiny—it could derail the whole thing."

He looks up at a group of hikers who have appeared through the trees and are making their way toward them.

"Now make a wish and take my picture like we're just a couple of old fruits come to dip our toes in the well, then let's get the hell out of here before anyone recognizes us."

9

MADDIE FRIAR'S MISSING PERSONS REPORT is filed at 12:46 p.m. and instantly triggers an alert in the Gloucestershire Constabulary headquarters in Quedgeley, about fifteen miles east of Cinderfield. It pops up on the screen of a desktop computer in a messy, and currently unoccupied office and goes unnoticed—for now. The report is also automatically forwarded to two national databases, the PNC—Police National Computer—and the UK Missing Persons Unit of the National Crime Agency—UKMPU. It is this that triggers a second alert which appears on a laptop currently lying open in a study overlooking the Thames at Tower Bridge. Apart from one wall of glass, the room is entirely lined with floor-to-ceiling bookshelves. These are crammed with books on criminology, law, forensics, and behavioral and social sciences, so many books they spill out onto the floor and collect in neat piles around a purple velvet Chesterfield sofa that rises like an island from the sea of words.

Sitting in the midst of all this, like a tiny bird in a nest of paper, is Dr. Laughton Rees, her small face and large, green eyes framed by a tumble of messy blond hair that makes her look more like the lead singer of an indie band than a professor of criminology. She looks up from the selection of autopsy photos spread out on the desk, her attention snagged by the ping of the alert, and speed-reads the contents of the email, making mental notes of the key details before clicking on the attached photo. She studies the smiling face of Maddie Friar bundled up in her scarf and coat, happily unaware in the moment the picture was taken that it would one day end up attached to her missing persons file.

"Mum!" The office door bursts open behind her and a teenage girl who could be Laughton's double barges in. "Have you seen my Converse?"

"Whoa, Gracie!" Laughton scoops the autopsy photos together and quickly turns them over. "What happened to knocking?"

"Sorry, I'm looking for my shoes."

Laughton turns and regards her daughter, dressed in the bottle-green sports kit of her school, her eyes dropping down to her feet. "You're already wearing shoes."

"These are for the beach, I need my Converse for going out."

"Right."

Gracie drops to the floor and starts hunting around, knocking over a pile of books on pagan folklore. Laughton had signed Gracie up for the surf trip to Cornwall when she'd moved to her new school back in January and Laughton was signing her up for pretty much everything in the hope that it would help her make new friends. Now that the trip has finally arrived and Gracie already has more friends than Laughton can keep up with, she wishes her daughter weren't going. She knows it's only Cornwall, and it's only five days, and that Gracie is sixteen now and the trip is fully supervised, but it'll still be the longest they've ever been apart, and the thought makes her feel an actual physical pain in her chest. She also knows it's her problem and that she needs to get over it and let go. But almost losing a daughter, as she had so nearly lost Gracie, will light a fire of anxiety in any parent that will never, ever be fully extinguished.

Gracie reaches under the Chesterfield and pulls out a black-and-red Comme des Garçons Converse like a rabbit from a hat. "Ta-da!!!"

"How did that get there?"

"Must have been when I did my homework in here the other night when you were out."

Laughton shakes her head. "I wish you wouldn't use my office without checking with me first." She glances back at the autopsy photos to make sure they're all facedown. "I have lots of sensitive and confidential material in here."

"Don't worry, I'm not interested in looking at any of your manky pictures."

"Good. Do you want me to walk with you down to the school?"

"No, it's OK." Gracie pulls the other shoe from beneath the sofa and stands back up. "Lily and Elodie are going to call round and we're going to walk up together."

"OK. Have you got your phone and your charger?"

"Yes, Mum."

"What about all your meds?"

"I'm all sorted, stop worrying."

Laughton forces a smile and steals a glance at the photo of Maddie Friar. It's hard not to worry when her working life is spent studying in detail the very worst things that can happen to people. She realizes her daughter is hovering and looking at her with that slightly guarded expression that usually means she wants something.

"Have you got any cash?" Gracie asks.

"Why do you need cash?"

"I dunno, food!?"

"I'm pretty sure they're going to feed you and I've already transferred forty quid to Mr. Ashford for spending money."

"Yeah, but what about snacks or emergencies?"

"Well, first, let's try and avoid the word 'emergencies,' shall we, and secondly, if you wanted some extra cash, you should probably have given me a bit more notice than two minutes before you're about to step out the door."

"Sorry. Have you got any though?"

Laughton closes her eyes and sighs. "There might be some in the kitchen drawer under the toaster in among all the take-away menus."

"Thanks, Mum. Love ya!"

Gracie skips out of the room and Laughton watches her go, wishing again that she'd never signed her up for the trip.

She turns back to the laptop and stares at the photo of Maddie Friar, barely older than Gracie is now and beaming with that same kind of open, wide-eyed, youthful trust and innocence that Gracie has.

And Maddie Friar is now missing.

"WHAT DRAWER DID YOU SAY IT WAS IN?" Gracie hollers from the kitchen.

"The one under the toaster."

"WHICH ONE!?"

"THE ONE . . . Oh, don't worry, I'm coming."

Laughton clicks on the photo to close it then drags Maddie Friar's missing persons file across from the email and into a folder on her desktop with a one-word title, written in caps: CINDERMAN.

10

ADELE WALKS AWAY FROM THE police station, feeling wrung out from her confrontation with the sergeant. She reaches the war memorial and her phone buzzes in her hand, setting her heart thumping. She shields her eyes against the sun, squints at the screen, but it's not Maddie, it's just an automatic notification asking if she wants to join the free Wi-Fi the council recently installed, along with a twenty-four-hour webcam live-streaming the High Street, which has to be the most boring thing she's ever seen. Nevertheless, the notification gives her an idea and she opens the connection request, fills in her details, then selects the video clip she filmed at the police station and starts uploading it to YouTube. At least this way she'll still have it if she loses her phone, and she may still need it. The sergeant said he'd filed the report but that didn't mean he actually had, and she flat-out didn't trust him. She didn't trust anyone. She waits for the video to finish uploading then sets the settings to private—for now.

She looks down the street, her eyes following the route the Midsummer Parade had taken the night before, past the shops and on toward the edge of town and the forest beyond. She should really head back to the campsite and finish off the morning cleanup, but something else draws her on, the idea that this was the last place her sister had been seen. She follows in her sister's last known footsteps until she reaches the edge of Cinderfield, where the forest rises up suddenly like a huge green wave frozen in the moment before it sweeps through the town and destroys everything.

Maddie had been heading to The Clearing, which meant she would have to have come this way and followed the pathway through the forest. Adele steps off the road and heads for the gap in the tree line where the path cuts through the woods. She reaches the threshold where sunlight turns to shadow and stops abruptly like she's bumped into an invisible barrier.

She listens to the creak and whisper of the forest and looks ahead to where dappled sunlight moves over the dusty pathway that winds beneath the trees. It looks pretty, peaceful even, and yet she can't take another step.

She takes a deep breath and blows it out slowly.

A forest is just a field with some trees in it. And the trees here at the edge are not even growing particularly close to each other. Maybe she should walk in just a little way, stay close to the edge so she can easily run back out again if she gets spooked. She paces at the edge of the trees, watching the sunlight shimmer on the dusty path.

This is the way Maddie would definitely have gone, she reminds herself, trying to psyche herself up

She was heading to the beacon party at The Clearing, and if I don't retrace her steps, who will? Not the police, that's for sure, the unhelpful sergeant had clearly already written her off as not worth the effort.

Adele continues to pace, trying to work herself up. Plenty of people thought Maddie was silly and shallow, but the truth was she was as strong as anyone. One of her strengths was her refusal to see the world in anything but optimistic terms despite everything they'd both been through. Adele was the opposite. Everything she'd survived had hardened her and made her more closed down. She shut out everything that might possibly hurt her, had even started pushing Maddie away. In the back of her mind she'd always known that if she truly wanted to leave her past behind, she'd have to leave her sister too. But now Maddie is gone and she feels guilty, like it's her fault for not watching out for her, like it was her who pushed Maddie away.

"Fuck it," she says, marching forward and passing instantly out of the sunlight and into the shadows

She feels the temperature drop the moment she steps into the forest, the trapped shade and cool air wrapping itself around her in a way that she would find pleasant in any other circumstance, but not here and now. Here it feels like something has taken hold of her, and she fixes her eyes on the way ahead and tries to ignore her discomfort.

Come on Adele, get it together.

She concentrates on the simple act of putting one foot in front of the other and takes deep breaths to try and calm herself, but the smell they carry, of dust and earth and rot, only serves to remind her of where she is and what she is doing.

She glances back to reassure herself that she's still close to the edge of the woods, that she's hardly gone any distance at all, but even in the few steps she's taken the trees seem to have closed in behind her and the houses at the edge of Cinderfield are almost entirely hidden. She can see shadows all around her now, shifting with the light as the leaves move in the breeze. It feels like they are deepening. Gathering.

Her breathing accelerates and she faces forward again, following the line of the pathway as it meanders through the woods, narrowing with distance until it vanishes in the gloom.

Her breathing gets faster and she feels hot despite the grip of the chilled air. The Clearing is too far away, way too far, and what is she going to find when she gets there anyway? A note from Maddie scratched into the dirt or carved into the bark of a tree? A shoe? A piece of clothing? Her body!?

The chances are that even if she does manage to walk all the way there she's not going to find anything, and she's already feeling light-headed as panic squeezes her chest. It's no good. She can't do this. She'll have to think of another way.

She turns and starts to head back, half running, half staggering as her vision blackens at the edges.

She tries to gulp more air but finds she can't breathe and her eyes go wide, like a diver who's swum down too deep in green, shadowy waters and is now kicking frantically for the surface. She's going to drown in this forest. She should never have stepped foot in here, neither of them should have. They'd agreed. They'd made a promise to each other.

She staggers on, a high-pitched whine sounding in her head now as the blackness at the edge of her vision grows like she's falling backward down a well. She's not going to make it. It's too far and the forest is too hungry. She looks down and tries to focus on the ground. If she can keep going and stay on the path it might just lead her to safety, like it did when they were kids. She had been running in blind panic through the forest, Maddie leading the way, Maddie always taking the lead back then, urging her on, telling her not to look back. But she had looked back. She'd heard the car and she'd looked back in time to see it appear on the other side of the cabin, sliding to a stop and throwing up great arcs of dirt. Then he had stepped out.

He had looked straight at her, like he knew exactly where she was and she could never escape him. She had felt herself shrink beneath his gaze, even at that distance, and she would have crumpled to the ground right there and then, just sat down and waited for him to come over, scoop her up in his arms, and take her back to the cabin like a sack of earth, like nothing. But Maddie had grabbed her arm instead and pulled her onward.

Keep running, she had said.

Keep running and don't look back.

And she had run. And she had never looked back.

Maddie saved her then, so she has to save Maddie now. Whatever it takes. Wherever it takes her. Somehow she has to find the strength.

Adele bursts back into the sunshine and takes huge gulps of air, crumpling to the ground and dropping her head down to get the blood flowing quickly back to her brain. She breathes, slowly and deliberately, until the blackness around the edge of her vision recedes and the high-pitched whine in her head fades away. She can hear birds singing again, the hum of insects, the distant sounds of people going about their day in Cinderfield.

Slowly she gets back to her feet and turns to face the forest. It looks like nothing again, just a bunch of trees crowded into a huge field, dry bracken on the ground, and a dusty path winding through it.

She takes a deep breath, one that doesn't taste of the forest, and thinks of Maddie, lost somewhere in all this vast greenery. Or maybe the sweaty police sergeant was right and Maddie went on a bender with persons unknown, overslept, and is now avoiding Adele's calls because she knows she'll be mad at her. If that's true she'll show up eventually. She can't ignore Adele forever. All her stuff is still lying in a pile in a corner of Adele's cabin and she'll have to come and get it sooner or later.

Adele frowns as a new thought strikes her and she starts walking along the edge of the forest, heading for the open fields.

Maddie was going to bring some dude with her to the beacon party, Ronan had said, some dude with a name he didn't know.

She reaches a gate, hops over it, and starts cutting through the fields, taking the most direct route back to the campsite, and her cabin, and the pile of Maddie's stuff lying in the corner. Maybe there is another way of finding out what her sister has been up to, and who she has been doing it with.

11

LAUGHTON STOPS OUTSIDE GRACIE'S BEDROOM and peers through the open door. She'd expected the combination of her daughter's excitement and her inability to find anything without emptying everything onto the floor first would result in some mess but not quite the devastation she now sees. The disarray gnaws at her OCD but there's no way she's going to tidy it up. She has seen pictures taken in the bedrooms of missing and murdered children in cold case files where casual mess like this has been preserved for decades and, in this moment, she understands why. The clothes on the floor and the unmade bed are all evidence that Gracie has been here. These are the last things she touched before walking out of the house, the last physical things that still connected her to home.

Laughton stands there for a moment in the gloomy shadow of these bleak thoughts then shakes her head and closes the door. What the hell is she thinking? Gracie has only gone away for a few days with school, not been abducted by a pedophile ring.

She stomps into the kitchen, making more noise than necessary to drive away the silence. She pulls her phone from her pocket, starts a thirty-second timer, turns on the tap, and picks up the kettle. Since moving to her father's old flat she's tried hard to use it as a fresh start and spring-clean her life, including trying to phase out her formerly crippling OCD rituals. So far she hasn't managed to stop any of them, but she has succeeded in reducing all her timed rituals from sixty seconds to thirty, which feels like some kind of progress. Right now, though, she is feeling a strong and superstitious urge to put it back to sixty, as if somehow that single act will keep Gracie safe. She stares at the seconds ticking down, holding the kettle ready until it hits zero and immediately moves the kettle under the stream of water to fill it. She blows out a long breath as she fills the kettle to the three-cup mark then sets it to boil.

On her phone she swipes away the timer app and finds Gracie in her contacts, her finger hovering over the call icon for a second or two before she puts it down and takes a mug from a neatly regimented cupboard instead. She doesn't need to check on Gracie. Gracie is with two of her friends, in broad daylight, in the heart of London.

Laughton drops a peppermint tea bag into the mug, scrolls through her contacts until she finds the entry for DCI Tannahill Khan and calls him instead. It goes straight to voicemail, prompting her to start tapping her fingers on the worktop in series of threes. She pours hot water into the mug from the kettle and heads back to her office, slumping into her chair and tapping the trackpad on her laptop to wake it so she can distract herself with work.

She clicks open the folder called "CINDERMAN" and creates a new "MADDIE FRIAR" subfolder then moves the missing persons file into it and double-clicks on the file to reopen it.

The smiling photo of Maddie Friar pops up again, a girl who actually has gone missing rather than disappearing for a fun, few days on a school trip. Laughton clicks the "action" tag on the file where all the details of everything that's currently happening in the investigation will be recorded and frowns when the page loads. It's empty: no additional photos, no information about where Maddie Friar lived or worked, no list of friends or relatives to interview, no record that any personal items like tooth- or hairbrushes have been requested to try and harvest DNA samples from. At the very least a statement should have been taken from the person who reported the person missing but there's nothing. Again.

She navigates back to the main report and scrolls to the end to see who reported Maddie missing and her frown deepens when she sees it was the girl's sister. Someone that closely related to the missing person should absolutely have been asked to give a detailed statement to help establish a timeline of her sister's last known movements and draw up a list of people of interest to interview. Why go to the trouble of filling in and filing a missing persons report at all if you weren't going to do anything to investigate it?

She searches through the pile of autopsy photos on her desk for a notebook, turns to a new page, and writes at the top:

"Maddie Friar—reported missing June 25."

Underneath that she adds, "Sergeant Millbrook responding officer—
<u>no</u> action taken," then reads through the report again, using the focus of
the task as a welcome distraction from the silent flat. Her mouth screws
over to the side when she spots the list of Maddie Friar's previous
arrests. Maybe that's why Sergeant Millbrook didn't feel she was worth
the bother. She reads through the charges, all small-time stuff and
misdemeanors, not that it will matter in the eyes of the criminal justice
system. In the overworked, underpaid, overstretched world of modern
policing, a victim with a record is always treated differently from a
victim who is squeaky clean. On each charge sheet it also notes that
Maddie grew up in social care, another thing that will count against
her. Laughton works through the file, adding key dates and questions
to her notebook.

1998—Maddie Friar born

> —*Age taken into care?*
> —*Reason taken into care??*
> —*Where did she grow up???*
> *2018—1st arrest—D&D (Aged 20)*
> *2019—2nd arrest—minor possession*
> *2020—3rd arrest—D&D*
> *2021—4th arrest D&D/affray/resisting arrest*
> *2022—reported missing*

She studies Maddie's photo again. She is wearing an old-fashioned
looking wool coat with a frayed collar, second- or third-hand most
likely, a charity shop buy judging by its age and style. Around her neck
is a colorful nylon scarf, not quite long enough to wrap around more
than once but new looking, something mass-produced and cheap. On
her head she has a wool hat that may once have been white or cream
but is now gray, with bobbles and snags around the edges. Chipped nail
polish is visible on two of the fingers of her left hand sticking out from
fingerless gloves. From the photograph it looks like she has little to no
money, which is another thing that will work against her.

There is a well-worn maxim in criminal investigations: "follow the money," meaning that if you looked for whoever stands to gain the most financially from whatever crime you are investigating, more often than not you will also find the perpetrator. But there is also a flip side to this, one that Laughton has learned herself firsthand, and that is, if you want to find the victim you only have to look where there is an absence of money. Because it's the powerless and the marginalized who tend to be the targets of crimes. They're also the ones who are less likely to see justice. And Maddie Friar's charity shop clothes and chipped nail polish have "victim" written all over them. Add that to a childhood spent in social care and a criminal record and she is a prime candidate for being swept under the carpet and forgotten about. But in the perverse nature of Laughton's own personal law, Maddie Friar is exactly the sort of voiceless, potential lost cause she feels compelled to help. Because Laughton was once one of those lost causes herself.

The sudden buzz of her phone makes her jump and she snatches it up in case it's Gracie with an emergency.

"Has she gone?" Tannahill asks the moment she answers.

"Yeah, about fifteen minutes ago."

"She'll be totally fine, you know."

"Yeah, I know."

"Do you though?"

"Yeah, 'course."

"So why did you call me the moment she stepped out the door?"

"I didn't."

"Yeah you did, I had a missed call from you exactly fifteen minutes ago when I was in a tunnel and didn't have a signal. I bet you're still standing in her room and staring at all her stuff, aren't you?"

"No actually, I'm in my office, working. Speaking of which, are you in Glasgow yet?"

"No, I'm still on the train. I get there in about half an hour I think."

Laughton nods. She'd hoped to distract herself from Gracie's absence by spending more time with Tannahill, only to discover that he was going to be away the same weekend at some dull, international crime seminar. "Have you finished your presentation?"

"Yeah, it's really boring though."

"You're at a dry police conference, not a comedy convention."

"Exactly, that's why I'm trying to work some jokes into it."

"What's the subject again?"

"Media management in high-profile murder investigations."

Laughton smiles. "Sexy."

She had met Tannahill while working with him on just such a case. Not the most traditional or romantic of backdrops, but it had somehow worked for them—at least so far. Since the case had ended, though, some major life changes and their various workloads had conspired to keep them apart, so things had progressed very slowly. For a super-compartmentalized, buttoned-down weirdo like her, it had actually been pretty ideal. Only now that he wasn't there when she really could do with his calm brand of quiet strength did she realize how much she was starting to depend on him.

"There must be some clips online of someone punching a reporter"—she opens a browser and googles COP REPORTER PUNCH—"just kick off with one of those. Everyone loves to see a journalist getting smacked, especially coppers."

"That's actually not a bad idea."

Laughton scans the results, most of which show the same clip of an Australian news crew getting attacked by police in Washington, DC.

"Or just keep it short," Laughton suggests. "No one really listens to any of the presentations anyway, they're all just desperate to get to the bar."

"Well, then I'm glad I spent such a long time preparing it."

"It'll be fine, they'll love it. How long did you say you were away for again?"

"Four days, why, you missing me already?"

"Well, obviously." Laughton looks again at the smiling face of Maddie Friar with her chipped nail polish, police record, and not a soul actively looking for her except maybe her sister. "But I was thinking I might go on a little trip myself."

"Really! Where to?"

"Cinderfield, it's an old market town in the Forest of Dean."

"What's in Cinderfield?"

"A mystery." Laughton clicks on Maddie Friar's file to close it and stares at the contents of The Cinderman folder. "A girl just went missing there."

"Someone you know?"

"No. It's part of a research paper I've been doing on the intersection between real crimes and folklore."

"That sounds *way* more interesting than my presentation."

"It is pretty interesting, actually. Every community has its own bogeyman, local legends designed to scare children into obedience and keep people out of particular places. In the Forest of Dean they've got one called the Cinderman, some kind of forest phantom who's believed to prey on young women, particularly around certain dates like the summer solstice. A myth, obviously, except plenty of women have disappeared over the years. Anyway, I put an alert on the MPU to flag up any new cases that might pop up, and a girl did go missing last night."

"Midsummer's Eve."

"Exactly. And looking at her file, it seems like the local law aren't exactly bending over backward to try to find her, which unfortunately is also a bit of a pattern. So, I thought I might go down there myself and do a bit of digging around, see if I can figure out what's going on."

There's a long pause on the line before Tannahill finally speaks, his voice low and serious now. "How many women have gone missing?"

Laughton scrolls through the contents of her Cinderman file, a long list of sub-folders, each labeled with a different woman's name. "Fifty-eight in the last twenty years, five of those fairly recently."

"Whoa!"

"Yep."

Another pause stretches out, train noise filling the silence until Tannahill's voice eventually cuts through it. "Maybe you shouldn't go."

Laughton smiles. "You worried about me?"

"Yes. I don't want you to end up being number fifty-nine."

Laughton's smile spreads wider. "I'll be fine, I don't believe in the Cinderman or forest demons, but there's definitely something weird going on down there. Tell you what, I promise I'll wear a crucifix and carry garlic in my pocket if that makes you happier."

But the train noise is gone, cut off by another tunnel, so Tannahill never hears her promise.

12

EVEN WITH THE HEAVY BLUE tint, the bright midday sky appears scorched through the plate glass windows of the Gloucestershire Constabulary building. Cool air hisses softly through vents in the floor, battling the full heat of the day now pressing against the building on all sides.

Chief Constable Russell Beech shuffles heavily into his stuffy, messy office and collapses into his chair with a tortured screech of springs. He briefly surveys the piles of paperwork and clutter he has neither the energy nor the resources to tackle adequately, then leans forward and starts reading through all the emails that have piled up while he's been meeting with the Earl.

His bloodshot eyes move rapidly behind his spectacles as he scans the largely irrelevant emails before coming to rest on the missing persons alert. He opens the email, reads through the contents, then yanks a drawer open and fishes out half a packet of Mentos. He swapped cigarettes for mints years earlier and, apart from the occasional grumble from his dentist, never considered it to be a serious enough habit to quit. He works a minty white oval out of the packet, pops it into his mouth, and rolls it around his tongue as he rereads the document again, all the way to the end, where the person who filed it is named. He opens the Gloucestershire Crime Archive Database, inputs his password, then copies the name ADELE FRIAR into the search field and hits Return.

Nothing comes back.

He types in DONNA/HELEN BAILEY.

Still nothing.

He opens the ONECHECK database, a personnel hub linked to various civilian archives such as the Census Office and the Electoral Register, and types DONNA/HELEN BAILEY into the search field.

A couple of pages of results come back, mostly copies of referral letters to various child services with the details redacted. He would need to formally request the files if he wanted to read the contents, and the last thing he wants to do is create an official paper trail. Besides, he already knows most of the details after his meeting with the Earl.

Beech scrolls down the results looking for anything else that might be useful and finds pdfs of their birth certificates. Both have the same mother listed—Anne Marie Bailey—and both have "Unknown" in the box labeled "Father." He checks the date of birth for Helen Bailey against the given DOB for Madeleine Friar on the missing persons file. They don't match, which is interesting. Often when people change their identities they keep some link to their past; same initials but a different name, same date of birth to make it easier to remember how old they're supposed to be. And though Donna and Helen Bailey appear to have adopted a scorched-earth policy in most respects, severing all data connections with their previous existences, they have also stayed in the area, which is odd. Why go to such lengths to distance yourself from your past but stay living in a place where you might be recognized?

He looks up and out of the window framing the hot sky, a car park, and the Forest of Dean spread green and thick over the distant hills, the rapid clicking of the mint against his teeth matching the pace of his thoughts. He pulls out his phone and makes a call using WhatsApp, nudging down the volume as the untraceable call connects.

"Hello?"

The Earl's voice still sounds frayed.

Beech moves the mint to the side of his mouth. "There's been a development. The girl has been reported missing."

"Already!? You said we would have at least a day or two."

"I know, I thought it would take that long for someone to miss her but it turns out her sister has already come forward and filed a missing persons file."

"Oh Jesus!"

"It's OK, it's actually a good thing."

"How!? How can that possibly be a good thing?"

Beech scrolls back to the bottom of the missing persons file where, beneath Adele's name, she has given her mobile phone number, her occupation—Cleaner—and also an address—c/o The Site, Cinderfield.

"Because we now know what she's called and where she lives. And the best thing of all is she's a nobody. She's not married, no kids, no family, and she cleans toilets in a local campsite. All of which means, as far as loose ends go, she couldn't be any easier to tie up."

There is a long pause on the other end of the line before the Earl speaks again in an exaggeratedly low whisper.

"What are you going to do?"

Beech smiles and shakes his head, clocking the "you" in the Earl's statement, like all of this is his mess to clear up.

"I'm not going to do anything," Beech replies. "I think maybe it's time our silent partner started pulling her considerable weight, don't you?"

13

THE BUZZ OF THE PHONE sounds like a large insect in the smoky gloom of the forest. Grizelda Hughes, making her slow, stiff way across the broad clearing that gave the place its name, feels the vibration in her pocket and pauses, leaning heavily on her staff as she pulls the phone free, her thick rope of gray dreadlocks swinging like a pendulum as she peers down at the screen. She holds it at arm's length so her old eyes can focus on the caller ID then curls her lip and shoves it back into her pocket unanswered. She can barely face talking to Beech at the best of times, let alone right now.

She continues on her slow way, her great bulk rolling like an earthquake beneath the shroud of her smock. The Clearing is utterly trashed after last night's beacon party, cigarette butts stamped flat into the dry earth, crushed cans and broken bottles glinting sharply in among the bracken. It will take weeks to tidy it all up, but the parties always bring in so much money the community can't afford not to have them. And there had been more people here last night than Grizz had seen in over thirty years of Midsummers, a fitting send-off for an era only she knew was about to end.

She passes a tall, sinewy man with long hair pulled back in a ponytail, his white beard and deeply weather-lined face the only indicators of how old he really is. He looks up from the shattered vodka bottle he's sweeping onto the blade of his shovel.

"Go sort out the toilets, will you, Merlin, I've just been in there and there's piss all over the planks. Get someone else to help if you can't face it yourself."

Merlin nods, tips the broken glass into a bucket then heads away, his shovel held horizontally like a spear, his back bent a little after decades of picking fruit and vegetables in the summer fields of southern England.

It's people like Merlin that Grizz feels sorriest for, the originals. He had drifted in from who knows where maybe twenty-five years ago, when the community was new and still clinging to the ideals of what it might become, before reality and the harsh need to survive turned it into something else entirely. And now it's about to transform again, and Merlin has no idea, nobody does—nobody but her. Merlin will soon be homeless again at whatever age he is now, and Grizz, who has hardened her heart against so much over the years, still feels bad about that. Maybe she'll look after him after the dust has settled on everything, find out where he is and make sure he's all right. She'll probably do that for a few of them, the older ones like her who once believed in something. The rest can look after themselves, like she's had to do her entire life. Just as she's still doing now.

The phone finally stops buzzing as Grizz leaves the clearing, and she relishes the return of the natural sounds of the forest as she picks her way carefully along a faint track, huffing and sweating with the effort of it as she heads deeper into the trees. The path is hidden by bracken, and summer dry ferns, and she probes the way ahead with her staff, an oak branch split by a lightning bolt in a summer storm maybe ten years ago now. Oak is supposed to represent strength, though it seems bitterly ironic to Grizz that she only needs it now that she is getting increasingly weak. Getting old is a curse for which she knows no remedy—death is the only sure way to cure it.

She looks back over her shoulder, making sure no one is following, then veers off the path and heads down into a dip in the ground where an ancient river once flowed. She follows the dry riverbed for a long, few minutes, cool shadow now running thick where the water used to be, until she reaches the exposed roots of a huge chestnut tree. She looks behind her once more then slips through a gap in the roots and into the dark earth.

Grizz pauses on the edge of the darkness, takes a matchbox from a pocket of her smock, and strikes a match. Light flares, revealing the entrance to a tunnel and a paraffin lamp hanging from a twist of root curling out of the earthen wall. Grizz takes the lamp, touches the match to the wick, then lowers the glass shade and holds it in front of her as she follows the curve of the tunnel down, the amber glow of the lamp pushing away the darkness until it opens out into a cave. The longtime residents of The Clearing call this The School, a place where lessons are learned.

In the center of the cave another paraffin lamp hangs from the low ceiling, casting its dim orange light over a large, raggedy bear of a man with wild hair and beard. The man lies on the ground, strapped to a board by thick leather bands, a gag in his mouth keeping him quiet and two blocks of wood ensuring his head looks directly up. His eyes follow Grizz as she walks across the space to where another man sits on the floor, so still and silent he almost seems part of the cave. Grizz nods a greeting and he rises up, smooth and sure, like he has been switched on. The man is weather worn and compact, hard like dry mud on a well-trodden path, his face expressionless, his close-cropped hair and army greens giving him a vaguely military air. His unsettling stillness only adds to the impression that he may have known action and seen and done terrible things. The people at The Clearing call him Dog because of his devotion to Grizz and his relentless skills as a hunter.

Grizz turns back to the man lying at her feet and steps forward so her shadow falls across his face.

The man on the ground looks up at her, his right eye swollen from a deep cut in his eyebrow.

"Do you know what I hate?" Grizz says, pausing to watch his face for a reaction. "Rudeness."

The look of mild fear in his eyes turns to confusion.

"Imagine, for example, someone goes to the trouble of organizing and throwing a huge party, then some joker comes along and starts behaving like it's their party, starts selling things there, and keeps all the profits for themselves rather than offering to share it with the people who actually threw the party in the first place. That's rude. It's rude, and it's also stealing." She looks down at him through the ropes of her dreadlocks. "And the thing of it is, if you steal from one of us, then you're stealing from all of us. It's like you walked into a village and robbed every single house, took the food right off every table. We're a village here too, you see, a community. And like any community we have rules to keep things in order. And when those rules are broken . . . we also have punishments."

Grizz glances at Dog, who steps forward, pulls a clasp knife from his pocket, and opens it with a snick.

"I don't know if you know this," Grizz continues, "but this part of the forest used to be a Royal hunting ground. Then the monks owned it for a while, before King Henry fell out with the church and took it back again and gave most of it to one of his suck-up lords, but part of it he gave to the people as common land, this bit we're in now, to be precise. Now, according to ancient law, the issue of crime and punishment on common land is left entirely to the occupier to decide and administer, not the police, and not the courts."

Dog holds the tip of the blade up to the flame of the paraffin lamp hanging from the low ceiling and starts turning it slowly.

"The commoners, or 'foresters,' as we prefer to call ourselves, are basically outlaws. We are literally 'outside the law.' It means we can't call the police if crimes are committed against us, which makes some people think we're an easy target. So, we have to make it very clear that we are not."

Dog takes the blade out of the flame and holds it up, the bright red blade reflecting in his eyes. On the ground the bearded man starts to hyperventilate, his chest rising and falling rapidly against his leather bonds.

"Now, I don't know why you thought it would be OK to come and take from us. But we can't have people walking around with that kind of attitude. We need to demonstrate that we're not a soft touch, we need to make an example, so I'm going to give you a choice."

Dog drops down and pulls the gag free from the man's mouth. "I'm sorry," the man says frantically. "I made a mistake. You can have everything, the money, the rest of the drugs, everything. I'll go away and I'll never come back, I promise."

Grizz looks down at him. "I'm going to give you a choice," she repeats. "A hand or an eye."

The bearded man looks up at her with confusion. "What?"

"Do you want to lose a hand or an eye?"

The man laughs and tries to shake his head, but the two blocks of wood won't let him. "You're fucking with me, right?" His eyes flick between

Grizz and Dog, who is now crouched by his side with the knife held ready in his hand.

"If you don't pick one, we'll take them both," Grizz says softly.

The bearded man starts to twist and strain against his leather bindings.

"You can't break free," Grizz says, "and down here this deep in the ground no one will hear you scream. So, stop struggling, face your punishment like a man, and tell me which one you want to lose, your eye or your hand."

The bearded man continues to struggle and buck, his breathing frantic now.

"I'M SORRY!!" he screams, "I SAID I'M FUCKING SORRY!!"

Grizz watches him struggle for a moment then takes the paraffin lamp down from the ceiling. "OK, take them both," she says, then turns and heads away back up the tunnel.

"NO!! PLEASE!! I CAN GIVE YOU MORE MONEY. PLEASE!! FUCK!! JESUS! FUCK!!! OK MY EYE!" the man screams. "TAKE AN EYE."

His screams rise then rapidly fade as Grizz follows the curve of the tunnel back up to the entrance. She sees the dim glow of sunlight ahead just as her phone buzzes in her pocket. She pulls it out and holds it up to the paraffin lamp.

Beech again.

Grizz sighs and answers. "Yes?"

"We've got a problem," Beech says.

"Do we!"

"Yes, we do."

Grizz pauses inside the entrance and turns the wheel on the side of the paraffin lamp to extinguish it.

"And can I assume by the fact that you're calling me like this, that the problem we have is about to become my problem?"

"Now, don't be like that," Beech says, the trace of a smile in his voice. "If anything goes wrong with this deal we all stand to lose, and it just so happens that this particular problem lies more in your area of expertise, or at least, the expertise of people you have access to."

Grizz hangs the lamp on a root and turns to look back down the tunnel where Dog is emerging from the darkness, carrying the other lamp. "What's the problem?"

"Someone's asking extremely unhelpful questions and needs to . . . disappear."

Grizz nods. "A Cinderman job."

"Yes, can you handle that?"

Grizz notes how the "we" has now become "you."

She watches Dog wipe the wet blade of his hunting knife clean on the bark.

"Yes," Grizz says. "We can handle that."

14

IT IS MID-AFTERNOON BY THE time Adele makes it back to The Site.

Everyone is up now and lounging languidly beneath awnings and in the shade of trees, staring at phones and iPads. Some are reading magazines, a few are reading books. An impromptu game of football is taking place near the edge of the forest, and a couple of young girls sit cross-legged on a patch of grass, picking daisies with their mother. Adele studies them as she makes her way across the field, jealous of the memory this family is making along with the chain of daisies. She has no sunny memories of her mother at all. All her memories are dark and cold and filled with pain.

She looks away and fixes her gaze on the door of the sanitation station instead, her heart sinking a little when she sees that the lock is still in place. If Maddie had showed up while she'd been away, to crawl into bed and sleep off her heavy night, it would be open.

She dials in the combination, the metal lock almost too hot to touch, and the door opens with a waft of bleach and dust. She heads inside, past steel racks of plastic bags, brushes, and stacks of cleaning paraphernalia toward another door, also locked, and feels the trapped heat of the thinly insulated shack closing around her as she opens it to reveal a tiny office. Bill had agreed to let her stay here for free as a perk of taking the campsite manager's job—if a tiny space that was an oven in summer and had ice on the inside of the windows in winter could really be classed as a "perk." It is free though, and only temporary. A means to an end.

She pushes open the door and takes in the empty room, sunlight leaking in through a thin, yellowing blind that she keeps drawn partly for privacy and partly to try to keep some of the heat out. Maddie's bedroll and sleeping bag lie in a messy heap next to a rucksack and a pair of old trainers she'd dumped on the floor when she'd turned up here a few days earlier asking if she could crash. It all looks untouched from this morning.

Adele sits on the edge of her narrow cot bed and plugs her phone into the charging cable next to it. Filming the sergeant then uploading the video had been too much for her ancient phone to cope with and she'd now been out of contact for almost an hour. Maddie could have called her back in that time. She presses the power button, gets the empty battery symbol, so puts the phone down and looks across at the wall opposite her bed instead. It is covered in a patchwork of handwritten notes containing inspirational quotes she has carefully collected over the years, like spells to help transform herself and her life. She reads them again now, so familiar she knows them by heart, though today, in the light of Maddie's disappearance, they take on fresh meaning.

THE PAST CANNOT BE CHANGED.

EVERYONE'S JOURNEY IS DIFFERENT.

THINGS ALWAYS GET BETTER WITH TIME.

HAPPINESS IS FOUND WITHIN.

POSITIVE THOUGHTS CREATE POSITIVE THINGS.

YOU ONLY FAIL IF YOU QUIT.

THE DISTANCE BETWEEN YOUR DREAMS AND REALITY IS CALLED ACTION.

THE FIRST AND MOST IMPORTANT PERSON YOU MUST BELIEVE IN, IS YOURSELF.

IF THE PLAN DOESN'T WORK, CHANGE THE PLAN, NOT THE GOAL.

SUCCESS IS NEVER GIVING IN TO FAILURE.

NEVER. EVER. LOSE. HOPE.

The phone buzzes on the bed next to her as it starts up and she grabs it and holds it as high above her head as the charging cable will allow.

The phone finds a signal and a message pops up telling her she has two missed calls. She opens the call menu hoping one of them is from Maddie so she can get back to the simpler job of being cross at her instead of worried, but one is from her boss, Bill, and the second is from Ronan. She calls Ronan back first, taking a deep breath that tastes of dust and bleach as she waits for it to connect.

"Yo!"

"Hey, Ronan, it's Adele."

"Yeah, man, I was just checking to see if Maddie showed up yet."

Adele feels herself wilt. "No," she says, "still no sign."

"Oh." She hears concern in Ronan's voice too, which actually makes her feel a little better. At least someone else cares.

"Maybe her phone broke or something," Ronan says. "Or she just ran out of juice and is someplace she can't plug in. She said she was gonna be with some dude, so maybe she's still with him. Maybe they decided they wanted to be alone instead of hanging out with a bunch of people and she's just, you know, having a nice time somewhere."

"Yeah, maybe."

Or maybe she's lying dead in a ditch, or tied up in the back of someone's van, or locked in a basement with a group of guys taking turns on her.

Adele looks up at the wall and finds the phrase she needs most right now:

POSITIVE THOUGHTS CREATE POSITIVE THINGS.

"You're probably right," she says. "It's not like Maddie's ever been particularly reliable or great at staying in contact, right?"

"Right!"

Her eyes find another phrase:

OVERTHINKING WILL LEAD TO SADNESS.

"And just because no one's heard from her doesn't mean something bad has happened."

"Exactly," Ronan says, his voice brightening a little. "I mean, like, I haven't talked to my brother in, like, a coupla weeks and I bet he en't worried about me. I know I'm a dude and everything but still . . . I mean, like, Maddie can look after herself, you know. She's not, like, some little kid or something."

"Yeah," Adele says, remembering a time not so long ago when she and Maddie *were* little kids and it was Maddie who looked after her. "She'll turn up," she says, her eyes dropping down to a new phrase, deliberately pinned low on the wall at eye level so it's the very last thing she sees when she's going to sleep and the first thing she sees when she wakes up.

"I'll make some more calls," Ronan says, "see if anyone knows where she is, try and find out the name of this new dude. I'll give you a bell if I hear anything."

"Thanks, Ronan."

Adele hangs up, her eyes still fixed on the phrase pinned low on the wall:

NEVER. EVER. LOSE. HOPE.

"She'll be OK," she whispers to herself.

Maddie IS OK. She's just being Maddie. She'll turn up. She always does.

Her eyes drop down to the tangle of Maddie's things on the floor. She reaches forward and picks up her backpack, expecting it to be heavy and is surprised and a little saddened to discover that there's hardly any weight to it at all. She holds it up with one hand, watching it turn and studying the scuffed exterior. Pretty much everything Maddie owns in the world is in this ratty-looking rucksack. All her belongings. All her secrets.

She lowers it gently to the floor then pulls open the neck and peers inside at the contents—a jumble of T-shirts and underwear, some makeup, a stick of deodorant, the cable of a phone charger. She reaches in and pushes her hand down to the bottom, her fingers pushing through the meager belongings until they touch something thin and plasticky. She pulls it out into the light and feels instantly bad about going through her sister's things. It feels intrusive and personal. She counts the number of pills that are missing from the blister pack of contraceptives then tucks it back where she found it, hoping Maddie won't notice it's been moved. She goes to close the bag then notices a pocket by the neck with a flap over it. She pulls it open, the rip of the Velcro sounding brutal in the dusty silence of the shack. Inside is a folded envelope. Brown. Official looking. Adele hesitates for a moment then slides it out and reads the name and address on the cover:

Ms. Madeleine Friar
c/o The Charcoal Burner Inn
Cinderfield

She turns the envelope over and feels a chill pass through her when she sees the return address:

Gloucestershire County Council Fostering Service
Shire Hall
Gloucester

They had promised each other this was a door they would always keep shut because there was nothing for them on the other side of it but pain and bad memories. Looking forward was good, and looking back was bad, they had both agreed on that. But this envelope suggests that Maddie had looked back, she had looked back, and returned to the forest, and now she is missing.

Adele opens the envelope a little and catches a glimpse of the letter inside—formal, typed, "Gloucestershire County Council" written across the top of the sheet. She opens it a little wider, enough to read the first line:

Dear Ms. Friar,
In response to your request for archival information regarding the fostering record of Donna and Helen Bailey,

The rest is hidden by the fold. If she wants to read it she will have to take the letter out of the envelope and read the details of a chapter in her childhood she has spent her adult years trying to forget. She will have to look back too. And though she really doesn't want to, it might help her understand what happened to Maddie. It might help her find her. So she reaches into the envelope and starts pulling out the letter.

The bang comes so loud and sudden it makes the building shake. Adele's head whips up just as an angry and familiar voice booms out:

"What the fuck is going on with the bins!?"

15

ADELE QUICKLY STUFFS THE ENVELOPE back into the rucksack as the door to her room flies open and Bill's looming figure fills the doorway.

"Look at the state of that." He thrusts his phone in her face, so close she has to lean back to see it. On the screen is a photograph of an overflowing bin next to the caption:

Come glamping at @TheSite #RubbishHoliday #campsitefail

"That popped up on Instagram fifteen minutes ago," Bill says with the same kind of grave seriousness someone else might use to announce that war had been declared. "It's already had two hundred likes and thirty comments!"

"I'm sorry," Adele says, pushing past him and snatching a fresh roll of bin liners from one of the shelves on her way to the door. "I'll go sort them right now."

"Now is not good enough." Bill pursues her across the creaking floor of the shack. "Now is too late because the damage is already done."

"It's only Instagram, Bill." Adele passes through the outer door into the too-bright afternoon sun.

"Only Instagram! This is exactly the kind of thing that goes viral."

"It's just a picture of a full bin," Adele says, sliding into the seat of the honey-wagon. "How many shares is a picture of a bin going to get? It's not even funny, it's just a bin."

"No, it's not, it's a picture of a bin on my campsite with two hundred likes, actually two hundred and four now, and . . . thirty-two comments! Do you know how many followers the person who posted this has? Four and a half thousand! This could be everywhere by teatime, it's a fucking PR disaster."

Adele releases the handbrake, floors the gas pedal, and races from zero to four miles per hour in almost as many seconds.

"I'm sorting it," she says to Bill, who is now walking alongside her, easily keeping pace despite his farmer's physique.

"How? How are you going to sort it?"

"By emptying the bins."

"That's not going to fix this, you fucking idiot."

Adele stamps down hard on the brake bringing the milk float to a sudden halt. "What do you want me to do, Bill? Something came up and I had to go into town and I'm really sorry that one of the bins I missed happened to be next to Bill Gates's tent, but I'm on it now, OK!? I don't know what else I can say to you."

Bill opens his mouth to say something then shakes his head as if he's never been more disappointed in anything in his life. Adele knows exactly what he's thinking. He's thinking he'd probably like to fire her because it would make him feel like a hardcore business executive, but he also knows there's no way he'd be able to replace her at such short notice, so he'd then have to empty the bins himself. And there's no way that's going to happen because that definitely won't make him feel like a hardcore business exec. He shakes his head some more, still trying to look like the most disappointed boss who ever had to put up with substandard work from substandard workers.

"Just get it done quick," he says, pointing at the campsite as if he's a general sending her into battle. "And when you've done that make sure the toilet blocks are spotless. I do not want to see any more notifications popping up on my phone unless they're five-star reviews on TripAdvisor. Understood?"

16

SHE FEELS THE BREEZE AND opens her eyes, blinks a few times to make sure they are actually open, then turns her head, feeling for the breath of moving air in the darkness. It had come from her left she thinks, away from the wall with the roots snaking out of it and deeper into the unknown dark.

She listens for a moment to the white-noise nothingness of the silence then reaches out with both hands and moves her arms in small circles as she feels the way ahead. It is too cold to stay still anyway, better to keep moving, keep exploring the space and looking for a way out. Besides, she learned a long time ago that the power of the dark to frighten lies not in the absence of light but in the fear of what it might contain. Knowledge is power, she read that somewhere too, so if she can discover what this darkness contains then she will remove its power to frighten.

Her hand touches something new and she fights the urge to snatch it away.

"Knowledge is power," she murmurs.

Not knowing is where the fear leaks in.

She stands perfectly still for a moment, heart hammering in her chest, then slowly she flattens out her hand until her palm is pressing against the object. It is perfectly flat and smooth, and the warmth of her skin reflects back from its surface like it's a plank or a wooden board.

Man-made, her mind whispers, and the realization that this dark place is not entirely natural makes the fear stir again in her chest.

An old mining tunnel might still have some old planks in it, but anything that has been underground for a hundred years or more would surely have rotted away long ago. And this plank, or whatever it is beneath her hand, feels dry and new.

She pushes it slightly but it does not move, so she moves her hand up and along its flat surface, feeling for a detail, anything that might give her a clue as to what it is. She finds the upper edge where the smooth surface meets the dirt wall, where it has been *fitted* into the dirt wall, and runs her hand along it until she reaches a corner then follows it down toward the dirt floor until her hand touches something new, something cold and hard, about halfway down and level with her hip.

It's a handle, and the thing she has found is a door.

Her hand closes around the cold metal and she twists it, half expecting it to be locked tight and not sure how she will deal with the discovery of that fact.

But the door is not locked, the handle turns and the door swings silently open, revealing more fathomless darkness beyond.

17

SWEAT STINGS ADELE'S EYES BUT she works through it, loading bin bags onto the honey-wagon as fast as she can despite the heat.

Discovering the letter in Maddie's bag had floored her. She had felt the distance widening between them over the last year, but she never thought Maddie would do something like that without at least talking to her about it first.

She glances up at the edge of the forest.

Never go back into the woods.

That's what she and Maddie had vowed to each other after they had escaped.

Never go back and never look back.

And Maddie had done both.

Adele takes a break and scans the tree line.

She freezes.

There's someone there, in the forest.

She blinks, wipes sweat from her eyes with the back of her hand, and looks again.

It's a woman, appearing in fragments and flashes of sunlight as she makes her way along the path, moving closer through the shadows. Adele takes an involuntary step toward the tree line, hoping that it's Maddie finally slinking back after her late night. Adele doesn't care, so long as she's safe, her anger from this morning all gone now, curdled and clotted into pure worry.

She remembers Maddie's bag, dropped on the floor by her bed, the neck still open, the letter half out of the envelope from when Bill burst in. She could hurry back and put it all as she'd found it, pretend she'd never seen it, not mention any of it to Maddie at all. But as the figure in the woods draws closer, she realizes that she would rather talk about it, scream and shout and get it all out in the open. Finding the letter had proved how wide the gap between them had become, and she wanted to close it again before that became impossible. So Maddie could scream at her if she wanted. Screaming was better than silence.

But the screaming would have to wait awhile, because the woman emerging from the forest, blinking in the afternoon light, is not Maddie. She glances over at Adele, her face screwed up against the brightness, her body wavering unsteadily.

"Hey," Adele says. "You OK?"

The woman nods her head slowly then looks like she instantly regrets it. Adele reaches for the water bottle on her belt then remembers she gave it to the other casualty earlier. The woman totters toward wherever she's going and Adele watches her, finding some small comfort in the fact that her appearance proves that people are still only now resurfacing after last night's revelries.

She hauls the last bin bag onto the back of the honey-wagon then slides behind the wheel and floors the gas pedal to start her slow and steady journey back to the sanitation station. As she draws closer she sees that Bill's Land Rover is no longer parked outside, so that's one less thing to deal with. It seemed crazy to her that Bill made her drive around in this clapped-out old truck for "good optics and brand consistency" while he drove around in his diesel Discovery, a car about as eco-friendly as setting fire to a pile of old tires.

She pulls to a halt in front of the bins and unloads before heading through the door of the shack, annoyed at Bill for not locking it before he huffed off to wherever he'd gone in his gas guzzler. She takes a breath and pushes open the door to the office, ready to face up to her past and read the letter in Maddie's rucksack. The door swings open and she stops.

Maddie's bag is no longer there. Neither are her bedroll, her trainers, her rucksack, or her sleeping bag. Everything Maddie owns in the world is gone.

Adele stands frozen in the doorway staring down at the empty space where Maddie's things had been. Maybe Bill had taken them, though she couldn't imagine why he would want to steal a ratty bag, a secondhand pair of shoes, and a sleeping bag. Maybe someone else had taken them, the door had been left unlocked after all. Maybe that wasn't all they'd taken!

Adele launches herself across the room, drops to her knees and reaches under her bed, feeling for the loose floorboard. It's still there. Still in place. She hooks her fingers under the gap on one side and prizes it up, reaching down for the tin she keeps stashed beneath the floor. She pulls it out, wrenches off the lid, and blows out a breath of relief when she sees it's all still there.

She closes the lid, puts the tin back under the floorboard, then sits on the floor for a moment, staring at the place where Maddie's things had been, a dusting of grit from her trainers the only evidence anything was ever there at all. She thinks about all the people who would possibly want to steal them and arrives at the obvious answer.

Adele pulls her phone from her pocket and dials Maddie's number for the umpteenth time that day and for the umpteenth time that day it goes straight to voicemail:

Hey, leave me a message and I'll call you back.

"It's me," Adele says. "Listen, I just got back to the shack and saw all your stuff has gone so I was wondering if you'd swung by and taken it because you didn't want to . . . because you were avoiding me, basically. If you did, I just wanted you to know that I'm not mad at you. I was mad earlier, but it's all good now, so you don't have to avoid me. You can text me if you don't want to talk. Just let me know you're okay. OK?"

She hangs up then sends Maddie a text telling her the same thing, only with added smiley face emojis to prove she's not mad. She sends it and stares at her phone, hoping it might buzz with a reply from Maddie, just a thumbs-up, or a heart, or even a middle finger.

Nothing.

She rises wearily from the floor and heads back outside into the afternoon sun, locking both doors behind her before standing in the shade of the shack, scanning the campsite and the fringe of the forest beyond. The girl who had emerged from the woods earlier is now standing by a bell tent, shoulders down, arms folded, while some hipster type—her boyfriend probably—talks at her, frowning and waving his arms about. Adele realizes this is probably what she looks like when she's bawling Maddie out and feels a pang of shame and regret.

She thinks about the letter in Maddie's bag, wishing now she had read it. It had been addressed to the Charcoal Burner Inn in Cinderfield, so Maddie must have been staying there before she'd come to crash with her.

She glances over at the bike shed where campers, or "clients," as Bill likes to call them, can hire mountain bikes during their stay. A couple of men's bikes lean against the rails. Adele walks over and dials in the combination code to unlock the smaller of the two then wheels it out onto the track. The Charcoal Burner Inn is around three miles away on the far side of Cinderfield. There is a shortcut through the forest but there's no way she's taking that, even if that's the way Maddie would most likely have gone.

She pushes off and starts pedaling toward the road in a standing position because the seat is set too high and she doesn't want to waste time adjusting it. If Maddie had snuck back to collect her things and is now on her way back to the pub, Adele wants to get there ahead of her.

18

SHE TURNS HER HEAD TO the side, feeling again for the faint breeze and listening for any sound coming through the open door.

Nothing.

She reaches out, feeling for the edge of the doorway, then takes a small step forward, the soft crunch of dirt underfoot sounding way too loud in the enveloping silence. The darkness beyond the door feels different somehow, as if it has more substance, as if it is less empty.

She takes another step, passing through the doorway then stands for a moment, breathing softly, listening to the silence. It sounds different here too. She clicks her fingers to test it, the sharp snap cracking like a dry bone and instantly swallowed by the dark. In the tunnel the sound was more open, but here it has no echo at all, as if this is a much smaller space.

She reaches out with her hands and takes another step forward, then another, feeling ahead through the darkness until she touches something hard and cold at hip height. She snatches her hand away in surprise, her heart hammering in her chest as she stumbles backward into something else that hits her from behind, knocking the breath from her lungs. She spins around and her hands hit a wall, but not like outside in the tunnel with roots sticking out and loose dirt pattering to the ground—this feels flat and smooth, and warm to the touch, as if this place has been lined with wooden boards, as if it has been built.

Again, she tries not to think about who made it or what its purpose might be and turns back instead to the unseen room. She takes a breath then steps forward, searching again for whatever it was she had touched in the dark. She takes another step and finds it. It feels thin and round, hard like a metal bar or a pipe cutting horizontally across the darkness. She grips it with both hands, feeling the cold of the thing against her flesh, and follows the line of it as it curves down to a kind of shelf with thick material stretched across it that flexes as she presses it, making the tubular frame creak.

It's a chair, one of the old canvas and tubular steel stacking chairs she remembers from her days at The Clearing. She and her sister used to set out chairs like these every month at the moon gatherings when everyone met up to talk about what needed doing around the place.

She turns the chair around so she can sit on it and it knocks against something with a dull, solid thud. She places the chair on the ground and reaches past it, feeling for whatever it had struck, and finds a small, rectangular table pushed up against another wall. She feels her way along that too, hoping she might find another door. Her leg bumps against something at knee height and she reaches down and touches the soft roughness of a blanket. She starts to run her hands across it when a noise behind her makes her head whip around.

A soft creak. A sense of slow movement.

The door she came in, swinging shut.

She launches toward it, stumbling through the dark, arms outstretched. She catches the edge of the chair and sends it clattering to the ground as she stumbles forward, lurching through the dark to catch the door and stop it from closing. But the darkness has turned her around and instead of the door she finds the wall, just as the door bangs shut to her right.

She scrambles across the wooden surface of the wall until the slapping of her hands changes to a deep, hollow boom that tells her she has found the now closed door. Her hands skim frantically across the surface, feeling for the handle but finding only an oval hole too small for her finger to fit inside.

Keyhole, her mind whispers, and she pushes against the door, hoping for movement, though she knows the door opens into the room she is now locked inside. Only it's not a room, is it? A room does not have a door with no handle that only opens from the outside.

But a prison cell does.

19

THREE HOURS!

That's how long the map on Laughton's phone is telling her it will take to get to Cinderfield. She looks up at the evening traffic crawling along the Westway. At this rate it could well be dark by the time she gets there, even with yesterday being the longest day of the year. An ambulance with sirens blaring screams past on the hard shoulder and the traffic comes to a complete standstill.

Not a good sign.

She attempts to connect her phone to the car speakers via Bluetooth, her eyes flicking between it and the stationary traffic. She'd downloaded an audiobook about the Cinderman legend before leaving her flat and figured she might as well do some research during the lengthening journey ahead of her. The car creeps forward a little and beeps as it pairs with her phone. She is about to start the audiobook playing when her phone rings, the sound of it loud in the car's speakers. She smiles when she sees who it is.

"Hey," she says.

"Hey yourself." Tannahill's voice fills the car, making her wish the rest of him were filling it too. "Listen," he says, his voice sounding serious, "I've only got a minute but I just wanted to say, I got talking to a DCI from Hereford here at the conference. He used to be based in Gloucestershire and says the whole of the Gloucestershire Constab is a nest of vipers, rotten from the head down. It's why he transferred out, couldn't deal with it anymore."

"So?"

"So, you said you were thinking of heading there and doing some digging about for your missing person and I'm not sure that's the best idea."

"I'm already on my way."

There's a pause. The traffic edges forward a little.

"You could always turn around," Tannahill says.

"No, I can't."

"Why not?"

"Because if I do that, then no one will be looking for this missing girl."

Another pause. "You could push things along remotely. Send a few emails, make a few calls."

"Emails are too easy to ignore. Phone calls go unanswered. I'm harder to ignore if I'm actually there."

"Yeah, that's what I'm worried about. Listen, why don't you wait until I'm back? I'm owed some days in lieu because of this conference, wait until I'm back then we can go together."

Laughton takes a deep breath, half touched and half annoyed by Tannahill's concern. "What do we know about missing persons cases?" she says.

"What do you mean?"

"I mean, what's the key factor about the start of any missing persons investigation?"

There's another pause before Tannahill reluctantly answers. "The first seventy-two hours are the most important."

"Exactly. So if I wait for you to come back it may already be too late. This girl went missing last night so we've already lost a day, and she's not the first. There's something very wrong going on here and someone needs to find out what it is."

"Agreed, but it doesn't necessarily have to be you!"

"Yes it does, who else is going to do it?" Another silence. Snakes of heat twist in the air above the stationary traffic. "Listen, I'll be fine. I'm a big girl, I can look after myself."

"I imagine that's what the missing girl thought too. And you're not a big girl, you're five foot nothing."

Laughton smiles. "I have a big person's energy though."

"You have an annoying person's energy. Listen, I've got to go. Promise me you won't do anything reckless, and promise you'll keep in touch. Don't you go disappearing on me."

"I promise."

"And call me the moment you get there so I can start worrying properly."

"Will do."

The phone clicks as Tannahill hangs up. Laughton presses Play on her audiobook and settles back in her seat as the rich, deep voice of the narrator pushes back the low hum of the traffic.

"*Green Men and Cindermen—Myths and Legends of the Forest of Dean.* Collected by the Reverend. E. L. Newboldt. Read by Hugh Ross."

Laughton nudges the volume up a little as the traffic continues to creep past the accident she can now see up ahead.

"Chapter One. The Cinderman.

"A long time ago, back in the days when good King Henry sat on the throne and was still happily married to the first of his six wives, there lived in the Forest of Dean a charcoal burner and his wife. All was prosperous in the land and the forest was alive with carpenters, cutting down the mightiest oaks to build the ships that would sail the globe and make England the greatest and most powerful country since Italy spawned the Romans.

"The charcoal burner prospered too, gathering all the discarded branches to arrange in artful stacks he would then cover in damp turf and fire using a technique his father had taught him. By this method the charcoal burner and his wife turned free wood into charcoal, which they sold for a pretty penny to all the blacksmiths and iron smelters who also thrived in the great and bountiful forest.

"A few years after they were wed, the charcoal burner and his wife, having saved enough to build a cottage in the woods, were further blessed with a child, a bonny baby with soft pink cheeks and golden hair. The child quickly grew into a beautiful young girl, as kind as she was fair, who learned how to mend and cook with her mother, and how to stack the branches around the mottle pins with her father, and tend to the smoldering mounds of turf over long, careful days that saw the worthless wood turn into the foundation of their fortune.

"When the girl was not yet ten, however, a curse fell upon the land. Good King Henry broke from God and Church, then cut off the head of the wife he had done it for. Storms shook the trees of the forest, bringing rain so heavy it flattened the crops and rotted them where they grew. And the king, warring with God Himself in heaven now, no longer had interest or money to spend on earthly weapons, so all the shipwrights and iron smelters and blacksmiths disappeared from the woods, and as suddenly as it had arrived the prosperity was gone.

"With famine creeping through the forest, the wife of the charcoal burner, once so soft and gentle, began to become hardened and sharp.

"'What are we to do?' she would whisper to her husband as they lay in the black emptiness of each bleak night.

"'How are we to feed ourselves when there is scarce enough food for one, let alone three?'

"'Something will turn up,' the charcoal burner would reply, for he had no other answer to give, no other trade to turn to but the one his father had taught him, and nothing but hope to cling to.

"'God will provide if we place our trust and faith in Him.'

"But the wife, being a practical woman who had known hunger in her youth and learned hard lessons at her own mother's knee, knew that hope was not enough to save them. As a girl she had seen hope stand idle while the hopeful starved, until her practical mother had taken it upon herself to save what she could of her family. Faced now with a similar problem, she came up with a practical solution of her own, one that had nothing to do with hope and everything to do with the strength of mind and determination she had seen her mother display.

"Midsummer came, yet the weather remained cold and wintry, and her husband, still carrying hope in his heart, set out on a few days' journey to try to sell some bushels of charcoal to the itinerant farriers at Cinderfield Fair. As soon as he was gone, the charcoal burner's wife told her daughter to fetch the best basket and follow her into the forest that they might collect what they could to boost their meager larder.

"The daughter, weak from hunger but ever dutiful, took her basket and followed her mother, head down against the rain, along the slick, muddy path that fringed the banks of Black Water Ponds and into the darkest and most remote part of the forest. On she trudged, though the pathways became choked with bracken and brambles that tore at her thin clothes and scratched her legs, until eventually they reached a small clearing. Here the weak light had managed to drip down to the forest floor to ripen a handful of berries and tempt a few clumps of slimy mushrooms up from the sodden ground.

"'Find what you can, child,' the mother told her, and the girl set to work, her sharp eyes spotting the tiny berries in the thicket, her nimble fingers plucking them from between dense thorns until the juice stained her fingers red. So intent was she on finding what food she might among the thorns and briars that she did not see her mother steal up behind her. She did not see the darkness in her hungry and determined eyes, or the sharp, heavy rock in her hand, rising up toward the small patch of gray sky framed by the high green of the forest. Up and up, then down and down.

"A few days later, as evening fell and the rare sun dipped below the clouds long enough to thread golden fingers of light through the smoke-shrouded trees, the charcoal burner returned home leading a donkey laden with supplies and bursting with news.

"'We are saved!' he exclaimed, and he grabbed his wife and whirled her round in the golden evening light as he told her how he'd met an iron merchant at the Cinderfield Fair who had bought every sack of charcoal on the spot and given him a golden guinea on account to deliver the same to his smelting works at Coleford before the rising of each new moon.

"'But where is the child?' he asked, breaking off from the dance and fetching a slab of honey cake wrapped in brown paper from one of the saddlebags.

"His wife let out a sigh, as sad as anything the charcoal burner had ever heard, then turned and walked into the cabin without reply.

"The charcoal burner followed, expecting to find his daughter inside, but all that stirred in the smoky cabin was a cauldron of soup bubbling softly over the fire.

"'You must be so weary from your travels,' his wife said in a strange, breathy voice he did not recognize. She took a bowl from the shelf, ladled some broth into it, and held it out to him.

"'Eat,' she said in her strange, uncanny voice. 'Eat the broth and you shall be restored.'

"The charcoal burner stared at the bowl but did not take it.

"'Where is the child?' His voice was low and brittle, for he dreaded what the answer might be.

"'What has become of our daughter?'

"His wife sat down at the table, showing no sign she had heard his question, and started to eat the broth, spooning the thin liquid in a strange and delicate manner then raising it to her lips, almost like a kiss.

"The charcoal burner, fearing his wife had been bewitched and dreading what she might have done, ran from the cottage, calling his daughter's name, pleading with her to answer and follow the sound of his voice so she might find her way safely home.

"All through that night and the following day he ranged through the forest, calling her name and searching for the tracks where his daughter had traveled. But the rain that had fallen almost without cease since he had set off for the fair had long since washed clean all trace of her final journey, as it now washed away the charcoal burner's tears.

"And in the cabin his wife wept too.

"She sat by the fire, stirring the broth, ready for her husband's return, clutching the guinea he had brought back, stroking its yellow surface and murmuring to herself: 'Such pretty gold hair she has, such golden locks as e'er was seen, nor e'er will be seen again.'

"And every time she heard her husband's voice calling out their daughter's name, it chipped another piece from her hardened heart, and her tears fell, adding bitter seasoning to her strange soup until she could bear it no longer and she rose from her stool and walked out into the rain. She retraced the last steps she had taken with her daughter, picking up stones and rocks as she went, tucking them into her apron pocket until she reached Black Water Ponds and the sound of her husband calling her daughter's name had melted away in the heavy hiss of rain. She stood for a moment, her eyes following the path that wound around the bank she had last trod with her daughter, then she walked into the ice-cold water, stroking the golden guinea as she went, murmuring over and over, 'Such golden locks as e'er was seen, nor e'er will be seen again.'

"She said it even as the water closed over her head, the rocks in her apron pulling her down into the black weeds, the words forming bubbles that rose to the surface and popped to make circles that spread and flattened until they reached the edge of the pond and the surface of the water became still once more.

"When the charcoal burner finally returned home, delirious with exhaustion, and found his wife too was gone, he fell to his knees and cursed God for betraying his faith and trust. He vowed never to rest until he was reunited with his wife and daughter, in this world or the next, then he sat alone at his humble table and supped on the broth his wife had made before setting out again into the vastness of the forest.

"On some nights people say they can hear him still, calling out for his lost loves, and generations of mothers have warned their daughters to watch out in the woods, especially around Midsummer, and never to walk there alone lest the charcoal burner find them and take them to replace those whom he had once lost.

"Some people say they have seen him, standing apart and watching from the summer shadows, the damp smell of smolder lingering in the air whenever he is close, though the charcoal burners have long since gone from the forest.

"And though the names of this tragic charcoal burner and his family have been lost to time, he has earned himself a new name, a name filled with equal parts mystery, and sadness, and fear.

"'Beware,' fearful mothers across the centuries have warned their wide-eyed girls. 'Watch out for the Cinderman.'"

20

THE CHARCOAL BURNER INN IS crammed with the early-evening crowd by the time Adele arrives. She wheels the bike over to the side of the pub, feeling sticky from the ride over and the accumulated grime of the day, and stashes it behind the bins before walking into the beer garden. The tables are all full, tourists mainly, some still wearing their costumes from the Midsummer Parade the night before. At one table a Green Man is asleep on his folded arms, surrounded by empty cider bottles, the ivy in his hair looking as wilted as he does. At another is a group of young men all dressed as Cindermen and somewhat ruining their overall look by vaping, though one at least is smoking an old-fashioned roll-up.

"Adele!" A voice cuts through the burble of conversation and she looks for the origin in the crowd. "Adele, over here!"

She spots a group of locals clustered around a table on the far side of the garden in the shade of a large sycamore tree. In the center is Merrick, one of the people she called earlier about Maddie, so she weaves her way over, past packed tables and people carrying precarious trays full of drinks until the thick, sweet smell of weed hits her as she arrives at the table.

"You found her yet?" Merrick asks.

"No." Adele looks around at the rest of the group and spots Shep, one of Maddie's crowd whom she'd also called earlier.

"Hey, Shep, did you get my messages about Maddie?"

Shep regards her through the coil of smoke rising from the glowing end of his roll-up then nods slowly.

"Any idea where she might be?"

He shrugs. "Maybe the Cinderman got her." He laughs at his own joke in a way that suggests he's drunk or high enough to find pretty much anything funny. A couple of others join in, clearly in a similar state.

Maddie stares at him, hard enough to kill the laughter.

Shep raises his hands in mock surrender, but with the smirk still spread across his face. "Sorry, bad joke. I'm sure she's just on a bender with some dude. It's Maddie, right?" He looks around the table and several heads nod in automatic agreement.

Adele wants to kick the smirk right off his face but he's on the other side of the table, and judging by the glassy state of his eyes, she doubts he'd even feel it.

She turns back to Merrick. "You seen Martin?"

"Yeah, he's inside."

"Thanks."

"She'll turn up," Merrick says. "You know Maddie, she always does."

Adele nods. "So everyone keeps saying."

She walks away from the table and the muffled giggles of Shep and his stoned mates, and enters through the low door of the inn, built almost seven hundred years earlier, when anyone over five feet tall was considered a giant. She had worked here one summer and developed a backache from all the ducking beneath beams and low doors. She stands in the entrance for a moment, letting her eyes adjust to the gloom, scanning the room for Martin, the landlord. A few more locals are propping up the bar, giving off unfriendly vibes. They glance over then turn away again and start having a whispered conversation, probably about Maddie. News travels fast in a place like this, and it pisses Adele off that everyone knows her sister's missing, and yet rather than do anything about it, they hang around in the pub and make jokes instead.

Her eyes settle on a stiff, well-dressed-looking family sitting at a table at the back of the room—a mum, a dad, and two teenage daughters. The parents look like they're in their sixties, though the age of their daughters suggests they must be younger. The girls look about the same age she and Maddie had been when they ran away from their last foster home. She looks away before the weight of her memories drags her down and spots Martin huffing through the door behind the bar, looking even more red-faced and sweaty than usual. He glances up at her as she heads over then looks back down, grabs a jug, and yanks a pump handle until foam sputters from the tap. Adele reaches the bar and waits for him to look up, but he keeps on angrily pumping beer and foam into the jug.

She clears her throat. "Hey, Martin, have you seen Maddie?"

Martin snorts. "No, I have not."

Adele registers the hostility. Martin is famously grumpy, but this feels like something deeper. "Are you expecting her at all?"

"I was until she dropped me in it. I only said she could stay here if she covered the evening shifts, and I've had to cover them myself, so she can whistle if she's expecting any wages owed."

He bangs the jug of beer down, grabs another, and hauls on the handle to resume pumping.

"Did something happen to make her leave?"

"No. She'd been here awhile, absolutely no problem. I was even thinking of offering her more permanent work, so thank God I didn't bother. She's her own worst enemy, your sister, and if she's sent you round to pick up her things you can tell her she can come get them herself."

"What things?"

"She left a bunch of her crap behind when she did a runner."

"Could I see it?"

"No. I told you, if she wants it she can come get it herself."

Adele takes a breath and tries to keep the frustration out of her voice. "Yes, I get that, but she's missing, so she can't come and get her stuff, and there might be something in there that will tell us where she's gone."

Martin bangs another jug down on the bar top. "I'm not letting you have her stuff, all right? She can stay lost for all I care."

One of the locals at the bar snorts, and Adele glares at him, her anger and frustration building inside her. "My sister's missing," she says.

The man snorts again. "Yeah, but it's only Maddie."

Adele's anger explodes inside her and before she realizes what she's doing, she grabs the jug of beer from the bar and hurls it at him. He cries out in pain and surprise as it strikes him hard on the shoulder and he falls back off his stool just as the jug hits the floor and shatters, sending beer and glass everywhere.

"Jesus!" Martin launches himself through the hatch in the bar, grabs Adele by the shoulders, and starts marching her out past the shocked little family, their forkfuls of food paused halfway to their mouths. "Get out!" he hollers, shoving her out through the door. "You're barred. And that goes for your sister too."

"Give me Maddie's things!" Adele shouts back at him.

"No!" he bellows. "And if you don't leave right now I'm going to call the police."

He glares at her for a moment then turns and walks back inside.

Adele feels like running after him, jumping on his back, raining fists down on his head until he gives in and lets her have Maddie's stuff. She looks around for some kind of weapon and realizes everyone is looking at her, including Merrick and his table of clowns on the far side of the beer garden. Shep leans over, whispers something to the dude sitting next to him, then they both start giggling. Adele feels the anger and frustration of her day expand inside her again like a slow explosion. She opens and closes her hands, making fists that she would dearly love to use, but she knows that's not the way to get things done. If she wants to succeed she needs to play to her own strengths, she needs to be smart.

She looks around, sees a bin crammed with crisp packets and sandwich wrappers, and picks it up to test its weight. It's not quite as heavy as she would like but it will do.

"Hey," she calls over to the table of Cindermen. "You got a light?"

The one smoking a roll-up picks up his lighter from the table and holds it out.

"Thanks." Adele takes it, fires it up, and holds the flame to the edge of a sandwich wrapper in the bin until it catches and thick, black smoke rises up into the blue sky as the rest of the bin catches light. Adele carries the smoking bin back to the pub entrance, places it on the floor, then uses her foot to shove it inside.

Screams echo in the bar as smoke starts to fill it, but Adele is already on the move, around the corner of the pub and heading to the service door at the back of the building. The door has been propped open to try to create a draft for the stuffy, superheated kitchens, just like it had been when she'd worked here. She reaches it and slows a little, checking first to make sure there's no one in the corridor before ducking inside and heading for the stairs. She can hear the sound of shouting out front as she takes the stairs two at a time to the upstairs landing, where she barges through the door into the small box room that used to be hers. It hasn't changed since she stayed here: single bed, chest of drawers, a pair of pale green curtains that don't quite meet in the middle of the small, barred window.

She steps inside, closes the door behind her, and yanks open the drawers. Inside she finds a couple of Maddie's jumpers bundled together with a pink scarf and a cream bobble hat that suggest she planned on coming back when the weather started to turn. The second drawer contains more evidence of Maddie, a lip balm, a notebook and pen, and a couple of envelopes both addressed to her. One is a credit card application, partly filled in with Maddie's childish-looking, block-capital handwriting. The second is brown and official looking, exactly like the one she'd found in Maddie's bag earlier. Adele rips it open, any reservations about what she might find now totally gone. She unfolds the letter, expecting it to be from the Fostering Service, and has to read it twice before her mind registers what it actually is:

Dear Ms. Friar,
We have pleasure in confirming your enrollment in the part-time Introduction
to Business Administration BTEC qualification. The course starts on August
28th at 7:30 p.m. and will take place at the Adult Education Center, 4–6
Commercial Road, Gloucester.

Adele sits down on the edge of the bed and stares at the letter.

Maddie had enrolled in night school.

Maddie!

She experiences a brief moment of pride and sadness: pride that her flaky, feckless sister had gotten it together enough to make some actual grown-up plans for once, and sadness that she had never thought to tell her about it. It also suggested that Maddie had no intention of disappearing. Why make plans for the future if you're not going to be around?

The sound of footsteps thumping up the stairs snatches her attention back to the present, and she looks up just as the door flies open. Martin glares down at her, his face so red and glossed with sweat it looks like a varnished beet.

Adele stands up and glances past him, looking for an escape, but Martin is too big and fills the doorway. He opens his mouth to speak and she braces herself for an earful but in the end he just shakes his head and slams the door shut. Adele hears the sound of a key being turned in the lock and leaps forward, hammering her fists on the door.

"Let me out," she calls out. "You can't lock me up in here."

"Really?" Martin shouts back at her, his heavy footsteps already receding down the staircase. "Save it for the police. They're on their way here right now."

21

SHE LEANS WITH HER BACK against the closed door, staring into the total darkness, the sound of her own heartbeat booming in her ears.

She can't be locked in. She can't!

She had felt a breeze. She was sure of it, which meant there had to be another way out of here.

She edges forward into the room, sweeping her leading foot in front of her until it kicks the chair, lying on its side where she'd knocked it over in her hurry to get to the closing door.

She picks it up and drags it back over to the wall then carefully stands on it and reaches up until her hands find the ceiling, which is flat and smooth, like the walls. She runs her hands along it, as far as she can safely reach in every direction, then carefully steps off the chair, moves it along a few steps, and repeats the process, over and over, gradually building a picture of the cell in her mind.

It is small, maybe twelve feet by eight, and contains only the table, the bed, and the chair. There is nothing else. The walls and ceiling are solid and featureless, clad in large sheets of wood that feel splintery in places. There are no vents, no hatches, and the only way out of the room is the door, which is now closed and locked.

She feels her way back to the bed and sits on the edge of it, staring into the dark, sweating slightly from her efforts, her arms aching from holding them above her head for so long.

Her mind tumbles with questions—

What is this place?

How did I get here?

How do I get out?

—and she feels the helplessness of her situation settle heavily on her. She lies down on the bed, the material of the blanket feeling scratchy against her skin. She stares ahead, knowing that the edge of the narrow single bed is right in front of her eyes. It shakes loose a memory, long buried and not welcome.

When she was a kid she'd had a bed exactly like this—metal frame, thin mattress, scratchy blanket. And every night she would lie in it and imagine a face rising up slowly from beneath the bed, inches from her own, eyes wide and staring. She would lie there, eyes shut tight, fighting the urge to open them in case the thing was really there. Sometimes it would freak her out so much she'd have to climb in with her sister, who would usually get mad at her for waking her up.

Lying here now, knowing the edge of the bed is right in front of her but unable to see it, is strange. It should be the scariest thing of all and yet, somehow, she is more intrigued by it than frightened.

Then she realizes why.

She did not check under the bed.

She reaches out, her left hand moving across the scratchy blanket, over the edge of the mattress and down below the bed, tensed for what might be waiting there—a grabbing hand, something cold and slimy, a vicious bite. Her fingertips touch the cold, dirt floor and she lets out a breath and pauses for a second before twisting her hand and sliding it under the bed as far as it will go. The springs of the bed creak as she sweeps her hand across the ground in a slow arc, reaching as far as she can.

Nothing there.

She rolls off the bed and lies flat on the ground, reaching further under the bed. If there is another way out of here, a trapdoor or a hatch, or any kind of hole in the wooden walls where the phantom breeze might have come from, then it has to be here.

Her cheek presses against the dirt floor as she stretches her hand out into the solid blackness then stops abruptly as her hand touches something.

There is something there.

22

THE CELLS BENEATH THE CINDERFIELD police station are dark and dank, a relic of a time when crime was met with punishment rather than any attempt at rehabilitation. They drip with damp and are encrusted with white crystalline streaks leached from the solid rock the cells were carved from when the police station was built, three hundred years earlier. Since that time these underground dungeons have hosted every stripe of local offender, from common drunks to con men, burglars, cattle thieves, two suspected witches, three confirmed murderers, and an infamous local clergyman who killed a child he believed to be possessed. The cells were decommissioned in the nineties, deemed no longer fit for purpose, but are still reopened each year for the Midsummer Fair to serve as a temporary jail, mostly for drunkards and vandals.

Tonight there is just one guest.

Adele paces the cryptlike space, feeling angry, uneasy, and increasingly uncomfortable. She reaches one end, turns and looks at the tiny cell, illuminated by a fly-blown strip of fluorescent lighting that casts a harsh, headachy light through the floor-to-ceiling bars and onto a thin ledge that runs along one wall, slightly too wide to be a bench, slightly too narrow to function as a bed. A battered zinc bucket is chained to the bars so it can't be picked up and used as a weapon. This is the "toilet facility," and Adele badly needs to use it, but can't quite bring herself to do it.

She looks up at the ancient closed-circuit camera fixed on the ceiling outside the cell and linked to a monitor by the sergeant's desk in reception, which Adele noticed when she was being booked. She had also noticed how the bucket was in the center of the frame, placed where the light was brightest. She steps over and slides the bucket across the floor with her foot, the rasp of metal over concrete stopping with a snap as the chain goes tight. It can't be moved, not away from the camera's gaze at least. Maybe a guy could use it and somehow manage to maintain some degree of privacy, but not a woman.

She takes a deep breath and catches the stench of mold, stale sweat, and disinfectant that was slopped over the floor earlier to try to mask the stench of vomit left by the drunken war memorial decorators who were sent on their way after they finally sobered up. She tries breathing through her mouth but ends up tasting everything instead, which is worse.

She kicks the bucket in frustration then waves her arms over her head.

"Hey!" she calls out, her voice echoing down the corridor and up the stairs.

"HEY!"

She waves her hands at the camera and takes a big breath of foul-tasting air. "HEEEY!!"

There is a thunk as the door at the top of the stairs unlocks, then the sound of deliberately slow footsteps coming down the stairs.

Adele steps back from the bars, instinctively crossing her arms across her chest as the unhelpful desk sergeant from earlier appears, his face fixed in an expression somewhere between boredom and annoyance.

"What?" he says.

"I really need the toilet."

He looks at her for a beat then nods at the bucket. "Off you go then."

"I can't go in that."

"Well, you're going to have to piss yourself then, aren't you?" He turns and starts to waddle away, his bulk shifting from side to side and almost filling the narrow corridor.

"Wait. Please." He stops and turns slowly back around. "You can't seriously expect me to go in a bucket."

"You're in a police cell, love, not a five-star hotel."

"I know that, but I'm pretty sure you're not allowed to keep people locked up in these kinds of conditions."

"Really? You an expert on the law now, are you? What are you going to do, film me on your phone and threaten to post it online?" He taps a sausage of an index finger against his lips in mock thoughtfulness then his bushy eyebrows shoot up as if he's had a revelation. "Oh, no, you can't do that can you because all your stuff is in a box upstairs because you got nicked for trying to set fire to a pub."

"It was a bin, not a building. How long am I going to be in here? My sister might be trying to call and I haven't even got my phone."

The sergeant takes a sudden step closer, which makes Adele take one back, despite the bars separating them. "Listen, love," he hisses, elastic bands of spit stretching at the corners of his mouth as he speaks. "No one cares about your sister and no one cares about you. You're just a pain in the arse causing problems. Now, I'm at the shitty end of a twelve-hour shift that started with you waving your phone in my face and making all kinds of threats. I've had to deal with a nonstop parade of whining tourists who seem to think this is a bloody tourist information center, I've got a pile of paperwork that seems bigger now than when I started, and I've had to mop up some puke. So if you think I'm going to drop everything to escort you to the bog so you can have a comfy piss then you're having a laugh. If you need to go"—he jabs a pudgy finger at the bucket—"there it is. Now I've got half an hour of my shift left and I don't want to hear one more word out of you, do you understand?"

Adele opens her mouth to say something, realizes it's pointless, and closes it again.

The sergeant nods. "Good!"

He turns and waddles away, leaving a faint smell of stale sweat behind to mingle with all the other unpleasant odors.

Adele watches him leave, the muscles in her jaw clenching so tightly it makes her teeth ache. Maybe she can hang on for half an hour until the shift changes and someone new comes in, someone more reasonable, hopefully. She looks back down at the bucket and feels like crying. Not because of the humiliation of her situation, or even the pain in her swollen lower stomach, but because she knows that as long as she's locked in this medieval cell, no one is looking for Maddie.

23

SHE LIES VERY STILL FOR a moment, her fingertips resting against the solid object beneath the bed.

She adjusts her position to reach further and the object moves, but only slightly, just enough to prompt a rush of disappointment. She had hoped it might be the frame of a trapdoor built into the floor, something that could give her a way out of this room, but it's not. It's just another object she cannot see, another mystery in the dark.

She reaches further under the bed and her fingers find an edge. She hooks them round it then pulls the object toward her. The thing is not big but has some weight to it and drags slightly on the uneven ground as she slides it out from under the bed. She runs her hands over it, feeling its shape, looking for details, building a picture of it in her mind. It is small, rectangular, made of wood. She picks it up and something shifts inside, making a soft rumbling sound. She shakes it and the rumble comes again along with a soft, dry rattle that makes her think of insects.

She places the box on the ground and starts feeling her way over the surface, searching for a way inside. The top edge is raised on three sides and there is a slight indentation in the middle of the fourth. Her finger fits neatly into it, and when she pushes toward the edge, the whole of the top slides neatly off.

She stares down in the dark at the spot where she knows the box lies open, listening again for the dry insect rattle or any other movement. After a few seconds of silence she takes a breath and reaches inside.

The first thing her fingers touch is something cold and round. She picks it up, sniffs it, then frowns when she realizes what it is.

It's an apple. A fresh apple. Which means it must have been left here recently. She puts it back, despite the growl of hunger that rumbles in her stomach, and feels around to see what else the box contains. Her fingers touch something waxy, a short cylinder or tube of some kind, tapering to a point at one end, and she lets out a gasp when she realizes what it is.

It's a candle, and there's a whole bundle of them in the box, ten maybe. She remembers the rattle earlier and plunges her hand back into the box, digging beneath the candles until her fingers close around the matchbox buried beneath them. She pulls out a match with trembling fingers and drags it along the rough edge.

The flare of the striking match is physically painful after being so long submerged in the darkness. She has to screw her eyes shut and wait for the flame to settle before slowly opening them again to get her first look at the room.

It is smaller than she had imagined, and truly frightening to behold. But it is not the cell-like nature of the room that makes fear take full flight in her chest, it's what's on the walls.

24

DOG DRIVES THE STOLEN MINICAB down the quiet, empty streets of Cinderfield, past all the new coffee shops and the Farmer's Market Emporium selling cheap local produce at inflated tourist prices. He slows a little as he drives by the redstone police station. There's a light on inside. He checks the time then cruises past.

A couple of miles out of town he pulls in by a large sign at the entrance to what used to be a patch of woodland. Skeletons of half-constructed houses are faintly sketched against the deep black-purple of the night sky. He kills his engine and the lights and sits, listening to the sounds of the night through his open window. It's so quiet he can hear the tick of the engine as it starts to cool and the rustle of something moving in the hedgerow, a bird probably, disturbed by his car and now settling back in its nest.

He looks up at the big sign.

FOREST ACRES

Set in the scenic Forest of Dean, with natural beauty on its doorstep.
3- and 4-bedroom homes for any lifestyle, from first-time buyers to families looking for their forever home.

SALES OFFICE AND SHOW HOME OPEN DAILY.

There is a picture of a modern, executive-style house surrounded by trees, with a smiling young family standing in front of it. He gets out of the car, hops the gate, and walks down the road among the silent row of identical houses in various stages of completion. The show house is nearest to the entrance, its garage turned into a sales office with warm lights glowing in the lower windows, as if the perfect family on the billboard have already moved in. He peers inside at a beige living room decorated with matching IKEA furniture; large, framed photographs of landscapes and mountains; and some artfully arranged twigs in vases.

He moves on and walks further into the site, the houses becoming less and less complete the further he gets from the road. He stops at a plot that has been marked out and had trenches dug for the pipework. The foundations have been dug too and a stack of rebar lies on some pallets over to one side, ready for the concrete foundations to be poured. He imagines the perfect family on the billboard moving into their new "forever" home, little realizing a body is entombed beneath it. Would they experience strange things in that room, he wonders, a cold spot in summer, a stain that can't be scrubbed away?

He checks the time again.

Half past midnight. The witching hour.

He walks back toward the road, gets in the car, and drives back into town.

She will be released just before one in the morning, the message had said: "Due to the lateness of the hour a minicab will be arranged to take her home."

25

THE DESK SERGEANT ADDS ANOTHER file to his Done pile then arches his back to stretch some of the tension out. He glances at the monitor. Adele is still pacing in the cell back and forth like a caged cat. He smiles at the thought of how annoyed and powerless she must feel. Uncomfortable too. She hasn't used the bucket yet so she must be fit to burst.

The sudden ring of the doorbell makes him jump. He checks his watch—quarter to one. Bit late for tourists. Maybe it's just some kids dicking around.

The doorbell rings again, longer this time, suggesting that whoever it is they're not going away. He hauls himself out of the chair and stomps across the reception area to open the door.

The person standing on the other side is small, bordering on tiny, her blond hair scraped back from a heart-shaped face and big eyes looking up at him with an alertness that seems at odds with the lateness of the hour.

"Can I help you?" the sergeant asks.

"Sergeant Millbrook?" the woman replies, surprising him a second time.

"Yes, I, er . . ."

"I'm Laughton Rees. Sorry for the late hour but I got a notification through the Police National Computer that you'd arrested an Adele Friar a few hours back for arson and attempted burglary." She holds up her phone so he can see the email.

He peers at it then looks back at her. "I'm sorry," he says, his brain trying to catch up. "Who are you, again, and how come you're getting alerts from the PNC?"

"Oh, yes, sorry, probably should have started with that." She ducks her hand into her jacket pocket and pulls out her Met Police ID card.

"I'm a criminologist and academic. I work directly for the National Crime Agency and am currently on secondment to the Met." She pulls out her NCA card too and holds both ID cards up for Millbrook to inspect. He peers at them, checking the spelling of her name, which he didn't quite catch.

"Professor Laff-ton?"

"It's LAW-ton. My dad's idea. Long story. Anyway, I'm working on a research paper that involves historic disappearances in this area, and I picked up the earlier missing persons alert about Madeleine Friar, also filed by you, I believe?"

He nods.

"Well, I was heading here because of that when I got the second alert that her sister had been arrested, so I thought I'd come straight here and talk to her if that's possible."

The sergeant blinks and leans against the half-open door. "You want to talk to Adele Friar?"

"Yes, please. I'd also like to confirm what's currently happening with the Madeleine Friar disappearance as there doesn't seem to be anything listed on the Misper."

Millbrook looks over her head and down the street, hoping to see his shift replacement hurrying along it to relieve him both of his duties and of this conversation.

"Sergeant Millbrook!" The woman's voice drags his attention back to her oddly penetrating eyes. "May I come in?"

He looks at his watch. There's still another ten minutes before his shift ends. Too long to stall.

"You need to get proper authority and come back in the morning." He moves to close the door but she shoots out a hand and blocks it with a surprising show of speed and strength.

"Whoa, whoa, wait a second." Laughton plants her foot in the gap between the door and the doorframe to stop him closing it any further. "What do you mean get proper authority?"

"I mean you need proper authority before I can give you details of any ongoing investigation."

She holds up her NCA card. "This gives me proper authority," she says. "Unless the investigation has been sealed for some reason. Has it been sealed?"

"No, but I . . ."

"Also, why would I need any special permission to talk to Adele Friar?"

"Well, you're not next of kin or anything."

"No, but I am an officially recognized and sanctioned officer of the law, just like you, and I presume you've spoken to her without the need to get any further authority."

The sergeant looks back at her, his mouth flapping open and shut like a freshly landed fish. He could try forcing the door shut on her but he might break her tiny foot and then he'd be in all kinds of trouble. He takes one last look up the empty street in the vague hope that salvation might be walking down it, then opens the door and stands aside to let the annoying woman with the weird name inside the station.

Laughton catches an odor like old towels and cheese as she squeezes past Sergeant Millbrook and enters the surprisingly shabby interior of the police station. It reminds her of some of the older stations in London; run-down, underfunded, and destined to be sold off to cut costs. The sergeant ambles past her, squeezes through an open hatch in the counter then unlocks a door on the far wall.

"Cells are in here," he says, heading through the door and holding it open for her to follow.

Beyond the door the station is even shabbier, old paint peeling off even older walls and enough broken or faulty lights to make Laughton have to concentrate on each step as she follows the sergeant down to a basement that is, thankfully, several degrees cooler than the floor above. The sergeant unlocks another door then holds it open. "End of the corridor on your right," he says. "Cell C."

Laughton passes through the door and enters a crypt-like chamber that smells like every police cell she's ever been in, a mixture of fear, decay, piss, and disinfectant. She walks along the line of cells getting a distinct *Silence of the Lambs* vibe as she approaches the end of the corridor and half expecting Hannibal Lecter to be standing waiting for her in a too-tight boiler suit. But the occupant of cell C is not standing, she is squatting in the corner by the back wall, her shorts bunched around her knees and a stream of liquid running away from her along the floor.

"Oi!" The sergeant steps forward and bangs his fist hard against the bars. "Stop doing that."

The woman in the cell looks up through a fringe of hair, her eyes almost feral. "Go away!" she snarls.

"You're going to clean that up," the sergeant says, pointing a fat finger at her through the bars.

"I won't!" she screams. "You should have let me go to the toilet when I asked. GO AWAY!"

Laughton wheels on the sergeant and pushes him backward. "Don't you push me," he huffs, a look of surprise on his face, grabbing at the bars to steady himself. "I'll have you for assaulting a police officer."

"She asked us to leave," Laughton says calmly but firmly. "She's clearly in a compromised and vulnerable situation, a position you put her in by the sound of it. Is that true you refused to let her go to the toilet?"

"No!"

"So, she's lying?"

"There's a bucket in her cell, I told her to use that."

"A bucket is not an adequate toilet facility. If she asked you for a comfort break and you refused then you've violated her rights."

The sergeant stares at her in disbelief. "What are you, her lawyer?"

Laughton considers his question. "One sec." She leans back and calls over her shoulder. "Hi, Adele, do you currently have any legal representation?"

There's a pause then a small voice replies from the depths of the cell. "No."

"OK, well then, I'd be happy to represent you."

Another pause, then the small voice rises again. "How much do you charge?"

"Oh, nothing, I'll do it pro bono, which is a fancy way of saying 'for free.'"

"OK," the voice says, moving closer now. Laughton turns to find Adele standing behind her on the other side of the bars. She looks Laughton up and down as she finishes fastening her shorts then nods as if coming to a decision. "You're hired."

Laughton turns back to the sergeant. "As Adele Friar's legal representative, I wish to petition for her immediate release. Also, as she is next of kin, you can explain to her exactly what is currently happening with the investigation into her missing sister, and, as her legal adviser, I will sit in on that interview."

Sergeant Millbrook stares down at her like he's just lost a game of chess and can't quite figure out how.

Somewhere above them a phone starts to ring.

26

SHE STARES AT THE WALLS, the wavering flame from the match casting a shifting orange light across them.

They are covered in marks. Hundreds of them. Tiny vertical lines in groups of four with a diagonal line drawn through each one. Someone has been here before her, trapped in this room, marking the time on the walls. She cannot believe the marks represent days. It's impossible to believe that. They have to represent something else.

The match burns her fingers and she drops it and is plunged once again into darkness. She fumbles another from the box, wondering who had been here before her, and how they managed to keep track of time in this permanent midnight. Did they make a new mark every time they woke from sleep, or lit a new candle? The candles are short and would not burn for long, and she holds on to this thought, because to think that each mark might represent a whole day makes her feel panicky.

She strikes a new match and lights a candle with it, touching the flame to the wick with trembling hands and turning it until it catches, then holds it up to survey the room. She forces herself to ignore the marks for now and looks instead for anything she might have missed—the hidden outline of another door, cameras fixed high in the corners or set into a wall that might suggest someone is watching her, but there is nothing.

She tilts the candle and drips wax on the surface of the table then holds the candle in the puddle until it sets. She lifts the wooden box off the floor and places it on the table next to the candle, feeling faint and light-headed from her awful discovery combined with her growing hunger. She picks up the apple and takes a bite without thinking as she surveys the room again.

So many marks.

She takes another bite of apple, moves over to the furthest corner of the room, and starts counting.

27

DOG WATCHES FROM THE SAFE shadows of the parked minicab. He sees the door to the police station open and spill light and the small blond woman into the night. He had been about to approach the station himself when she had arrived, prompting him to hang back and wait. His instructions had been clear— The girl will be released from Cinderfield police station just before 1 a.m. The streets will be empty. Be there to pick her up. Don't let anyone see you.

He watches her descend the steps now, wondering what prompted her late-night visit to the police station: missing car, missing husband, didn't really matter, so long as she was now on her way somewhere else.

A second figure steps through the door and he leans forward in his seat. She is taller than the first woman, with dark hair, wearing a T-shirt and cut-off jeans. He had recognized Adele Friar the moment he was sent her photo earlier identifying the girl he was supposed to collect and make disappear. He remembered her living at The Clearing, her and her sister both, though neither of them had been there for a while.

The door to the police station closes and Adele walks down the steps to join the other woman on the street. They talk for a moment, or rather the small blond woman talks and Adele listens. Something seems to be agreed then they walk away together, down the street toward a parked car that flashes its lights as it unlocks.

Dog watches them get in then drive off and head out of town. He waits for a few beats then starts following them at a safe distance, their lights making it easy to see them on the otherwise deserted road.

He smiles. He thought this was going to be a simple snatch-and-grab, easy but boring, a Cinderman job. Now it was turning into something more interesting. The thrill of the hunt was always directly related to the intelligence of the animal being hunted: the smarter the animal, the more challenging and rewarding the hunt.

And there was no smarter prey than people.

28

LAUGHTON LEAVES THE WELCOME GLOW of Cinderfield's streetlights behind and enters the looming darkness of the country lanes.

Adele sits next to her in the passenger seat, the crook of her arm hanging out of an open window as warm night air floods into the stuffy interior of the rental car. "Thanks for the lift," she says, "and for getting me out of jail."

"I didn't get you out," Laughton says, peering ahead, not used to driving down dark, unlit roads, or any roads at all for that matter. "That call that came in was an order to let you go, I just happened to be there. You might need to get yourself a lawyer to represent you over the arson charge though."

Adele turns to her. "Aren't you my lawyer?"

"No. I know the law, but I'm not a lawyer." Laughton can feel Adele's eyes studying her.

"So what are you? A copper? A journalist?"

"God no, I'm an academic. I teach criminology, do research projects, and write books. You need a proper lawyer who knows the courts and the judges, though you should be able to plead so it never gets that far. The extenuating circumstances of the stress surrounding your sister's disappearance will certainly help your case, especially as the police are massively adding to that stress by not investigating it properly."

The conversation with Millbrook about the ongoing investigation into Madeline Friar's disappearance had been depressingly short because there wasn't anything to talk about.

"So, what are you doing here?" Adele says, staring out at the dark countryside, her fingers drumming restlessly on the handrest.

"I've been working on a research paper off and on for the past few years examining the overlap between crimes and folklore, and through that I discovered an unusually high number of missing persons reported in this area, often attributed to a particular local legend."

"The Cinderman."

"Yes."

Adele shakes her head, thinking of all the times people have already told her that maybe the Cinderman took her sister. "That's just a story people tell their kids to stop them from going into the woods. My sister was not taken by the Cinderman."

"No, and neither were any of the other missing women I've discovered, and it is mostly women, which is also weird."

"Really, why?"

"Nationally, seventy-five percent of people who go missing are men. Here it's the other way round, so I came to try to find out what happened to your sister, and also why the police don't appear to be doing anything about finding her or any of the other women who've gone missing here. I'm going to make some calls in the morning, see if I can speak to someone senior and get more of an overview. In the meantime, can you think of anyone who might have wanted to harm your sister in any way? Anyone she might have pissed off?"

"Maddie pisses off plenty of people, but not enough to make them want to do her harm. I mean, I'm probably the person she pisses off the most, and I certainly don't hate her."

"Are you close?"

Adele considers the question. "We've been through a lot together, enough that if she was planning on leaving suddenly, she would definitely have told me first."

"What about boyfriends? Any jealous, violent types in her past?"

Adele snorts. "Maddie tends to go for the wet, stoner types. I doubt anyone of them would dare even raise their voice to her."

"That doesn't mean we shouldn't consider them. Just because someone isn't physically strong doesn't mean they can't be dangerous. There are plenty of crimes committed against strong women by weak men because they feel inadequate." She glances over at Adele. "Not that I'm saying anything has happened to your sister, I'm just saying we shouldn't rule out ex-boyfriends because they don't seem the type. Often the ones who don't seem the type are exactly the type, if you see what I mean."

Adele nods. "I get what you're saying, but I still don't think any of Maddie's exes would have the energy or the . . . balls to do anything bad to her."

She pictures Ronan, with his floppy hair and spaghetti arms. "Actually, someone did mention that Maddie was supposed to meet a guy last night," she says, remembering their earlier conversation.

"OK, that sounds like a good place to start."

"I'm just in here." Adele points at a sign ahead and Laughton slows down and flicks on her indicator out of habit, though they haven't passed another car on the entire journey. She turns on to a gravel drive by a sign with THE SITE spelled out on it in cut pieces of wood, then crunches slowly along it, the car's headlamps sweeping over tents and old VW minivans sitting silent and still, like strange creatures sleeping in the night. They follow the track to a scruffy shed that looks like it's about to fall down and Laughton pulls to a stop next to an equally rickety-looking vehicle.

"Thanks for the lift," Adele says.

"You live here?" It comes out sounding more abrupt than Laughton had intended.

"Yep." Adele fumbles at the door handle. "Living the dream." She attempts a smile but turns away quickly and seems to crumple before Laughton's eyes, her head dropping, her shoulders starting to shake.

Laughton reaches out, hesitates, then lays a comforting hand on her shoulder. "I'm sorry, I didn't mean that to sound . . ." She can feel Adele trembling. "I was just surprised. Listen, I used to sleep on the streets on pieces of cardboard spread out in shop entrances, so I'm really not being judgy. You go ahead and have a good cry. Crying's healthy, gets rid of emotions that would otherwise fester. You'd be weird if you weren't crying given the day you've just had. Do you want me to come inside with you, make sure you're OK?"

"No, honestly, I'm fine. Anyway, this place looks even worse on the inside."

Laughton smiles and opens her car door. "I've got a teenage daughter, I doubt there's any mess you can show me that would come even close to her bedroom."

She gets out and walks over to the shed, giving Adele no option but to follow.

Dog watches them through the night-vision scope of his illegal hunting crossbow. He centers on Adele as she gets out of the car and keeps her in the crosshairs until she disappears behind the edge of the building.

He climbs up out of the dry ditch and moves into the campsite in a low, crouching run, keeping his steps short and quiet. He reaches one of the trees and tucks in behind it, sinking lower to the ground before edging around it. He can see them again in the distance, lit by the light from a phone. He raises his nightscope and the two figures jump into view. Much closer now. He settles into position and watches, waiting for the short, blond woman to leave so he can make his move.

Adele dials in the combination code then pushes open the door and switches the light on as she steps inside.

Laughton follows. "Jesus, it's hot in here."

"You get used to it." Adele moves over to another door with another combination lock. "At least it's free."

She opens the door, revealing a room not much bigger than a cupboard, and heads over to the narrow cot bed to plug in her phone. Laughton steps up to the open door and looks across at the written pages stuck to the wall.

"Oh that's—" Adele flaps her hand at the wall. "It's silly, it's just positive mental attitude crap."

"It's not silly at all. When I was living on the streets I used to write inspirational things on my hand in pen because I didn't have a wall."

"Were you really homeless?"

"Yep, for a time."

"How did you turn things around?"

Laughton thinks for a moment. "Well, the long answer is I got clean, went back to school, got a job, worked really hard for years, but the shorter answer and the real reason is I got pregnant."

"Really!?"

"Yeah. I was in a self-destructive spiral. Lost. Ran away from home. Cut off all ties. Didn't care what happened to me. Didn't care if I lived or died. Then all of a sudden I was responsible for something other than just me. That's when I started writing things on my hand." She thinks about Gracie, out there in the world now, on her own, and it makes her feel such a sudden and overwhelming sense of protectiveness that when she looks up at Adele sitting on her single bed with its thin mattress, she can't bring herself to leave her here.

"Listen, why don't you come and stay with me? I've booked an Airbnb that's way bigger than I need because it was all I could find at such late notice. It's got two bedrooms, two bathrooms. You'll probably know exactly where it is, too, whereas I could easily spend the rest of the night driving around looking for it."

Adele looks down at the floor, seeming like she might be about to cry again.

"It makes total sense," Laughton says. "We'll need to work closely with each other to find your sister and time is precious. The first seventy-two hours in any disappearance are crucial, and we've already lost a day. If we were in the same place, it would make things a million times easier."

Adele looks up at her. "Are you sure?"

"Oh my God, absolutely. You'll be doing me a favor, I'll cack myself all alone in a cabin in the woods. I'm a city girl. All this darkness and silence gives me the creeps."

Light spills out into the night as the door to the shack swings open. Dog watches through the nightscope as the driver of the car steps out. He is close enough to see her face now and he lingers on it for a moment, tracking her movement as she walks over to her car. She turns and looks back at the shack and he pans across in the direction of her gaze to catch Adele stepping out of the door. She switches off the light then closes the door and starts walking over to the car.

Dog centers the crosshairs on her chest and slightly to the left, his finger curling round the trigger, ready.

It looks like she might be leaving with the other woman, which complicates things. If he's going to do it, now might be his best time.

Don't be seen the message had said. And no one had seen him.

He takes a breath then starts letting it out slowly.

"Sorry." Adele turns abruptly and hurries back to the shack. "I forgot something."

She reenters the stifling dark through the door she'd left unlocked and moves across the creaking floor, not bothering to turn the light on, because it feels better somehow to do what she's about to do in the dark. She reopens the door to her room and hurries over to her bed, dropping to her knees and feeling underneath for the loose floorboard. She prizes it up with her fingernails, lifts the tin out from under the floor, then grabs the bag she's been living out of, like, forever, and hurries back out again, stuffing the tin inside.

Dog watches Adele reemerge from the shack carrying a bag over her shoulder. He recenters the crosshairs on her chest and follows her movement. But if he shoots her now, the other woman is bound to scream. She'll scream, and the couple of hundred other people sleeping in this field will instantly wake. Many of them will choose to ignore it, leave it for someone else to deal with, too scared to investigate themselves, but not everyone. There's always one hero in every crowd. Someone would respond, and the alarm would be raised, and then there would be an investigation, maybe some local press, maybe even national if it's a slow news day. Someone getting killed by an arrow in a campsite in the middle of summer is a good story.

He rests his finger on the side of the trigger guard and watches Adele through the scope. Maybe she'll hand the bag to the other woman, say her goodbyes, then return to the shack. If she's on her own it will be easy, he can take his time, wait for her to fall asleep then break in and deal with her in a way that will make it look like she took off on her own. No screams in the night. No have-a-go heroes. No investigation. No story on the national news.

He tracks Adele all the way to the car and watches her get inside. The car starts up and reverses slowly away from the shack. He unnocks the arrow and holds it in his hand as he sprints back across the campsite, keeping low and away from the lights. He heads to the track where he left his car, ready to follow them wherever they might go.

29

THE SOUND OF TIRES ON tarmac filters in through the open window as Adele reads the directions on the booking confirmation email on Laughton's phone, trying to figure out exactly where the Airbnb is. She used to know all the holiday rentals in the area, had cleaned quite a lot of them, but there are so many more appearing each year, and Cedar Lodge is new to her.

"Take the next left," she says, mentally adjusting the directions which are from Cinderfield, not the campsite, as she tries to figure out where they're going. Laughton slows down and makes the turn. Adele glances up as the headlamps sweep round the corner to light up a long avenue of trees ahead, their branches arching overhead to create a tunnel.

The forest!

They're driving into the forest.

It hadn't occurred to her that Cedar Lodge might actually be in the woods because until recently, no new building was allowed on forest land. The car speeds up and Adele pushes back in her seat, staring ahead, eyes wide in panic, the headlamps lighting up the trees all around as they pass into the tunnel. Adele makes fists with her hands. It feels like the forest is swallowing them, swallowing her. It makes her want to open the door, leap out, and run back up the road to safety. She searches for the door handle with her hand, eyes wide and staring ahead at the looming tunnel of trees, then they emerge as suddenly as they entered and pass back into open fields. She blows out a long breath of relief, causing Laughton to glance over.

"You OK?"

Adele nods. "Yes, I just . . . I don't like the forest."

"Why not?"

"Too many bad memories." She starts to relax a little and they crest a slight rise in the road, the headlights sweeping down to reveal a large figure, standing in the dead center of the road.

Laughton sees it too and stamps on the brakes, sending the luggage in the back crashing into their seats as they lurch to a screeching stop. The car stalls and silence floods in. The thing stands in the road, its eyes reflecting golden in the headlights as it stares straight at them.

"Jesus," Laughton says, half laughing with relief.

The stag tilts its head as if sniffing them or just showing them it isn't afraid, then it turns, jumps through the hedge, and disappears into the night.

"You don't get that in London." Laughton restarts the car and puts it in gear. "Drunks, yes, but not deer."

They move forward, Adele's heart still thumping from the double scare of the forest and the stag. She can see the edge of the forest ahead, drawing closer again, and looks back down at Laughton's phone, checking the address on the booking confirmation email, trying to figure out if it's actually in the forest or not. She looks back up, her heart hammering harder. Then she sees the sign—"Cedar Lodge."

"There," she says, and Laughton pulls off the road and comes to a stop beside a very new and modern-looking log cabin. A single light burns by the entrance, but the windows are dark, making the cabin look a tiny bit spooky against the backdrop of looming trees. It looks nothing like the sunny, dappled photographs she'd been seduced by when she booked it. She looks back over at Adele, who is not looking at the lodge at all, her eyes fixed on the wall of trees behind it.

"Is this too close to the forest?"

Adele shakes her head. "No, it's fine, it's . . . I'm fine."

"OK, good. Let's get inside then and draw the blinds so you can't see it."

Laughton gets out of the car and pulls her bags free from where they've piled up against the backseat. Adele gets out too and follows her over to the cabin, listening to the sounds of the forest whispering and creaking as Laughton taps the code into the key safe next to the door.

"What's that?" Laughton points at a small, handmade cross of twigs by the door hanging from a string of dried berries on a red thread.

"It's a rowan cross," Adele replies, "a protection charm. If you hang it on a door or above a fireplace of a house it's supposed to stop bad luck from getting in."

Laughton opens the key safe and takes the key from inside. "Does it work?"

"Lots of people around here think so, but they believe in all sorts of things. Forest folk are pretty superstitious."

Laughton fits the key in the door and unlocks it. "Do you believe it?"

Adele shrugs. "I've never had a house of my own to keep bad luck from entering," she says, "so it doesn't really matter what I believe."

Laughton opens the door and flicks on the lights to reveal a large, open-plan living-dining space with stairs leading up to a mezzanine.

"Well, this is your home for the next few days." She points up the stairs. "Bedrooms are up there I think, take your pick, I'm not fussed."

Adele is momentarily overcome with emotion. She's cleaned places as nice as this before but never stayed in one. She nods her thanks and smiles, afraid her voice will betray her if she tries to speak, then steps through the door, takes a couple of steps toward the stairs and . . .

Movement . . .

On the far side of the room . . .

Someone there!

She whips her head around, heart hammering, and stares at her shocked self, reflected in the black mirror of the floor-to-ceiling windows.

"Jesus," she says, clutching her hand to her chest.

Laughton follows her gaze and sees her own reflection next to Adele's.

"I think we're a bit freaked out after our near miss with Bambi back there." She closes the door behind them, shutting out the creaking whisper of the forest, then heads over to the window and draws the blinds, banishing the reflected images of their ghostly selves.

She turns and takes in the interior: stripped pine table, two benches, a sofa, a TV, a small wood-burning stove and a stack of logs that they definitely won't be needing. Adele heads up the stairs to the mezzanine above the small, neat kitchen with a welcome basket and folder lying on the countertop. Bookshelves line one whole wall and Laughton drifts over to read the titles: *Flora and Fauna of the Forest, The Good Pub Guide, Secret Forest, Green Men and Cindermen—Myths and Legends of the Forest of Dean.*

She takes this one down and studies the cover, a black-and-white, vintage-looking photograph of a dark, hooded figure wreathed in smoke and standing in the shadow of a tree. She opens it and flicks through pages of collected Cinderman stories, peppered with sketches and drawings of the same shadowy figure from the cover. She closes it and heads over to the kitchen to inspect the welcome basket—three tiny jars of local jam and marmalade, a variety of tea bags, a small pouch of coffee. She is tempted by the coffee but grabs a chamomile tea bag instead. She drops it in a mug then turns on the tap, adjusting the flow so it's slow and steady, and starts the thirty-second timer on her phone, moving the kettle under the stream of water the moment it hits zero.

"I'll take the single room if that's OK?" Adele calls from above.

"Take the double if you want, I honestly don't mind. You want tea? There's peppermint and chamomile if you don't fancy caffeine."

"Just water would be great, thanks."

Laughton sets the kettle to boil then heads over to the door, picks up her bag, and carries it over to the dining table.

Everyone has a routine when they check into a new place—some people check the bathrooms, others turn on the TV—but the first thing Laughton always does is set up her office. She unzips the bag and takes her mobile printer and laptop out and places them on the table, fishes out the cables and switches them on, then copies the Wi-Fi code from the welcome folder into her network preferences and checks her email.

Nothing from Gracie. Nothing from Tannahill.

She emails Gracie telling her she hopes she's having a nice time, then opens a new email to Tannahill. She types "FAVOR" in the subject line, then pecks out a message, the clicking of the keys mingling with the sound of Adele's footsteps as she descends the staircase.

Hey you,
Arrived safely in Cinderfield. Police here being criminally unhelpful. Could you run a quick cell tower check on a phone number for me? I know it's cheeky but the police here should have done it anyway so I figure it's not treading on anyone's toes. Number is . . .

Laughton turns to Adele. "What's your sister's mobile number?"

Adele places a battered-looking tin on the table then leans in and types Maddie's number into the message. Laughton looks at the tin, dying to ask about it, but decides to wait and see if Adele volunteers the information instead. She signs off the email, adds some kisses, then hits Send.

"OK, so what I've just asked for is a mobile cell-tower trace on your sister's number. Every phone pings the nearest tower every time it comes in range and the networks keep records. By triangulating the strength of signal between different towers and matching it up with the time stamps, we can track her phone and therefore her movements."

"Could it show us where she is now?"

Laughton stands up and heads into the kitchen. "It might, but I wouldn't get your hopes up, everyone who's listened to a true-crime podcast or watched a cop show on TV knows you can trace mobile phones, so the trail is most likely to go cold at the same time she disappeared."

She fills her mug with hot water, finds a glass in one of the cupboards, then fills it at the tap and carries it over to Adele. "Listen, I'm going to be honest with you. In all likelihood we are looking at three possible scenarios here: one, your sister has voluntarily disappeared for some reason, maybe she was in some kind of trouble and decided running away was her best option, in which case it's unlikely the phone data will reveal anything other than where she was when she switched it off."

Adele shakes her head. "She wouldn't go away without telling me."

"OK, then the second scenario is that she is lost somewhere, maybe she fell in the woods, broke her leg, hasn't got any phone signal. In that case her phone data will help us locate her and bring her to safety."

Adele nods. "And the third option?"

"The third option . . ." Laughton catches the edge of the tea bag and dips it up and down in the hot water. "The third option is that someone took her. I know that's a horrible thing to contemplate, but in order to stand the best chance of finding out what happened to her and getting her back, we need to consider and investigate every possibility."

Adele nods but says nothing.

Laughton carries her tea over to the table and sits down next to Adele, tension coming off her like heat now that the elephant in the room has finally been mentioned. "Also," Laughton says softly, aware that what she is about to say is not what Adele wants to hear, "this is not the first time a woman has gone missing around here."

She leans forward and clicks on the Cinderman folder on her laptop. It opens to reveal numerous subfolders, each with a different person's name and date. She turns it so that Adele can read them all, starting with Maddie's on the top.

"How many are there?" Adele murmurs.

"Fifty-eight, and these are just the cases I've found going back twenty years, so there could be more."

Adele nods and stares at the screen, her face slack with the realization that her sister may be in much bigger trouble than she had allowed herself to admit.

Laughton clicks on the folder below Maddie's labeled "Scarlett Banks" and opens the files inside—five pdfs of news articles and a copy of a missing persons file. The news articles are all from local papers, each showing a photo of a smiling young woman with short, black hair and a crop top. The caption beneath the photo identifies her as Scarlett Banks, nineteen, known as "Star," because of the star-shaped tattoo on her neck. Laughton points at the headline: "ANOTHER VICTIM OF THE CINDERMAN?"

"Just like in Maddie's case, the police seem to have done little to nothing to investigate any of these." She scrolls to the section of the missing persons file where details of the investigation are recorded. Apart from a few dates and a note of the initial witness statement it's practically blank. She scrolls down to the oldest folder, "Rachel Cooke," and opens that too, scrolling to the action page of her missing persons file, which is just as blank as the others.

"I was starting to look into these cases in more detail earlier when the alert popped up about your sister, and when I saw the same lack of investigation, I decided it was a good opportunity to come down here and see what was going on for myself."

Adele continues to stare at the screen blankly, then something seems to break the spell and she leans in, squinting at the signature of the police constable who took the initial statement on the Rachel Cooke case. "I know that name," she says, "He's in charge of everything, the big chief or whatever you call him."

"The Chief Constable?"

"Yes."

Laughton reads the name of the officer printed beneath the signature at the bottom of the Missing Persons Form—Russell Beech, only a sergeant back then, so he clearly had a pretty meteoric rise to be chief now. She clicks on a shortcut link to the National Police Database, types "Chief Constable Russell Beech" into the search field, and hits Return.

A personnel file opens up with an official photograph showing a man in full dress uniform, round face, neat auburn beard, reddish hair cut short, and receding slightly at the temples. He looks solid, heavy almost, like a rugby player whose playing days are behind him, a career copper with a hint of cynicism and weariness around the eyes. She turns to Adele. "How do you know this guy?"

"Well, I don't really know him. My boss at the campsite is always dropping his name like I'm supposed to be impressed. I think he knows him through some business thing."

Laughton skim reads Chief Constable Beech's résumé charting his rapid rise from uniformed PC to head of the Gloucester Constabulary, more impressive for its speed than its distinction. There's nothing flashy about it, no high-profile cases that propelled him to the top, just a steady series of promotions and several citations from senior officers and local politicians for efficiency, low crime figures, and for setting up and overseeing a large number of subdepartments within the force, including a revamped Missing Persons Bureau. He seems more like a manager than a policeman, steady and careful, the type who's clearly got on by keeping his head down, causing few ripples, and knowing the right people. A networker. Laughton scrolls to the bottom of the file where his contact details are listed and clicks on the link to email him.

"Let's see if I can get a meeting," Laughton says. "He seems to be a man who likes rubbing shoulders with the top brass, and my dad was pretty high up in the Met, so he probably knew him, or at least knew of him. I'll drop some other names of high-ranking police officers I know, see if that hooks some interest."

A new email opens up with Beech's email address already pasted in. Laughton types MISSING in the subject line, then:

Dear Chief Constable,
You don't know me but you may have met my father, John Rees,
former Commissioner of the Metropolitan Police. I think you may
also know my godfather, Keith Rivett, District Commander of
Avon and Somerset Police.

I'm currently in the area as part of my research tenure in the
Criminology Department at London Metropolitan University
and wondered if I could talk to you about a historical missing
persons case you dealt with back when you were in uniform. I'll
be here for the next couple of days and would really appreciate a
moment of your time.

Sincerely,
Laughton Rees

She adds what she calls her "wanky" signature on the bottom with all the letters after her name and a list of her academic posts, hoping that the weight of her accumulated learning, coupled with her Olympic-standard name-dropping, might be enough to generate a response. She hits Send then sits back and looks over at Adele, who remains still and quiet.

"Maybe you should turn in for the night and get some sleep. It's going to be a busy day tomorrow, lots of ground to cover. Hopefully we'll get the phone data back first thing, which will give us a starting point for our search."

Adele nods but doesn't get up. She places her hand on the tin instead. "I need to tell you something," she says, "about me and Maddie's past. Something that . . . might be relevant to why she disappeared."

"OK," Laughton says. She nods over at the sofa. "Why don't we go and sit over there. And take your time, I'm not going anywhere, I promise."

30

LAUGHTON KICKS OFF HER SHOES and settles in the corner of the sofa, ready to listen to what Adele has to say. Adele sits next to her and places the tin on the sofa between them. She draws her knees up to her chest and lifts her glass of water like she's about to take a sip but stares into it instead, like it's a crystal ball or a window into the past.

"Maddie is not really her name," she says, her voice low, like she's afraid to say the words. "Her real name is Helen. Helen Bailey. And mine is Donna. We are real sisters, that's true, but everything else is something we made up to try and get away from . . . who we were and . . . what happened to us."

She looks down and frowns, struggling to share the thing she has kept secret for so long.

"I can't really remember our mother. Maddie says she can remember her a little, but she was seven when we were taken into care, and I was only five, so all I can remember are fragments. I remember moving around a lot, I remember being hungry and cold, but I was never scared because I always had my sister to look after me, even though, looking back now, she was not much more than a baby herself."

She glances up at Laughton then back at her glass. "Our mother was an addict. I don't know who my father was or even if my father was the same as Maddie's. I assume he must have been, as we look so alike. Not that it matters. Maddie was the only family I ever had. The only real family.

"We lived in Gloucester back then, jumping around from place to place, sleeping on sofas and on floors, sleeping outside sometimes. Our mother would make us beg on the streets when things got really bad, or send us into shops to steal food. That was how we got picked up by social services. She'd sent us into a supermarket to get something for tea, which included a bottle of vodka, and I dropped it as we were running out. I cut my feet really badly because the shoes I was wearing were my baby shoes with the toes cut open. Maddie was already out of the shop. I remember looking up at her and crying because I was in pain and knew I couldn't run. She could have got away and left me there, but she didn't, she came back for me and so we both ended up getting caught." She frowns. "Funny that I call her Maddie, even though she was still Helen back then. She's been Maddie for so long now that it's hard to think of her as anyone else.

"Anyway, we both got taken somewhere and they cleaned and bandaged my foot and asked us loads of questions about who was looking after us and where we lived and then some people went around to wherever we were staying that week and found our mother off her face or blackout drunk and that was it. I think she did try to get us back at one point. I have a memory of sitting on the floor in the corner of some room somewhere with a box of books and a few toys while she cried and hugged Maddie and told us she loved us and that she was going to get clean and find a place for us all to live. That was the last time we saw her.

"After that we moved around a lot, bouncing around between various children's homes. The only thing I can really remember about that time was being scared all the time: scared of the bigger kids, scared of the people looking after us, who always seemed to be angry, but mostly I was scared of being split up from Maddie.

"Once, after we'd been there a few months, I was taken in a car to a house with a bunch of other kids in it and an old couple who gave me a bowl of Cocoa Pops for my tea and said I could stay with them if I liked. I asked them when Maddie was coming and they said she was coming later. So I stayed there for one night and when Maddie didn't come the next day I jumped out of a window and walked the streets until I found a shop. I went inside, picked up a bottle of vodka, and smashed it on the floor because I thought that would then get me back to the place where Maddie was. And it worked. I remember when I was taken back to the home a woman sat me down and told me that if I behaved myself and was a good girl, I had a real chance of getting a new family, because people always wanted younger kids like me, not older ones like Maddie.

"Well, after that I made sure I wasn't a good girl anymore because I didn't want to be split from Maddie again. I played up all the time, broke things, never did what I was told—and so no one took me away in a car again, and even though every home we stayed in was horrible and scary, I was with Maddie, and that made it OK.

"But then one day, when I was eight and Maddie was ten, we were both called into the office and told that someone wanted to give both of us a new home. It was a couple who lived in the forest who'd been turned down for adoption several times, but seeing as my sister and I were so hard to place, they decided to bend the rules a bit, so they filled in the paperwork and off we went.

"Our new house was deep in the woods. I remember that first night our new mum put us to bed and read us fairy stories about all the horrible things that lived in the woods—witches and goblins and Cindermen and how terrible fates befell children who ran away. She told us never to go in the forest because there were bad things in there, worse than we could imagine. But it turned out our new home was worse than any fairy tale, and our new father worse than any monster.

"We suffered every sort of emotional and physical abuse in that house. Our father was a very sick man and Maddie did what she could to keep me from being alone with him, even if that meant putting herself in harm's way. Our mother would always take one of us on errands, and Maddie would volunteer to stay behind, saying, 'Take her, she can go.' As if it was nothing. But I knew what it was, and so did Maddie. Sometimes our mother would talk about a daughter they'd had who died, though our father never spoke about her.

"Our only escape from it all was school. It was in a little village called Blackchurch that taught kids from all over the area. Every day we got picked up by a bus at the end of our forest track and dropped off again in the evening. Every Friday I would get a knot in my stomach when the bus dropped us back and drove away, knowing for the next two days and three nights it would be just us, alone with them, in that house.

"Then one day, when I was twelve and Maddie was fourteen, the head teacher called our mother in for a meeting. I think she'd started to suspect something was wrong and assumed our mother didn't know and would want to protect us if she did. Instead she locked us in our room the moment we got home, called our father, and told him we'd been making up wicked stories and that he needed to come home right away and punish us.

"I don't think I'd ever been more scared in my life than I was at that moment, knowing our father was coming, and that the big secret of our messed-up family was no longer a secret anymore. I think that was the worst thing for me, the feeling of incredible shame, like it was my fault somehow. I remember thinking that he would kill us for sure when he got home and that a part of me was relieved that it would soon be over.

"It was Maddie who broke the lock on the bedroom window, Maddie who made sure I climbed out first and told me to run into the woods. I remember looking back and seeing Maddie running after me with our father's van speeding down the long dirt road through the trees behind her. It was Maddie who grabbed me and told me to keep running, we had to keep on running, no matter what terrors lay in wait for us in the woods, because anything was better than going back.

"We ran until it got dark, further and deeper into the woods with no food and no idea where we were going. That night we slept in a hollow under a tree, cuddling together to keep warm. I remember Maddie whispering in the dark, telling me it was OK, that everything was going to be fine because whatever happened we were never going back to that place and that to make sure they never ever found us we had to leave everything behind, including our names. That's when we became Adele and Maddie, there under that tree, in the middle of the night.

"The next morning I woke shivering, not just because of the cold but because I heard footsteps crunching through the leaves and getting closer. I thought our father must have found us, or maybe it was the Cinderman come to drag us down to hell. But it wasn't either of them, it was a woman with long dreadlocks who looked like a witch. This was Grizz. She took us to a place called The Clearing, where there were lots of other people who gave us food and asked us lots of questions about where we'd come from and where our parents were. Maddie told them everything, everything except our real names, and Grizz said we could stay there as long as we wanted. So The Clearing became our new home, and we thought we were safe at last. And we were, but there was a dark side to that place too."

Light floods into the room and Adele's eyes fly wide in surprise and fear. "There's someone there."

Laughton spins round and stares at the bright, white blinds, lit from behind by security lights. "Where?"

"Over there, in the corner," Adele whispers. "Someone was standing behind the blinds, I saw it the moment the lights came on, then it was gone."

Laughton gets up from the sofa and moves silently across to the window. Outside she can hear the faint whisper of wind in the trees, muffled almost to nothing by the double glazing. Something screeches in the night in the far, far distance, then she hears something closer, much closer, the soft crunch of a footstep on the dry ground.

There is someone out there.

She steps closer and moves her eye to the gap at the edge of the blind, being careful not to disturb it as she peers through.

Outside the night burns brightly, everything lit from above by a harsh, white light fixed high on the side of the house. She can see a picnic table and two benches, the edge of the forest beyond—and three deer grazing on the grass between the cabin and the woods.

"What is it?" Adele whispers.

"Bambi's back," Laughton says. "Only this time he brought friends."

Adele gets up from the sofa and joins Laughton at the window.

"Are you sure you saw a figure?" Laughton says, widening the gap in the blind and looking along the front of the cabin.

Adele shakes her head. "I don't know, it was so brief. Maybe I'm just tired."

Laughton continues to study the night, watching for movement beyond the grazing deer. "Perhaps we should turn in for the night."

Adele shakes her head. "No, I want to tell you everything now."

Laughton takes one last, long look outside, then lets the blind fall back into place and heads back to the sofa.

Dog hears the blind tap twice against the window as it settles.

He is standing to the right of the window, his back pressed against the wooden siding of the house, arms flat against a wall that is still radiating the trapped heat of the day.

Following them had been easy, the moon bright enough for him to drive without lights on and the glow from theirs allowing him to follow at distance until they stopped and parked by the cabin. He had parked too and run the rest of the way along the road using the moonlight to guide him.

The cabin was perfect, so much better than the last location, no field filled with sleeping campers, no other people at all. It was remote, isolated, and as close to the forest as you could get without actually being in it. He couldn't have picked a better spot.

He'd done a wide recce of the place, keeping well back as he checked for any alarms and made a note of all the entrances and exits. He'd spotted the security lights fixed beneath the eaves of the roof on each side and approached the house slowly in a blind spot, creeping closer a few centimeters at a time to make sure not to trip the motion sensors.

He'd tried to listen through the wall, but it had proved too thick and well insulated, so he'd moved across and pressed his ear to the glass patio door instead and listened to them talk. He'd heard all the names of senior policemen the blond woman had dropped too, suggesting that she was connected. Potentially someone who could cause major problems if he didn't play this thing right. He'd been texting Grizz with an update when the security lights had tripped. It was sloppy. He'd taken his eye off the ball and it had almost ended badly.

He looks at the deer now, the stag lifting its head and turning in his direction as it sniffs the air. He focuses on the spot behind its front leg where an arrow would pass straight through into its heart and kill it instantly. Fucking deer! He raises both arms and waves them above his head, spooking the stag and sending all three skittering back to the safety of the forest.

He waits for the security lights to click off again then sends the text to Grizz. Then slowly, carefully, he moves back to the window, inching to his right until he is standing fully in front of the glass door. He turns his head and presses his ear back to the glass.

He listens.

31

"AT FIRST GLANCE THE CLEARING seemed idyllic, a kind of forest community made up of runaways like us, dropouts, misfits, ex-prisoners and ex-military who couldn't adjust to civilian life, civilians who couldn't adjust to any kind of modern life." Adele takes a sip of water then smiles at a memory.

"Grizz always said we were outlaws, like Robin Hood and his merry men, only we didn't steal from the rich and give to the poor. We were the poor and everyone was required to do their bit to contribute to the community. We were organized into labor gangs and hired out for cash jobs doing whatever needed doing. A lot of it was seasonal work, picking fruit through the summer, vegetables in the autumn, laboring on building sites, year-round gardening work.

"Every penny earned went into the communal pot, which paid for whatever we needed, food mostly. We grew some of our own but there were a lot of mouths to feed, especially in summer. Sometimes it seemed like there were hundreds of people, other times maybe just a couple of dozen. It was hard work and hard living and most people couldn't stick it. It was tougher on the women, I think. Younger women like us often only stayed a few days then left. But we didn't leave because we felt safe there. Grizz never left either, she never left the forest, never really left The Clearing.

"She explained it to me once when I was a bit older, how the land The Clearing stood upon was ancient common land and that anyone who lived on it had the right to remain there freely. She said there had once been lots of communities like theirs but that one by one they had been lost as people left, until The Clearing was the only one left.

"I remember being scared when she told me this, scared that we'd be kicked off the land one day, but Grizz reassured me that would never happen to us. She said as long as she remained on the land, the authorities could never evict them, and that was why she never left. Grizz always had an angle on everything. She comes across as this sweet, earth mother type but she's very smart . . . And she's ruthless."

Adele glances down at the tin lying on the sofa next to them.

"In what way?" Laughton prompts, wanting to keep the flow of Adele's confession going.

"Well, like, if ever anyone broke a rule, the punishment was always swift and brutal. Grizz called them 'crimes against the collective,' like we were some kind of . . . political movement or something. She would exile people, literally drive them away, and she would cut people to mark them as criminals if they stole even the tiniest thing, I mean, like, cut off fingers, even hands. I guess it was her way of keeping order in a place where everyone was an outlaw. And it worked. There were hardly ever any incidents at The Clearing because everyone was scared of Grizz. But they respected her too because she always managed to provide for us; no matter how many people there were, she always gave us what we needed—food, shelter, a safe place to hide from the rest of the world. But then something happened that was . . . It was too much, and me and Maddie never felt safe there ever again.

"We'd been there maybe four or five years. It was winter, so there were a lot fewer people around, maybe twenty or thirty, no more. Winters are hard in the forest, so we tended to be less busy. We still got people turning up every now and then, people who'd heard about The Clearing and maybe had nowhere else to go, but they would usually stay a few days then leave again, especially the women. It was the cold that drove most people away. 'Winter visitors,' Grizz used to call them. It was one of these it happened to.

"He walked out of the woods one evening, sat down by the fire, and didn't say a thing to anyone, no introductions, no conversation at all. He looked ex-military, that kind of type. Grizz spoke to him, asked him where he was from, told him he was welcome to stay so long as he respected the place and the people in it, and that he would be expected to earn his keep through work—the usual speech every new arrival got. Only he turned out to be not the usual kind of guest at all. There was something off about him. He reminded me of our father, not in the way he looked but in the way he was, like there was a darkness in him, like there was something broken inside.

"That night I woke to the sound of screams. While we slept this man had forced a woman to go into the forest by holding a knife to her throat. He had tied her to a tree, raped her, then left her there, almost naked, in subzero temperatures. It was only because she managed to work her mouth free and scream that she raised the alarm. If she hadn't she probably would have died.

"Grizz sent someone out to find the man and bring him back. There was this guy who was like her right-hand man who everyone called Dog. He was always the one who doled out the punishments and so we were all a bit scared of him. He was Grizz's man, not really part of the community. He was a good hunter too, always used a crossbow and would bring back all sorts to help feed the camp—rabbits, birds, deer. Anyway, it was him she sent out to find the man and bring him back. A few hours later Dog returned with the man limping along behind him. He had a crossbow bolt in his leg and his hands tied together.

"Grizz gathered us all together in the main clearing where the man stood, tied to a tree along the edge. He didn't seem at all bothered by any of it, smiling even when Grizz told us what he had done, like he wasn't afraid of us. Maybe that was what did it, the thing that finally made Grizz lose her cool and reveal another side. She took the knife he'd used on the woman and stabbed him right between the legs. I remember the look of surprise on his face, like he couldn't believe what had happened. None of us could. Then she stabbed him again, and again, jabbing him between the legs while he was tied helplessly to the tree, just like he'd done to the woman.

"He bled out right in front of us. So much blood. And when it was over Grizz held up the knife and told us that what we had just witnessed was natural justice, the only kind available to outlaws like us. She reminded us that any crime against our community was a crime against us all and had to be punished by all of us collectively, and that if anyone spoke about what we had witnessed it would also be a crime against the community, because the authorities would use it as an excuse to shut us down. That was how she kept everyone in line, by making you believe your identity was tied in with everyone else's, and that the community was more important than any one individual. It was why it was so hard for us to get away."

"But you did get away," Laughton says.

"Eventually. Spring came, then summer, and we finally went to Grizz and said we wanted to leave. Everyone else seemed to come and go, so we didn't see why it should be any different for us. Even so, it was a scary thing to do, go and ask her like that. It felt like we were rejecting her in some way, turning our back on her and everything she had built, which, in a way, we were. It was like going up to God and saying we wanted to leave heaven.

"Grizz reminded us how she'd taken us in and protected us when we were all alone, and how we basically owed her our lives, which was true. She told us we could leave but only after we'd paid her what we owed. She wanted six thousand pounds, a thousand for every year we'd been there. But we didn't have any money, nothing at all, so she might as well have asked us for six million. Every penny we'd ever earned had gone straight to the collective. So now we had this unpayable debt hanging over us, and both of us knew what Grizz did to people who didn't pay what they owed.

"Maddie got really down after that meeting. I think she thought we would never get away from that place. I think it made her realize, made us both realize, that we were slaves and would never earn the money to buy our freedom. I'd never seen her like that before. She was always so upbeat and . . . strong. It's a funny thing about Maddie, everyone thinks I'm the strong one, the one who's more together and that she's away with the fairies half the time. I wish they knew who she really was. I wish they knew about that little girl who had done everything she could to protect her sister. Everything I am today is only possible because of what Maddie did for me back then.

"So when I saw her so down I decided to do something for her. I went back to Grizz in secret and did a deal with her. I said if she let us go right now I would pay her two thousand pounds every year for five years, ten thousand in total. I had no idea how I was going to earn that money, I just knew we had to get away from that place. And Grizz agreed, but on two conditions. One, we had to stay close to the forest until we paid the debt. Two, we were never allowed to say anything about who we were or where we had come from. So we agreed and left the forest for what I hoped would be forever.

"I never told Maddie about the deal I made, because I didn't want her to feel like any of it was her responsibility. It was my way of paying her back for everything she'd done for me. I just told her Grizz had changed her mind, that we were free to leave but only if we promised never to set foot in the forest again. But after we left the forest Maddie struggled far more than me. Maybe it was because her identity had always been tied up with looking after me and I didn't need looking after anymore. I had my secret mission, which gave me purpose.

"So, every New Year's Day for the last four years I've gone to a spot on the edge of the forest and left two thousand pounds in an envelope in a hollow tree for Grizz to collect, because she can't leave the forest and, ever since we left it, I've had a fear of going back in. Everything that happened in those woods left me traumatized to the point where I can barely even look at the forest, let alone step foot in it. As soon as our debt was paid I planned to leave this place and go and live in a city, or by the sea, anywhere where there are no trees. And we were so close. Sooo close."

She pushes the tin toward Laughton. Laughton picks it up and feels something shift inside. She hooks her fingernails under the lid and prizes it off to reveal a thick stack of banknotes.

"That's the last payment," Adele says, "our freedom money, due at the end of the year. One thousand, five hundred and seventy-six pounds, everything I've managed to scrape together over the last year by working hard and living as cheaply as possible." Tears brim in her eyes and spill down her cheeks. "After that we would have been finally free to leave this place. But now Maddie is gone and I don't know what to do."

Laughton looks at the stack of folded notes in the tin. Maddie and Adele's freedom money.

"Do you think maybe Grizz took Maddie because she doesn't want to let you go?"

Adele shakes her head. "I've stuck to my promise, made all the payments, and Grizz is a woman of her word if nothing else. And she wouldn't need her for work, it's the middle of summer, there's tons of people around at this time of year."

"What about your foster parents, the ones you ran from. Could they have somehow found Maddie and taken her back?"

"No!"

The force of Adele's reply takes Laughton by surprise.

"Are you sure?"

"Maddie has not been taken by anyone." Adele grabs the tin and fumbles the lid back on, like she's closing the discussion too. "I have to keep believing that. She's just gone away with whoever this mystery person is." She clutches the tin to her chest, like it's a shield against whatever might threaten her. "If we can find out who he is and where they went, then we'll find my sister."

32

ONE THOUSAND, ONE HUNDRED AND eighty-six.

That's how many marks there are on the walls.

She has counted them three times to make sure the number is correct, nibbling her apple nervously to the core as she counted. And if each mark represents a day—which it can't, it just can't—then that's the equivalent of three years and three months. She's done that calculation three times too.

She sits down on the edge of the bed, the weight of this number and the awful implications of it suddenly too much for her to bear. Her mind trembles with fretful thoughts.

Did one person make all these marks?

If not one, then how many? Two? Three? Twenty?

She draws her knees up to her chest and stares at the room from behind them, the candle bathing everything in a soft golden light that would be soothing if it were shining anywhere but here. She looks at the flame, so still it could be a photograph. No breeze disturbs it. Whatever draft drew her here has gone now or was of her own imagining.

She lies on her side, knees still shielding her from the heavy reality of the room. The bed smells like the earth but it's not damp and not entirely unpleasant, though the gray blanket feels scratchy.

How many people lay on this bed before me? she thinks, and then, before she can catch it, another thought slips in after it. *And where are they now?*

She stares at the room, feeling trapped in its stillness, like an insect in amber, her head so heavy she can no longer lift it. Her arms and legs feel heavy too, like the room has its own gravity, one she is not built to withstand.

Her eyes flutter and start to close. She tries to open them again, surprised by the sudden tiredness pressing down on her. She tries to sit up but her body refuses. Tries to move her arms but they won't move either. Then she realizes as her eyes close again and the heaviness pulls her down into a deeper, darker place.

The apple.

There was something in the apple.

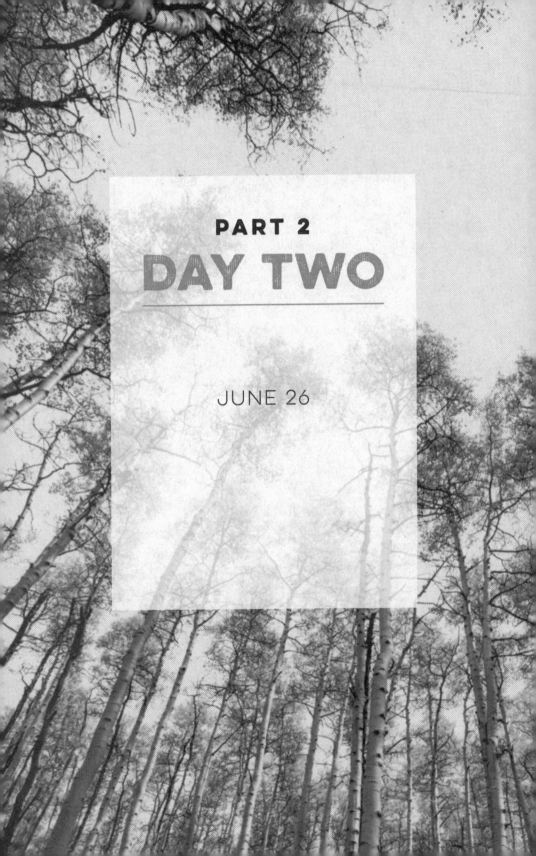

PART 2
DAY TWO

JUNE 26

33

THE SKY BEGINS TO LIGHTEN long before dawn.

Mist pools in the valleys and blankets the forest, snagging on branches and swirling like crowds of ghosts. The birds rouse too, fluttering in the predawn dark to loudly restake their daily claim on their particular patch of the forest.

Grizz is also awake. She lies in her caravan, snug in her bed piled high with blankets and quilts, savoring the last moments of warmth before her bursting bladder forces her to leave it. She pulls out her phone to check what time it is and sees the message Dog sent in the night.

Target was picked up at the police station by another woman. Followed them to a cabin on edge of woods and listened to them talk. The unidentified woman seems connected, overheard her say her dad was high up in the Met. What do you want me to do? Continue? Abort? Deal with both?

She closes her eyes, the message making her feel bone weary before the day has even begun. Poor Adele, she had tried so hard to break free from the shitty hand life had dealt her, but bad luck had too strong ahold on her. Maybe Maddie would just turn up and all this would go away.

She rolls from beneath her covers and rises stiffly, feeling the morning chill in her joints as she works her arms into her smock. Once dressed, she waddles outside and shuffles away into the woods rather than face the foul-smelling hut containing the composting toilet.

Grizz had always had a soft spot for Adele and Maddie, maybe because she'd once had a sister too, though they had never watched out for each other the way Maddie and Adele did. Her sister had screwed her over big-time, helped her set up The Clearing, then vanished with all the money they'd managed to scrape together just before the first year was out. It had nearly finished her, not just the abject poverty she'd found herself in in the middle of the harshest winter on record, but also the betrayal. It had hardened her. She'd never trusted anyone after that, which was probably what had enabled her to survive. Only Adele and Maddie had managed to get close. They were like she had been forty years earlier, or maybe like the daughters she'd never allowed herself to have. She had even protected them back when she was plying a darker trade to keep The Clearing safe and well funded, though what good had that done, ultimately? Despite everything she had done they were back in trouble's way. She wouldn't protect them again. It had been weak of her to do it in the first place, a relic of her former, weaker self. And she was weak enough as it was.

She walks stiffly past the outer ring of tents and caravans and enters the trees that surround the clearing. When she was young and had first dreamed of a place like this, it had seemed idyllic, living on and from the land, following the natural rhythms of nature instead of the unnatural ones of society. Now it's just painful. People may have lived like this in the past, when cripplingly hard work, or disease, or malnourishment, or combinations of all three carried them off before they reached forty, but it wasn't meant for someone like her, who was now decades past her use-by date.

A winter guest had talked to her about this once. She'd been a nurse out in the world before a breakdown had sent her down a different path. She'd said there were numerous biological factors that proved we weren't supposed to live past forty. Women ran out of eggs and stopped being able to have children, all kinds of cancers kicked in, even the fact you couldn't go through the night without needing to piss was part of it, something to do with an enzyme that ran out when you reached your forties. She said once you got past forty you stopped aging and effectively started rotting. Grizz believed that was true. She could smell the rot on herself sometimes.

She finds a tree, lifts up her smock, and leans against it to steady herself while she squats down as far as her old knees will allow. The pain in her bladder begins to ease as she looks back through the trees at her kingdom, a ragged patchwork of tents sprouting from the ground like mushrooms. The only people in the past who had lived into comfortable old age were the landowners and the wealthy in their dry houses and soft beds, with servants to bring them food and tend to warm fires that never went out. The Earl and his ancestors never had to live like this. And, in a few months' time, neither will she.

She finishes and stands upright then raises her phone and types a reply to Dog, her fingers so ingrained with the dirt of the forest that the skin on them has changed color.

Keep watching. Will get more info about the new woman then let you know how best to proceed.

She forwards his message to Beech and adds three question marks.

Let him do some work for once. Make him get some dirt beneath the nails of his soft, pink, unworked hands.

Russell Beech sits at his breakfast table next to one-year-old Sophie in her high chair and opposite five-year-old Ella, who is trying to shake some Cheerios into a bowl with the same kind of focus as someone defusing a bomb. Beech attempts to coax a spoonful of mashed banana porridge into Sophie's mouth but gets most of it on her face. A yipping sound cuts through the burble of the *Today* program.

"Can you let the dog out, hon?" his wife calls over her shoulder.

He looks over at her standing at the cooker, stirring the pan of porridge mixed with flaxseed she insists he eat every morning because it's good for his heart. Jenny is twenty years his junior and as sunny as his ex-wife was gloomy.

He turns back to Sophie, all blond curls and her mother's eyes. "Can you be trusted with the spoon while I go and let Pickle out?"

Sophie nods and takes the spoon as Beech slides out from behind the table. He heads out of the cramped kitchen-diner into the tiny hallway where the family spaniel sits by the frosted glass door, sweeping the floor with his tail and waiting to be let out.

Beech hates this small house, all he could afford after the divorce, though he does enjoy the forced intimacy it creates. He had always been so removed in his first marriage, distant with his wife and two boys, playing the traditional authority figure, out early to work, back late, bringing home the bacon while his wife did everything else. He'd thought that was what marriage was supposed to be like, you work hard, you bring up your kids, you have your two weeks' holiday in the sun and you don't expect too much else. Then, just as the boys were finally leaving home and he was thinking about early retirement, his wife had left him and hired an expensive Rottweiler of a divorce lawyer—using his money—who had helped her go after the rest. He'd lost the house, half his savings, and a big chunk of his pension pot and was still having to pay spousal support. All that graft, a lifetime of work and sacrifice, only to end up with nothing.

Actually, not nothing.

He met Jenny when the divorce was being finalized, and God knew what she'd seen in him because it certainly wasn't his money, but she's shown him what marriage is supposed to be like, and what being a real father should be like too, meals around the table, books at bedtime, all the little shared moments that he'd missed first time round. She deserves the best for doing that, and he is determined to give it to her.

He opens the door and the dog dashes out and starts sniffing around for the perfect place to pee. Beech stands in the doorway, looking out at all the other identical houses on the road, the only difference being the color of the front door and the make of car parked on each tiny, identical drive. They were starter homes really, cheaply made and cheap to buy. He knows three other policemen who live here, every one of them way more junior than him, which is humiliating.

He checks his messages and blows out a long breath of frustration when he reads the one from Grizz. He couldn't really have made things any easier for them, arranging for Adele Friar to be released from Cinderfield jail in the middle of the night so that Grizz's man could come along and make her disappear. But then some mystery woman had appeared out of nowhere to fuck everything up. Either way it means he now has two problems instead of one, another person to check out, identify, and possibly deal with.

He looks up just as Pickle lets out a long stream of pee onto the back wheel of his car, then scrolls through his emails, deleting most of them. He is about to delete one from a name he doesn't recognize when he notices the time. It had been sent at almost two o'clock that morning, about an hour after Adele Friar was picked up by the mystery woman at the jail.

He opens the email, reads it, and frowns when he gets to the sender's name, which seems familiar. He googles "Laughton Rees," and the pages of results that come back solve the mystery for him. She was the woman at the center of the Murder Mansion case the year before, the estranged daughter of John Rees, former commissioner of the Met.

He thinks for a moment then hits Reply and checks the time. He could be in the office in less than twenty minutes.

I have a window this morning at 8:45 if that suits?
Best,
R. Beech
Chief Constable, Gloucestershire Constabulary

Let's see if this Laughton Rees is as keen to see him as he now is to see her.

34

THE EMAIL FROM BEECH PINGS into Laughton's inbox but goes unnoticed at first, the alert sound drowned out by the chattering of the printer spitting out a hundred flyers with Maddie's photo and Laughton's phone number on them.

Laughton is on the phone to Tannahill, a big smile on her face and a satellite map of the Cinderfield area open on her screen covered in red dots.

"How the hell did you get this processed so fast?"

"Someone at the DFT owed me a favor," Tannahill replies. "At least they used to owe me a favor."

"Awww, you cashed it in for me!"

"Well, what do you get the girl who has everything?"

Laughton smiles. "I'll take this over a bunch of flowers any day."

"You are so weird."

"And that's exactly why you like me. How did your presentation go last night?"

"Ah, it was amazing, I took your advice and just showed a bunch of clips off YouTube and it brought the house down."

Laughton smiles. "Who knew media management in high-profile murder investigations would be such a crowd-pleaser. What are you up to today?"

"I'm about to go into a small, airless room to listen to a couple of nerds talk about the latest face-recognition technology."

"Sounds exciting."

"No, it doesn't."

"Sounds exciting to me."

"That's because you're a nerd too."

"Well, that is also true."

"Listen, after this face-recognition nerd-fest I'm doing, I've got the rest of the morning free, so why don't you send over all your case files, I'll go through them and see if there are any officers' names on your missing persons' that correspond to the list of delegates here. I can also track down my DCI friend from Hereford who told me Gloucestershire Constabulary was a shit-pit and try and get him to elaborate."

"Oh, if you do happen to talk to your friend, ask him about the Chief Constable here, Russell Beech."

"What's his story?"

"That's what I'd like to find out. His name is on most of my Mispers."

"OK, I'll ask. I've really got to go now, the gig's about to start."

"Take lots of notes."

"I'll film the whole thing on my phone for you if you like."

"Great, I'll buy popcorn. We can watch it when you're back and make a night of it."

"Deal. Talk to you later. And send me those files."

"Will do."

She hangs up just as Adele arrives next to her with two mugs of black coffee. "Sorry," she says, "couldn't find any milk."

Laughton takes a mug. "Don't worry, black is probably what we both need after the night we've had."

Adele sits down next to Laughton on the bench and studies the map displayed on the laptop.

"OK," Laughton explains, "so this is a cell tower map of the last recorded movements of your sister's phone." Adele leans forward and studies a satellite image of the area around Cinderfield that is peppered with red dots. "Each of these dots shows a place where Maddie's phone was pinged by the cell towers and has a time and date stamp showing when it happened." She points at the dots along Cinderfield High Street. "These confirm that she did go to the parade. The rest will hopefully tell us where she went next."

Adele follows the line of the High Street with her finger and continues up to a vast area of green to the north of the town. "This is the way she would have gone to get to The Clearing, and she was pinged here at 8:43 p.m." She points at a red dot near the top of the screen.

Laughton zooms out, the area of green grows larger, and one more dot appears over to the left, surrounded by a large area of featureless green. Adele frowns.

"She wasn't heading to The Clearing at all." She points at a different spot higher up the map with a thin line meandering through the green toward it. "That's The Clearing, and that's the path that leads to it from Cinderfield." She points back at the red dot showing Maddie's last recorded position, way over to the left. "She was going somewhere else."

Laughton zooms the map out further and more details appear—roads, a town, and a clearing in the forest with what looks like a large church in the center of it, surrounded by smaller buildings. "What's that?"

Adele leans in, tracing the lines of the roads to figure out where it is.

"That's Cinderfield Abbey. It's a big stately home and kind of a local heritage center where they do forest crafts, basket weaving, blacksmithing, that kind of thing."

"Like a museum?"

"Not exactly. The Earl of Dean and his family still live there, but they also rent the house and grounds out for events, weddings mainly."

"Would they have had a Midsummer party?"

"Maybe. There are loads of beacon parties on Midsummer's Eve."

Laughton googles "Cinderfield Abbey" and clicks on the official website. A photo opens up, a large and impressive-looking building made from the same local redstone as the police station, looking more like a small cathedral than a house.

"Someone actually lives there?" Laughton says.

"Yep, the Earl and his family. The Abbey has been in the family for hundreds of years."

She clicks on the "What's On" tab in the menu and scans through the list of weddings and summer events. "There's no Midsummer beacon party listed, though I suppose there could have been a private one." She taps her fingers on the table for a moment, thinking, then turns to Adele. "Does the Earl have any kids?"

"Yes, a son."

"How old?"

"I don't know, late twenties. Thirty maybe."

"Is he a catch? I mean, apart from being in line to inherit a massive mansion."

"I don't know, I've never seen him."

"Well, let's have a look, shall we?" Laughton opens the Wikipedia page for Cinderfield Abbey and scans the sidebar listing key facts about the place, including details about the current Earl and his heir.

Earl of Dean is a <u>title</u> in the <u>Peerage of England</u> held by members of the Kingston family. The current Earl, <u>Mallory Stoker Hawthorn Kingston (b. 1970)</u> is the eighteenth member of the Kingston family to hold the title after inheriting it from his father, <u>Ashleigh Delmar Kingston (b. 1942)</u>, eldest son of the <u>sixteenth Earl</u>. The current <u>Earl of Dean</u> inherited the title after his elder brother, <u>Greville Pearson Kingston (b. 1968)</u>, was deemed unsuited to run the family estates. The heir apparent is the present Earl's only son, <u>Sebastian Mallory Hawthorn Kingston</u> (b. 1997).

There is a photo showing a slightly ruddy-faced man in a tweed jacket standing in front of the Abbey with his arm around a thinner, darker, slightly sickly-looking teenager.

Laughton clicks on the blue highlighted link to open the son's Wikipedia page, and the skinny teen is now a thin and haunted-looking young man with black hair and hollow eyes. He's wearing some kind of formal evening wear and an old-fashioned, ruffled shirt and has been photographed in arty black-and-white in front of a peeling wall.

"He looks like a strong breeze would break him in half," Laughton says. "Do you think maybe he could be our mystery man?"

Adele regards the photo and nods. "He's definitely Maddie's type."

Laughton copies his name into a new search field and pages of results come back, links to galleries mostly. She opens the top one and clicks through pages of portrait photographs of aristocrats, artists, and a few celebrities.

"Looks like he's a photographer, based in London with a studio in Kew. Let's say hello, shall we?"

Laughton clicks on the contact link and a blank email opens. She types "Maddie Friar" in the subject line then:

Dear Lord Kingston,
I'm investigating a missing persons case—Maddie Friar—who
lived near Cinderfield Abbey and was last seen heading in that
direction yesterday evening (Midsummer's Eve), and I wondered

if you knew her. I have attached a photograph.

Look forward to hearing back from you.

Best regards,

Laughton Rees

She attaches the photo of Maddie from the Missing Persons File, and hits send.

Next, she sends an email to Tannahill with her Cinderman file attached and is about to close her mail down when she spots the new message in her inbox from Chief Constable Beech. She opens it. Reads it. Checks the time.

"How quickly can I get to Gloucester from here?"

"Forty-five, fifty minutes—probably a little longer if you hit traffic."

"Shit!" Laughton leaps up from her chair and starts stuffing her laptop and the flyers into her bag. "I need to go. Beech says he can talk but I need to be in his office at eight forty-five, so I need to leave, like, five minutes ago. What are your plans this morning?"

Adele thinks of the campsite and the list of jobs she should already be doing. "Nothing," she says. "I'm going to call in and say I can't work today. I want to help in any way I can."

"Good." Laughton takes a swig of coffee, grabs the car keys from the table, hoists her bag onto her shoulder, and heads to the door. "Because I have a job for you."

35

DEEP, DEEP IN THE FOREST, where almost no one ever goes, he stands in a shaft of sunlight, the smoke from the smolder pile thickening the air and clinging to the branches and bracken that fringe the hidden hollow.

He is naked and clean, his scarred and scaled skin still singing from being submerged in the pure, icy water that bubbles from the depths of the earth and forms a pool at the edge of the hollow.

He picks up a staff of yew then pushes the baked and smoking sods aside with the point of it and drags ash from the center of the pile, spreading it over the ground to cool.

The ash is from a selection of woods, each chosen for their individual properties: Birch for new beginnings, oak for courage and strength, and yew again for death, rebirth, and long, long life.

He had died in a fire once, been buried in the earth beneath the burning wreckage of his former life. But he had been reborn in fire too. Reborn and re-formed.

He takes a handful of dirt and ash, still warm from the fire, rubs it between his hands, then places each on an opposite shoulder and draws them down across his chest, all the way to his hips, leaving the smeared sign of a cross.

It is the pagan cross, older than Christ, almost as old as the forest itself.

He takes a second handful of ash and dirt, rubs it between his palms, then covers his face with his hands and draws them down, the mulch of decayed leaves and gray embers mixing with the water still trapped in his beard to form clumps of grayish-brown paste. He licks these away and swallows, savoring the bitter taste of rot and loam, seasoned with smoke and the taste of the fire, as he renews again his place in the circle of birth and death and rebirth.

The sun makes the trees.

The trees make the fire.

And the fire made him.

Swallowing the ash and the dirt means the fire and the forest are inside him now, just as he is the fire and also the forest, reborn and ready. Ready to harvest. Ready to plant and nurture and reap.

No beginning. No end.

An endless cycle of rebirth.

And of death.

36

LAUGHTON FOLLOWS THE SATNAV, DRIVING as quickly as she dares down narrow country lanes that are only slightly less scary in daylight.

"Here's what I need you to do." Laughton glances at the time, keenly aware that she'll practically have to kick Adele out of the car while they're still moving if she stands any chance of making the meeting with Beech. "Now we know for sure that Maddie did go to the Midsummer Parade in Cinderfield you need to flyer the whole route. Put up as many as you can, on lampposts, on road signs, everywhere people might see it. You'll need to buy a stapler and some cable ties from somewhere so you can attach them to telegraph poles and things, get some clear plastic covers too if you can find some, it'll make the flyers last longer. I'll give you money for all this."

"No, it's fine. I've got money." Laughton waves her off.

"Also, you should go in all the shops, cafés, and pubs, and ask the owners if they remember anything. Show them the flyer, ask them if they've seen Maddie, and if they have, then take names and numbers so we can arrange to take proper witness statements. I'll give you a notebook to write everything down."

Ahead of them a tractor pulls out of a gate and turns onto the road, towing a trailer full of hay bales that leaves a blizzard of straw behind it. Laughton slows and falls in line as it crawls past a sign saying, "Welcome to Cinderfield."

"Also, try to get the shops and pubs to put a flyer or two up in their windows. Anything posted in a fixed location is much more likely to get noticed, and they also tend to spark conversations. The more we can get people talking about Maddie, the more likely someone's memory will be jogged and the better chance we have of getting some leads. At the moment, apart from the people you've contacted, I doubt many people even know she's missing, so we need to change that."

She edges out to see if she can pass the tractor, but a stream of traffic coming the other way makes her fall right back into the blizzard of straw.

"Another thing I want you to look out for is cameras. Any CCTV cameras you can spot along the route, security cameras on buildings or traffic lights, cameras on residential properties, doorbell cams, anything that might have caught Maddie walking by. If you see any cameras on shops, ask the owners about them, and see if they're happy for us to look at their footage from the day. They might not be, in which case we'll need to get a warrant, but most of the time people want to be helpful, particularly on a case like this."

She sees the war memorial appear up ahead. "Duck in the back there and get the flyers out of my bag. Take all of them, we can always print more. And grab a notebook and a pen too, there's a pack of both in there. You're going to need to jump out as soon as I stop if I have any chance of making this meeting."

Adele leans in the back to gather what she needs.

Laughton looks for a place to pull over, feeling annoyed that they're having to do all this in such a rush. The police should have set all this in motion the moment Maddie was reported missing. They should already be reviewing CCTV footage and doing door-to-door inquiries. She remembered what Tannahill had said about Beech, how there were cases that got attention and others that didn't, and Beech was the one who decided which was which. It made her mad. It also made her determined to make the meeting with him so she could look him in the eye. She pulls over into a bus stop and looks across at Adele, her arms filled with images of her sister's smiling face, and feels annoyed all over again that she's having to leave her to do this alone.

"Listen," she says, "this kind of legwork is tough, so if talking about Maddie to people who quite possibly won't seem to care becomes a bit overwhelming, be kind to yourself and stop doing it, OK? There are other things you can do that will be just as useful. You can start making a list of people of interest, anyone your sister might have annoyed or rubbed up the wrong way, no matter how petty or small it may seem, write it all down. Also, you could start putting together a timeline of events leading up to her disappearance, dates, times, places she went, people she saw, phone calls, text messages. If we can piece together a detailed picture of the days and hours leading up to her disappearance, we have a much better chance of figuring out what might have happened to her."

Adele nods. "No, this needs doing, and I'd rather get on with it. I'll be fine, honestly."

She opens the door, steps out into the sunshine, then nudges it closed again with her leg.

Laughton looks at her, the flyers with her missing sister's face clutched to her chest. She imagines her own daughter's face on the flyers and feels a sudden surge of maternal protection toward Adele. "Listen, one more thing. Have you ever heard of a hope diary?"

Adele shakes her head.

"A hope diary is a way of focusing your mind on positive thoughts and positive outcomes. Basically you think about what you hope will happen and write it down. It might sound a bit hippie-dippie but it helps keep you positive. It works in the same way athletes previsualize a race or the shape of a shot to ensure they get the outcome they want. You're going to have a lot of negative thoughts crowding in on you in the next few hours and days which could easily drag you down, so you need to stay focused and you need to stay positive, OK?"

Adele smiles. "OK." She looks up the road where the long procession of cars is still filing past. "You should be fine for time, once you get past that tractor it's a pretty straight run all the way to Gloucester, and the police HQ is this side of it, so you won't have to go through the town center."

"Thanks," Laughton says. "Good luck. I'll call you when I'm out of the meeting and let you know how I got on."

Dog watches in his rearview mirror as Laughton pulls out and rejoins the back of the convoy. When she'd pulled over it had taken him unawares and there was no room or time for him to pull over too so he'd driven on, past her parked car, hoping to find a chance to pull over somewhere soon. And now he had another dilemma.

The arrival of the other woman had complicated things the night before, but now they'd split up again, it posed another problem.

Which one to follow?

The initial target was alone again, but she was also in the middle of a busy high street, in the middle of a busy morning. Taking her without anyone noticing was going to be difficult, bordering on impossible. There was a chance that if he followed her for long enough she might end up somewhere more secluded, but there was an equal chance she was going to work in a shop all day and wouldn't be alone again until nightfall.

Whereas the other woman, the one now behind him in the car, was an altogether different proposition. Following her might provide some answers to questions that had been turning in his head, such as:

Who the fuck was she?

What the fuck was she doing turning up in the middle of the night and ruining his nice, easy job?

And possibly most interesting of all—

What the fuck had she meant when she'd said her dad was someone high up in the Met?

Ahead of him the tractor pulls over to the side of the road and the line of cars starts to spread out as they pass it by and speed up. He checks in the mirror again to make sure her car is still behind him then indicates left and turns off the main road and into a side street. He pulls over quickly and watches the junction until her car drives past, then he backs into a driveway, turns his car around, and rejoins the main road. He is now a couple of cars behind her instead of a couple in front and driving a nondescript car that blends in far more than the minicab he'd been driving the night before.

He hangs back a little to give her more space.

He can find the other woman again later.

For now, he's more interested in where Goldilocks is going.

37

ADELE WATCHES LAUGHTON JOIN THE queue of cars behind the tractor and drive slowly out of Cinderfield.

She heads over to one of the benches by the war memorial to sort the stack of flyers into a neater pile after having had to grab them in such a messy hurry. She shuffles them together, places them on the bench, then puts the notebook on top to stop the light breeze from snatching them and sending them fluttering away down the High Street. She runs her hand over the smooth black cover of the notebook, remembering what Laughton had said about writing—what had she called it? A hope diary. It actually hadn't sounded hippie-dippie to her at all. The phrases she'd collected and pinned to her wall over the years had always helped her, focusing her mind on positive things rather than all the bad stuff that swirled around inside it that made her want to curl up in bed and never get out again.

She pulls her phone out and checks the time.

8:02.

She should have already started her morning cleaning round at The Site, but clearly that isn't going to happen. She finds Bill's number and calls him, resting her hand on the stack of flyers and listening to it ringing, hoping he doesn't answer so she can leave a message and avoid a confrontation.

He answers on the third ring.

"What!?" He already sounds pissed off. Behind him she can hear the hiss of road noise, suggesting he's driving.

Adele clears her throat. "Hey, Bill, it's Adele. Listen . . . I can't work today. I'm really sorry, but something came up . . ."

"So, who's going to clean the camp?"

"I'm sorry, Bill, I just can't do it today. I'm sure you'll be able to find someone . . ."

"Who!? Who am I going to be able to find at this short notice?"

"Aren't there agencies you can call?"

"Agencies!? Have you any idea what they charge? I don't need no agency cleaners, I just need you to get to work right now."

"I can't. I'm not at The Site."

"Where are you?"

She thinks about saying something like "the hospital" to shut down the conversation but then feels annoyed at herself for not having the courage to just tell him the truth. She looks down at the stack of flyers, her sister's face peeking out from behind the notebook. "I'm still trying to find Maddie."

She hears a loud exhalation and can picture him rolling his eyes. "If you're telling me you're leaving me short-staffed with no notice just because of your bloody sister then you can pack up your stuff and move out right now."

Adele takes a deep breath and blows it out slowly. "OK," she says.

"What!?"

"I said OK. I quit. I'll come around later and pick up my stuff and the wages I'm owed."

"You can't quit!"

"Why not?"

"Because I'm firing you."

Adele shakes her head. Talking to Bill was exhausting. His ego was so large and yet so incredibly fragile.

"OK," she says, deciding to go with the flow because it was easier. "You fired me. I'm fired. Are we done now?"

"Yes. Actually, no. I got a call from the bike hire people this morning saying they came to collect the last lot and there was a bike missing."

Adele closes her eyes and shakes her head. "Yes, sorry, I know where it is. I'll bring it back when I come and collect my things."

"Right! OK then. I mean, you can't drop me in it like this and expect me to do nothing."

"Absolutely. I deserve to be fired and, well, you fired me, so that's that. I'm going to go now, Bill."

"Wait . . . Can you think of anyone who might want your job?"

Adele shakes her head in disbelief. "No, Bill, I can't." She pictures her old room and wonders why she put up with it for so long. Then a new thought strikes her.

"Hey, yesterday when you were at The Site, did you see anyone hanging around the shack?"

"You mean the sanitation station?"

Adele closes her eyes. "Yes, the sanitation station."

"No. Why?"

"Someone came in and took Maddie's stuff, and I wondered if . . ."

"Didn't see anyone."

His response is clipped, almost defensive. Why would someone who'd just fired her be defensive? Unless . . .

"Did you take Maddie's stuff?"

"Me? No."

Again, the answer seems too quick. Too defensive. She decides to try to push it.

"Why did you take Maddie's stuff, Bill?"

"What!? . . . I'm not . . . Listen, I have to go, I need to find someone to take over your job."

The phone clicks as he hangs up.

Adele stares at her phone for a second then stabs the number to call him back.

Straight to voicemail.

She looks up at the High Street, the steady stream of cars and people going about their day. Why would Bill take Maddie's things then lie about it?

She opens the notebook to the first page, unclips the pen and writes:

<u>PEOPLE OF INTEREST</u>

BILL DOWNHAM ???

Then she picks up the stack of flyers and heads over to the hardware shop on the corner to buy a staple gun and cable ties and to ask the owner if he has a CCTV camera, or if he remembers seeing her sister at the Cinderfield Parade.

38

BEECH IS FIVE MINUTES AWAY from work when his phone rings. He checks the number and groans inwardly when he sees who it is. Ordinarily he would ignore it but given the situation, and the early hour, and the fact that the call is coming in on WhatsApp instead of on an open line, he answers.

"Bill!" he says, as if his call is a pleasant surprise. "To what do I owe the honor?"

"Sorry to bother you like this but, er . . . I just . . . you know that thing you asked me to do? The thing with the backpack."

"It's OK to talk about it, Bill, no one's listening."

"OK, so you know you asked me to clear Maddie Friar's things from The Site? Well, I think her sister knows it was me that took her stuff."

Beech stares ahead at the road for a beat, his lips compressing to a tight line.

"And why do you think that, Bill?"

"So, what happened is . . . she called me, not to talk about that but we kind of got on to the subject of her sister and she asked if I'd seen anyone around The Site yesterday, and I said I hadn't, but then she came right out and asked me if I took her sister's stuff. I told her I hadn't, but I'm . . . well, I'm not sure she believed me."

Beech nods. He's not sure he would believe Bill either.

"How did you leave it?"

"I ended up firing her."

"You fired her!?"

"Yes. Not because of that. She didn't turn up to work today, which at this time of year is a nightmare, so I fired her."

Beech shakes his head. Asking Bill to tidy up this loose end had been a mistake. He'd hoped that getting rid of Maddie's things would make it look like she had gone off somewhere. Now it was something else that might seem suspicious.

"Listen to me, Bill." He flicks his indicator on and makes the turn into the sprawling car park surrounding the Gloucestershire Constabulary building. "It doesn't matter what she suspects, because she doesn't know anything and she certainly can't prove anything. Now, there's a hell of a lot at stake here and we all stand to benefit from this deal, so we can't have nobodies like Adele spoiling everything by bringing unwanted attention where it isn't needed. So, for the time being, don't talk to her. If she calls you, don't pick up. If you bump into her on the street or in a pub, tell her you're still pissed off with her and don't want to talk. All you need to do is keep your head down for the next day or so and things will sort themselves out, OK?"

"OK, cool. Yeah, no problem."

Beech's phone starts beeping with another incoming call.

"I've got to go now, Bill. Just keep a low profile and forget all about this, OK?"

He hangs up, pulls to a stop in his reserved spot, then looks at the phone, his mouth screwing back into a tight line when he sees who it is.

"Morning!" he answers with the same upbeat tone he used with Bill.

"We have a problem." There is nothing upbeat about the Earl's voice. It sounds tight and dry, like he hasn't slept much.

Beech squeezes out of his car and feels his usual pang of annoyance that his is the oldest and most basic model parked in the reserved spots.

"What kind of problem?" He takes his phone off speaker, clamps it to his ear, and heads to the entrance.

"I just got off the phone to my son and he is extremely distressed. EXTREMELY distressed."

Beech shakes his head. It never ceases to amaze him how bent out of shape entitled people get when the world fails to line up in their favor for once. They also automatically assume their problems are things other people need to sort out for them.

"What's made him so distressed?"

"An email," the Earl says with the same kind of venom he might spit out the word "whore." Beech waves at the receptionist as he passes through reception. She smiles back and buzzes him through the security gate. "An email asking him if he knows Maddie Friar!" the Earl hisses, his voice barely more than a whisper like he's afraid of being overheard. "It even had a photo attached."

Beech presses the button to call the lift. "Have you seen this email?"

"Yes, Sebastian forwarded it to me. I can send it on to you if you like."

"No! Don't do that. Don't send it to anyone else. It's a pity he sent it to you, but you could argue he was just sharing it to see if you knew her, seeing as you live locally. Who sent it?"

He hears fumbling noises as the Earl checks the mail. "It's from a Laughton Rees. Any idea who he is?"

"Yes," Beech says as the doors of the lift slide open. "And 'he's' a 'she.' I'm actually about to have a meeting with her."

"Really!? Why are you meeting with her?"

"Not sure yet. Let me see what she has to say then we should all meet up and discuss what needs to be done. Things are getting messy, and we all need to agree on how to clean things up. I'm not making this decision on my own. This is something for all of us to decide."

39

LAUGHTON PULLS OFF THE MAIN road at 8:42 exactly and enters a large car park surrounding a strange-looking building with a curved roof. She cruises up and down the packed rows looking for a space, surprised by the number of cars. The systematic budget cuts that had slimmed down the London Metropolitan police force had seemingly not affected this place at all judging by the number of people working here. She spots an empty bay, backs the hire car into it then shimmies out, hugging her laptop tightly to her chest as she heads toward the building with a curved, blue roof that makes it look like a big, plastic rowing boat that has been upended. She pushes through the entrance door into a reception area with a large board listing the building's occupants that solves the mystery of the packed car park:

G—Planning and Development
1—Council Tax and Parking
2—Sanitation and Recycling
3—Police
4—Police

This police department hadn't escaped the cuts at all, they'd just become uncomfortable roommates with other municipal departments in this hideous new building, probably so the council could sell off whatever lovely old stone headquarters they used to occupy in the center of town.

"Can I help you?" The receptionist smiles up at her, hiding her Starbucks Venti under the counter at the same time.

"Yes, I have an appointment to see Chief Constable Beech."

"Can I take your name?"

"Laughton Rees." She spells it out because, after a lifetime of being asked, she knows it's quicker to volunteer it.

The receptionist makes a call and starts preparing a visitor's pass. Laughton looks past her into the depressing, partitioned, open-plan splendor of the inner building, wondering what the old police headquarters would have been like. Similar to the ones in London, she imagines, beautiful old stone mansion blocks built to house a growing police force at the end of one century only to be sold off at the end of the next and turned into luxury flats most police officers couldn't afford. Not the honest ones, at least.

"Here you go." The receptionist hands her a lanyard with her pass. "Take the lift to the fourth floor, someone will meet you there."

Laughton smiles her thanks, takes the lanyard, and manages to slip through the closing doors of an upward-bound lift filled with people.

The "someone" who meets her on the fourth floor turns out to be the person she's here to see. Chief Constable Russell Beech looks much older and heavier than he did in his online photo, his auburn beard more salt than pepper, his hair thinning and brushed forward in the Romanesque, "I'm-not-really-balding-I-just-like-it-this-way" style. He stands with fists on hips and legs apart, barrel chest and beer belly straining against a pale blue shirt, like a Henry the Eighth lookalike who's lost his costume. He looks her up and down as the lift doors slide open then frowns slightly as he meets her eye. "You're shorter than I thought you'd be," he says, with a vague air of disappointment, like he's just lost a bet.

"Laughton Rees," she says, ignoring his remark and stepping out of the lift with her hand extended. "Thank you for seeing me at such short notice, sir." She braces herself for the kind of crushing handshake that usually accompanies men that look like him but instead he takes her hand quite gently, shakes it once, then turns and strides away down the corridor.

"I did it out of respect for your old man, really. I met him at a police conference a few years back. He was the keynote speaker, bought me a pint at the bar after. Good man, good copper too, even if he was from London."

He barges through a door with "Chief Constable RUSSELL BEECH" written on it and into an office so messy and teetering with piles of paper-work it looks like it might have been recently burgled.

"My sympathies for your loss," he says, collapsing into the black leather executive chair behind the desk and gesturing for her to sit opposite. "Though I gather you two weren't particularly close."

"We patched things up at the end," Laughton says, feeling her usual discomfort when talking about the man she'd spent most of her life hating and the last days of his sleeping in a chair by his bed, holding his hand and hoping he'd somehow pull through.

"Really?" Beech's eyebrows shoot up into the trench-lined no-man's-land of what used to be his hairline. "That's not how it looked in the papers. Seemed to me you stuck the knife in all his life, then twisted it for luck once you'd buried him."

Laughton studies Beech's face, trying to figure out if he's deliberately trying to rile her or if he's just one of those men in a position of power who has lost any filter he may once have had.

She smiles. "I'm sure you know better than most, sir, that you should never believe everything you read in the papers."

He nods slowly. "Indeed. So, how can I help?"

"I have no doubt you're very busy, sir, so I won't keep you long. I just wanted to pick your brains about an old case you worked back when you were still a sergeant, the Rachel Cooke case."

"Oh Christ, you really are digging back into ancient history now. That case is closed as far as I recall."

"Yes, it was, by you—though Rachel was never found."

Beech leans back in his chair and folds his hands over the mound of his stomach. "Lots of people drop off the grid, especially round here. The forest is like a magnet for all kinds of people wanting to go back to nature or whatever, turn their back on the evils of the modern world."

"Is that how you would characterize Rachel?"

"I can't really remember, like I said, it's a long time ago. As far as I can recall she had no close family, which would suggest she may have been somewhat . . . untethered. I imagine once we'd gone through the usual motions and didn't find any evidence that a crime had been committed, there wasn't much else we could do."

Laughton opens her laptop. "Actually, that's one of the things I wanted to talk to you about. I have a copy of the case file here, but I can't see any of the usual procedural evidence you'd expect to find in a missing persons inquiry; no witness statements, no tapes or transcripts of any interviews with friends or relatives, no timeline of events leading up to Rachel Cooke's disappearance. All there is on file is the initial missing persons report, filed by the girl's aunt, who expressed concern that her niece may have been taken by the 'Cinderman.'"

Beech snorts. "Well, there you go, I told you this place was a looney magnet."

Laughton turns her laptop around for Beech to see. "That initial statement was taken and signed by you, and a summary sheet officially closing the investigation two years later was also signed by you. Other than those two documents, there's nothing in the file, no evidence of any further investigation at all."

Beech leans further back in his chair and regards Laughton coolly. "What are you implying?"

"I'm not implying anything. I'm just telling you what there is in the file and hoping you might remember some more details about the case that may not have been recorded at the time, particularly who she associated with. I'd also like to know if you ever came up with a working theory about what might have happened to her?"

Beech leans forward with a shriek of springs and pulls open a drawer in his desk. "Well, like I say, it was a long time ago. I can barely remember where I was last Wednesday without looking at my damn phone." He takes a packet of Mentos out of the drawer and holds it out to her. "Mint?"

"No, thank you."

He works one out of the packet and pops it into his mouth. "Why are you so interested in this particular case?"

"Actually, it's not just this case." She opens her Cinderman folder and turns her laptop round so Beech can see all the named subfolders inside. "It's actually fifty-eight, going back twenty years. I discovered them as part of a research paper I'm working on exploring the overlap between folklore and crime, where people are sometimes more inclined to believe supernatural explanations for disappearances over more earthly ones, especially in closed and remote communities like these."

"'Closed and remote communities'"—Beech does air quotes with his fingers—"is that how you see us, inbred country bumpkins who believe in ghosts and goblins?"

"Not at all, you can get closed communities anywhere there are people, cities too. Spring-Heeled Jack was widely believed to stalk the East End slums way before Jack the Ripper appeared on the scene. Jewish communities in every major European city feared the Golem long before the Nazis turned up as real-life monsters. Superstition is a state of mind more than a state of place, but it doesn't grow in a vacuum. If something bad happens in your community and no one can tell you who did it or why, then people look for other explanations, because the mind craves order and fears chaos. They'd rather believe in a monster than nothing at all."

Beech regards her for a moment, rolling the mint around his mouth, like he's trying to make up his mind about something. "And what do you believe?"

"I believe in facts and evidence. That's why the lack of any in the Rachel Cooke case and many of these others bothers me. I also find it concerning that history continually repeats itself. Two days ago, the latest young woman went missing. Madeleine Friar, aged twenty-four, vanished in the forest on her way to a Midsummer party. Her sister, Adele, filed a missing persons report yesterday at lunchtime, but so far the only thing the police have done in relation to the case is arrest Adele for disturbing the peace yesterday evening and throw her in a jail cell."

Beech nods. "Until you came along and harangued my sergeant into letting her go."

Laughton frowns. "That's not what happened. She was being released anyway, and I wasn't haranguing your sergeant, I was querying the conditions he was keeping a female prisoner in, which were frankly appalling. Thank you for clearing up one thing for me, though."

It's Beech's turn to frown. "What's that?"

"It explains why you thought I'd be taller."

Beech snorts. "Yes, I really need to have a word with my sergeant about growing some balls. Let me give you a little bit of background on Maddie Friar and her sister. I looked them up before you arrived because, yes, I heard about your little scene in Cinderfield last night and figured this meeting might be related.

"Firstly, Maddie Friar is a flake and so is her sister. Maddie Friar's got a record as long as your arm."

"No, she hasn't, she's been picked up a few times for minor offenses, and her sister had no record at all until yesterday."

"Either way, Maddie Friar is still what we would term an 'unreliable victim.' She may not even be a victim at all, and we have to weigh all that up when deciding whether to allocate scarce resources to any investigation. I don't know what it's like in London but we're stretched pretty thin here. We don't have the kind of resources or budget the Met has, which is why we're crammed into this building with a bunch of other departments. I've got one thousand, four hundred police officers covering an area of over a thousand square miles; that includes cities, towns, royal palaces, Cheltenham Racecourse, and large tracts of forest with very complicated jurisdiction. Fourteen hundred officers is nowhere near enough police to cover that kind of area, so I'm sorry if you're unhappy that I'm not setting up a special task force to comb the woods looking for a girl who may or may not even be missing, but I just don't have the manpower."

"So, just so I understand this correctly," Laughton says, weighing her words carefully. "You're saying that if you had more manpower, you would have launched a full investigation into Maddie Friar's disappearance."

"If I had enough manpower I would investigate everything that came across my desk."

Laughton nods. "So, why didn't Rachel Cooke get a proper investigation twenty years ago? Why did none of these historical cases get investigated when so many of them predate the budget cuts in police spending?" She waits while Beech leans back in his chair again with a slow screech of springs, works another Mento out of the packet, and pops it in his mouth. "Your name is on all of these reports, Chief Constable, mostly to sign them off, but with Rachel Cooke it was you who took the initial statement. Did you personally decide twenty years ago that she was an unreliable victim and therefore not worth wasting police time on?"

Beech shifts the mint from one side of his mouth to the other and lodges it in his cheek, "Well, like I said, it was a long time ago. I can't remember the details."

Laughton closes her laptop and looks directly at Beech.

"You know, in the course of my work I've interviewed thousands of police officers about all kinds of cases, cold cases mostly, some going back half a century. And the one thing I've noticed with all of those interviews is how remarkable the recall is about the little details—the names, dates, times, leads, suspects—everything. It's like they're talking about a case that happened yesterday. A retired detective inspector explained it to me once, he said it's the ones you don't solve that stay with you."

Beech nods slowly. "That's true, but I would also add that some cases carry more weight than others."

"And the Rachel Cooke case carries no weight in your mind?"

He shakes his head. "A missing persons report does not mean a person is actually missing."

Laughton holds his gaze for a beat then looks away so he can't see the contempt creeping into her eyes. She looks instead at the mess of his room, the teetering piles of case files, each containing the story of someone's life, and, in many instances, death—the justice of each in the hands of this man who does not even seem to have the decency to pretend he cares. She shakes her head then stands to leave.

"Thank you for your time, sir," she says, her mind already racing with people she could call and favors she might pull to go over his head and make this maddening excuse of a policeman do his actual job. Then it strikes her. The solution is simple.

"I'll run the investigation," she says, turning back to face Beech.

"You?"

"Yes, I'm qualified, I'm available, I'm already being paid to be here by my research grant, so it won't come out of your budget. I just need your authorization."

Beech folds his arms across his chest and looks at Laughton with a slight frown. "I'm not sure that's a good idea."

"Why not? You said it was a manpower issue and I've just offered to work for you for free."

"Yes, but . . . It's not just a personnel issue, I also don't think Maddie Friar being missing for a few hours is worth wasting any time over."

"With respect, sir, I disagree. The first three days of any missing persons case are the most crucial, and we've already lost nearly half of that. In addition, it's my own time I'm proposing to waste, not yours, so I don't see what possible objection you can have. Unless for some reason you don't want Maddie's disappearance investigated."

"Be careful," Beech says, his voice low. "You're getting dangerously close to being insulting."

"My apologies," Laughton says, forcing a smile. "My passion is getting ahead of me. Of course, it's ridiculous to think you wouldn't want to investigate a possible crime in your district, which is why you're obviously going to let me do it."

Beech regards her with a peculiar look on his face, something between annoyance and curiosity.

"OK," he says. "If you want to waste your time, be my guest, but I want a daily update of what you're up to and a list of everyone you want to interview before you talk to them. I don't want you annoying anyone important because of some local nobody who got drunk at a party and lost their phone, understood? Now if you don't mind, I've got another meeting in five minutes."

Laughton stands up but doesn't make a move to leave. "I'll need a warrant," she says. "Something on headed paper signed by you, confirming I have authority to investigate this case. We wouldn't want the chain of evidence to be compromised if I find something, would we?"

Beech looks up at her and crunches his mint loudly between his teeth. "No," he says, pulling his keyboard closer so he can write her a letter of authorization. "We would not."

40

ADELE REACHES THE END OF Cinderfield High Street, where the shops peter out and the houses are set too far back for any cameras fixed on them to be any use. She feels like crying, or breaking something, or crying while breaking something.

She is frustrated at how few cameras she has found, and how hard it has been to try and persuade the shops that do have them to let her see the footage. Even the flyer with her sister's photo on it has failed to have the effect she thought it would, and rather than softening hearts, her story has been met with folded arms and shaking heads. Hardly anyone let her put a flyer in their window, their excuses ranging from vaguely apologetic claims that it's not their shop so not their decision, to stern refusals along the general theme of "We don't want to advertise that bad things happen around here in case it spooks the tourists."

In angry response to this Adele made it her mission to decorate every lamppost, sign, and vertical pole she could find with as many flyers as she could fit on them. She walks back down the High Street now, Maddie's face smiling out at her everywhere she looks, until she arrives back at the war memorial, her fury still simmering. She sits on the ground in the shade of the statue of the unknown soldier because the benches are now full of the tourists who must not be frightened. She feels like walking up to each one of them and thrusting a flyer into their hands and saying, "You could vanish here and no one will do a single thing about it."

She checks her phone to see if Laughton has called or left a message then opens the notebook and goes through the list of CCTV cameras. Laughton said they'd get warrants for the footage if the owners wouldn't volunteer it, so she is very much looking forward to going back later and watching their faces fall as they are told they have to show them their precious footage, whether they like it or not.

She leans back against the plinth, enjoying the feel of the cold stone against her back, and closes her eyes. Taking deep breaths, she repeats in her head some of the phrases she's collected, to try to calm the cocktail of rage and frustration boiling inside her:

Positive thoughts create positive things.

You only fail if you quit.

Never. Ever. Lose. Hope.

Hope . . .

She opens her eyes again, the word reminding her of something Laughton had said, and turns to a fresh page in the notebook. A "hope diary," she had called it, a way of focusing your mind on positive thoughts to help bring about positive outcomes.

She uncaps the pen, taps it against her lips for a moment, then writes:

Maddie has gone away for a few days to clear her head. That's why she didn't say anything to me and that's why she hasn't made contact with me yet.

She reads it back then crosses it out angrily.

Just writing a bunch of wishful nonsense in a book isn't going to change anything. She needs to keep it close to the truth of what happened and find the positives in it.

She thinks again then writes:

Maddie went for a walk in the forest. She'd promised she wouldn't because she knew it was dangerous but something drew her there. And just because her phone lost signal does not mean that she is lost. Just because she is missing does not mean she is gone. She may have fallen. She may be hurt. But she would never give up and neither will I. Whatever has happened to her. Wherever she is. I will find her.

She underlines the word "will" several times, and just the simple act of doing this, of pinning her promise to a page, makes her feel better.

"Believe in what you want so much that it has no choice but to materialize," she murmurs, recalling another of the phrases fixed to her wall.

She looks back up the High Street at the hateful shops and the flyers of Maddie fluttering in the breeze along with the bunting left over from the Cinderfield Parade. Then she sees something else, fixed to the top of the clocktower, a camera she had missed.

She sits forward and checks her signal, making sure her phone is connected to the free Wi-Fi then googles "Cinderfield Webcam." A high, wide view of the High Street loads up on her screen. She raises her hand

and waves it above her head and on the screen she sees herself do the same. She scrolls to the bottom of the page where a number of links are listed, archived feeds of notable dates in the town, a kind of greatest hits of the Cinderfield Webcam: New Year's Eve, Bonfire Night—

—and the Midsummer Parade.

41

LAUGHTON HANDS HER LANYARD BACK to the receptionist and heads out of the building, folding the signed letter she'd extracted from Beech and sliding it into her laptop to keep it safe. Her meeting with him had left her feeling unsettled. She had expected him to be defensive, unhelpful even, but not to the level she had just experienced. She couldn't work out if he was lazy, or negligent, or whether there was something more sinister at the heart of his clear reluctance to investigate Maddie Friar's disappearance or talk about any of the other fifty-seven missing persons cases she'd found.

She heads across the packed car park over to where she thinks she parked, making a list in her head of all the things she needs to set in motion now she's leading the investigation into Maddie Friar's disappearance. Not that she's really leading anything—she and Adele are the investigation.

She spots a small, silver car in the middle of a row and heads over to it, fumbling the keys from her pocket and pressing the unlock button on the fob, but nothing happens. She takes a few steps closer, pointing the fob directly at the car, and presses it again. Still nothing. She spots the "Baby on Board" sticker in the back window and realizes she's trying to unlock the wrong car then looks around, trying to remember where she parked and realizing that silver cars are quite popular.

She starts working her way through the car park, firing the key fob at every silver car she comes across, the heat of the day already rising and doing little to improve her mood.

From his fourth-floor window, Beech watches Laughton zigzagging through the parked cars, pointing her hand in different directions like she's firing an invisible gun. He holds his phone in front of his mouth, listening to the trill of the Google Meet ringtone until it cuts out and connects.

"Yes?" Grizz's voice sounds clipped and unfriendly.

"Listen, we have a problem."

"Is this a different problem from the one we already have?"

"It's the same problem only worse, a lot worse. I just had a meeting with someone who's looking into historic disappearances in the area, missing persons cases that I signed off."

He hears a deep sigh on the line and can picture Grizz closing her eyes and shaking her dreadlocked head.

"Who is this person?"

"She's an academic who does some consulting work for various police departments, the Met mainly. She's called Laughton Rees. Google her, she was all over the news a while back."

Down in the car park the hazard lights flash on a small silver car and Laughton heads toward it. Beech squints against the sun to read the number plate and scrawls it down on a Post-it note.

"How do you want to handle it?" Grizz asks.

"Just scare her off, make her back off to buy us some time. Once the deal is done and dusted she can investigate all she likes and we can deal with any loose ends then."

Down in the car park Laughton squeezes through the door of the silver car and closes it behind her.

"Where is she now?"

"She's about to drive out of police HQ car park, I imagine she's probably on her way back to Cinderfield."

"Is she in a silver Ford Focus, registration number NU22 DRB?"

Beech looks at the number he wrote on the Post-it note. "How do you know that?"

"Because my guy has already been following her for the last hour. Don't worry. I'll handle it."

Then Beech's phone clicks as the line goes dead.

42

LAUGHTON FOLLOWS THE SATNAV DIRECTIONS on her phone back to
Cinderfield, the morning sun casting the shadow of her car in front of her
as she heads west through rolling countryside. She waits until she hits the
main road, still turning the meeting with Beech over in her mind, then
picks up her phone and holds it to her mouth.

"Hey Siri, call Tannahill."

"Calling DCI Tannahill Khan. Mobile."

Siri reciting his full title reminds her that she keeps meaning to edit
his contact to something less formal than how she'd entered it when they
first met and their relationship had been entirely professional. The fact
that she hasn't changed it yet is testament to how new everything still is.
She listens to the ringtone mixing with the white noise of her tires on the
road until he picks up.

"Hey," Tannahill says, the burble of overlapping conversation loud in
the background. "What's up?"

"I just had a very weird meeting with Chief Constable Beech."

"What's he like?"

"He's kind of an old-school, eighties-throwback, career-type copper.
Chews mints like he's chain-smoking, which means he probably used to
be an actual chain-smoker. Looks like he's one sausage roll away from a
coronary."

"You've just described a large chunk of the people at this conference."

"Yeah, I imagine he's been to a few of them. Maybe ask your new
buddy if there's any gossip."

"What kind of gossip?"

"I don't know, anything dodgy that didn't end up on his record, skeletons
in his closet . . . there was definitely something slightly off about him. He
responded to my request for a meeting immediately but then was pretty

closed down and borderline hostile from the moment I arrived. I thought it might just be the usual bullshit male-female, big-man-in-authority-doesn't-like-being-questioned-by-tiny-woman kind of thing, but I think there was more to it than that. When I asked him about a historical missing persons case he worked, he said he couldn't remember any details."

"That's odd."

"That's what I thought. He was still a sergeant when he worked it, so you would have thought it would be one of those early-career cases that lodged in the memory, but he said he couldn't remember anything about it, couldn't tell me what the operating theory was, couldn't tell me why there was no evidence of a proper investigation. Nothing."

"You think he's hiding something?"

"Yes, I do. The most worrying thing is that exactly the same thing is happening again with this new case I'm looking at. I had to pretty much back him into a corner and force him to authorize me to run an investigation because he clearly wasn't planning to. He kept saying that he couldn't spare the resources and that she probably wasn't missing anyway. He didn't seem remotely interested, but then when I suggested I investigate her disappearance, he only agreed on the condition that I report directly to him. He went from total disinterest to personally overseeing it. What's that all about?"

"Could just be a territorial thing. Old silverbacks like him tend to be touchy about outside agencies trampling on their patch and questioning their methods. He definitely won't have liked being told what to do by someone down from London."

"Yeah, well, if he did his job properly I wouldn't have needed to."

"Let me ask around, see if anyone here knows him and can give some background. He could just be a shitty cop, nothing more sinister than that. I'll try and find my new friend from Hereford again and ask him about Beech."

"Thanks. I really appreciate all this, you know."

"Ah, it's fine. It'll give me something to do in the evenings when everyone else is down at the bar trying to outdrink each other. These conferences are not really set up for the nondrinker. Downing pints of mango juice doesn't really impress that many people."

Laughton smiles. Tannahill is an interesting product of his mixed heritage, brown skin and black hair from his Pakistani father, but blue, Irish eyes from his mother. He also has a very un-Celtic dislike of alcohol that means he drinks pints of fruit juice instead of Guinness.

"What are you up to now?" Tannahill asks.

"Driving back to Cinderfield."

"Cinderfield! Is that a real place?"

"Yep. Most of the towns and villages around here sound like they should have hobbits living in them."

"Be careful."

"Why, because of orcs?"

"No, because people in rural areas don't generally take too kindly to city folks poking around in their business."

"Don't worry, I'm always careful."

"I wouldn't call pissing off the chief constable of a regional division being particularly careful."

"Oh, he was pissed off before I even stepped into his office. He looks like the sort who wakes up annoyed and goes to sleep furious."

"Either way, just tread lightly. Remember, lots more people in the countryside have shotguns. I've got to go now, there's someone here I want to talk to about your missing persons."

"Which one?"

"All of them. Got to go, I'll call you later."

He hangs up, leaving Laughton wondering what he's up to. She checks the time. Nine thirty, which means it's probably safe to call Gracie. She glances in the rearview mirror at the traffic then holds the phone up to her mouth.

"Hey, Siri, call Gracie."

It starts to ring. On the satnav she sees a large patch of green appear, which means she's getting close to the forest again. The phone clicks and her smile broadens as Gracie's voice fills the car.

"Hey, Mum."

"Hey, gorgeous girl, how's Cornwall?"

"It's pretty."

"What about the surfer dudes, are they pretty too?"

"They're OK."

"Any interest?"

"It's not like that."

Laughton smiles. "Yeah, it is. Give us some gossip, I could do with a distraction."

The satnav indicates a turn up ahead and she flicks on her indicator and follows the curve of the exit road into a tunnel of trees so deep in shadow it makes the automatic headlights turn on.

"Rose got really drunk last night and ended up in a port-a-loo with some sketchy-looking local."

"Eeew."

"She's spent all today throwing up and claiming she can't remember a thing, but we all think she shagged him."

"Classy."

"I know, right? Helena definitely fancies our windsurfing instructor and is being really flirty with him, which is chronic and gross because he's, like, thirty or something."

"Wow, he's practically dead."

"I didn't mean . . . you know what I mean. So, what's happening . . . forest, you. . . . nice time?"

"You're breaking up. I'm driving through some trees. Hold on."

She emerges from the shadows into bright sunshine. "You still there?"

"Yeah, I'm here. I asked if you were having a nice time."

Laughton reflects on everything that's happened in the last twenty-four hours. "I wouldn't exactly say I'm having a 'nice' time. There's a young woman here who's not much older than you and her sister went missing. She's on her own here and she's . . . well, she reminds me a little of . . . doesn't matter. I think I might stay here a few more days, seeing as you're away."

"OK."

She rounds a corner and the road dips down into another tunnel of trees.

"Listen, I might lose signal again. Have fun, but be careful around Rose, she's the kind of girl who'll drag you into a bad situation then leave you high and dry the moment a boy or something more exciting comes along."

"Are you saying I'm not exciting?"

"Oh, honey—you know I think you're really boring."

"Thanks."

The car enters the tunnel of trees and is instantly plunged into deep shadow.

"Seriously, though, she's toxic, probably literally after that port-a-loo incident."

"Yeah, I know. Don't worry. Listen I gotta go, we're all heading down to the beach for breakfast."

"Nice. Enjoy. Love you, G."

"Love you t . . ."

The phone beeps three times, telling her she's been cut off.

Laughton thinks about Gracie skipping off for a beach breakfast. Then she thinks of Adele, only a few years older, living in a shed, alone and practically homeless. She realizes that the person she reminds her of is not Gracie, it's herself at Gracie's age, equally lost and alone. She had never had anyone looking out for her. Maybe that's why she feels such a strong sense of duty to look after Adele now. She glances down at the satnav, but that has lost signal too and is now showing an arrow floating in the middle of an expanse of green.

"Welcome back to the nineteen eighties," she murmurs, then peers ahead through the gloom to see if she can see a road sign or anything that might tell her she's still on the right track. Behind her a car appears over a rise in the undulating road, headlights full and dazzling. She flips up the rearview mirror to cut the glare and spots a junction up ahead beyond a sign with a large, leafy branch in front of it, making it impossible to read. Laughton slows down as she approaches it to try to read it and a loud horn sounds behind her, startling her and making her automatically speed up. She whizzes past the sign without seeing what it says.

She glances back at the satnav but the screen is still grayed out and frozen. Left, she thinks. She's pretty sure that's what it had said before she lost signal. She indicates and starts slowing down. Again the horn blares behind her.

She glances in her side mirror to see who's in such a hurry, but the car behind is right on her bumper now, headlamps on full beam and blinding.

She reaches the junction. Looks left past the wall of trees.

Was it left? The road seems narrower that way.

The angry horn sounds behind her and she heads left anyway, committed now and hoping Mr. Angry behind her turns right.

She flips the rearview mirror back down and sees the blazing headlights
turn in her direction and start following her down the narrow lane, speeding to catch up with her.

"Great," she murmurs, focusing on the way ahead. The road rises
and falls as it follows the undulating ground, curving this way and that
through the shadowy forest. She glances down at her phone. Still no
signal.

Behind her the horn blares again, a series of blasts this time, ending
with one long, angry note.

"Oh, just piss off," Laughton mutters, then feels bad. Maybe whoever's
behind her has a genuine emergency.

She looks ahead for a place to pull over to let them overtake, but the
lane is too narrow, barely wide enough for two cars to pass. She slows a
little as she eases round a blind bend and is rewarded with another volley
of blasts on the horn. Ahead she spots a small gap in the trees where a
track joins the road. She indicates. Starts to slow down and gets another
long lean on the horn as a reward.

"I'm pulling over to let you pass, you moron!" She squints against the
blinding lights filling her rearview mirror.

She reaches the gap and turns in, feeling the thin wheels of the rental
car bump and slip as they leave the road and meet the soft, baked dirt of
the track. She stamps on her brakes and jerks to a halt, then looks to her
right so she can glare at the driver as his car blasts past.

Only it doesn't.

In the side mirror, she sees the car stopped on the road about ten feet
behind her, the headlights blazing so bright it's hard to see anything
beyond them. Laughton lowers her window, reaches out with her arm,
and waves it on.

Still the car does not move.

With her window open she can hear its engine now. A low rumble.
Idling. No sign it has any intention of moving. She holds her hand up to
try and shield the worst of the glare and can just make out the outline
of a figure sitting behind the wheel. She can feel him watching her. She
assumes it's a "he."

She waves him on a second time but still he doesn't move. He just keeps staring at her, his engine rumbling beneath the rustling leaves and distant coo of wood pigeons. Laughton doesn't know much about cars, she's never even owned one, and the dazzling headlights make it impossible to see what make this one is, but whatever it is, it sounds powerful, way more powerful than her economy rental. Even if she had the driving skills and local knowledge, she would never be able to outrun it.

She considers getting out of the car and walking over to him to ask what his problem is but feels instinctively nervous about leaving the safety of the car. She's a woman alone, in a remote spot with someone who has already demonstrated aggression toward her and is continuing to show aggression with this strange, stalking behavior. Getting out of the car to try to chat is too much of a risk. It's also exactly the kind of thing people do in books and films the moment before they get killed.

She looks back down at her phone. Still no signal. Picks it up in the faint hope it might make a difference. It doesn't. She's in a dip in the road surrounded by dense forest. She'd probably have to climb a tree to stand any chance of getting a signal. She looks back at the car. But he doesn't necessarily know that.

She holds her phone to her ear and counts to three in her head like she's waiting for it to connect, then says loud enough that the driver might hear if his window is open, "Hi, yeah, someone's following me and driving extremely dangerously on the A48 between Gloucester and Cinderfield. They've just run me off the road and they've now stopped and are blocking traffic. The registration number of the car is . . ." She holds her hand up to shield her eyes from the worst of the glare and squints to read the number plate.

But there isn't one.

Instead of the usual line of number and letters there's a line of black tape.

Laughton looks back at the figure of the driver, the skin tightening on her face as she realizes the implications of this. The driver is still looking right at her. He doesn't look away, doesn't look down to check if his phone has a signal. He knows she has no signal. Which means he knows her call was a bluff. He revs his engine, a deep and menacing growl.

Laughton locks the door, winds her window back up.

Outside she can still hear the engine revving, the sound penetrating her bubble of safety and revealing exactly how thin it is.

She looks left down the dirt track that runs through the woods, ruts of winter mud baked hard by summer sun. There's no way her city runabout hire car would get far if she tried going that way. She doesn't even know where it goes, and the last thing she needs is to end up somewhere even more remote than here. The only way out is forward, down the narrow road through the woods to wherever it goes.

She grabs the steering wheel, slams it in first gear, and stamps down on the accelerator. The wheels spin as the engine engages and the car slips sideways, dirt flying as the tires struggle to grip on the dry, loose ground. She eases off the accelerator a little, fighting her panicked urge to flee and the car lurches forward just as the other car appears directly in front of her, blocking her way. She stamps on her brakes, narrowly avoiding a collision, gets her first proper look at the driver, and a silent scream sounds in her head.

The man has no face.

43

LAUGHTON STARES IN HORROR AT the space where the man's face should be, the camouflage veil beneath the peak of his cap making his head blend in totally with the background, almost like he's part of the forest. The only human element visible are the cold, hard eyes that stare out at her through a narrow slit.

She jams the car in reverse and looks behind her, searching for a way out. She eases her foot off the clutch too fast and the car lurches backward then stalls.

She frantically turns the key in the ignition and the car lurches backward again.

Still in gear. Need to focus. Mustn't panic.

She stamps in the clutch. Restarts the engine and jams it in reverse.

The parking sensors beep. Her foot shakes as she forces herself to lift it slowly and the car eases backward. She hauls down on the wheel to turn the car and the parking sensors start screaming. She feels a bump as the rear bumper hits something and she puts the car back in first gear and looks forward again.

The faceless man behind the wheel is still there, still staring at her through the slit in the green veil, like the forest itself is looking at her. But it's not the forest. It's just some dick wearing military gear and getting off on the fear. Fuck this guy. Just fuck him and whatever his twisted deal is.

She looks down at the dashboard for the light switch, finds it on the end of the indicator stalk, twists it on, then puts it on full beam. She revs the engine as loud as she can, and the man behind the wheel shifts slightly, like he's momentarily unsettled and not sure what she's going to do.

She thinks about ramming him. Lifting her foot off the clutch and letting her car slam right into the side of his. But his car looks bigger, more solid. She would probably do more damage to her own car than to his, cripple herself even, and then be trapped here with this lunatic. The man shakes his head slowly, like he's gone through the same thought process and has come to the same conclusion. She imagines him smiling behind the veil and the thought makes her want to slam into the side of him anyway and fuck the consequences. Her hands tighten on the wheel and she revs her engine again, flooring it until it screams.

The man with no face holds her gaze, like he's daring her to do it.

Then he looks suddenly away and behind him, back up the road.

Laughton looks too. Another car has appeared, slowing down as the driver sees the way ahead is blocked.

Laughton yanks on the handbrake, throws her car into neutral, and is out of the door and running before she even realizes this is her plan.

"Hey!" She waves her hands above her head to flag the driver down. "HEY!!"

Behind her she hears the deep roar of the big engine and looks back, afraid it might be reversing. Grit stings her face instead as the car takes off, its wide wheels throwing dust and dirt into the air as it fishtails away. She narrows her eyes against the flying grit, trying to see the rear number plate, but black tape covers this too.

She watches the car, getting smaller as it moves away at speed, and she tries to commit as much detail as possible to memory before it disappears around the bend. It is black or very dark gray, and she can't see the make in the shadowy half-light of the forest. It also looks fairly new, some kind of 4x4, which means she wouldn't have stood a chance if she'd attempted to escape by heading offroad.

"Are you OK?"

Laughton turns to find a man who looks like a retired schoolteacher half out of the open door of his car, face etched with concern and his wire-rimmed glasses magnifying wide and anxious eyes.

"Yeah, I'm . . ." She shudders as the adrenaline starts curdling in her bloodstream. "I'm OK, thanks."

"You look quite pale. Let me get you a mint, I think I have some in my car." He ducks back inside and starts rooting around in the glove box. Laughton looks back up the road, but the car has gone now, though she can still hear the deep roar of its engine being steadily swallowed by the forest.

"Here you go, I knew I had some." The man holds out half a packet of Polos.

Laughton doesn't really want one but takes it anyway.

"What happened?" the man asks, peering at her car backed up against the bracken. "Did you have a crash?"

"No, I just pulled over to let that car pass but it boxed me in instead and wouldn't leave."

"Oh, dear, that's awful. I'm so sorry. Did you get a look at the driver?"

Laughton shakes her head. "His face was covered." She works a mint out of the packet, pops it in her mouth, and hands the packet back.

"Keep it. You're probably in a bit of shock and could use the sugar. I'm so sorry you had such an awful experience. I imagine it was probably just a local youth who decided to do a bit of tourist baiting. I'm assuming you are a tourist."

She shakes her head. "Not really. I'm here on business."

"Oh really? What kind of work do you do?"

"I'm, er . . . I'm a criminologist."

"That sounds interesting." He glances back up the road in the direction of the departed car. "You don't suppose that was someone you'd arrested, do you? You know, someone out for revenge or something."

Laughton shakes her head. "I'm an academic. I study crimes, I don't investigate them. Not usually."

"Oh, right!" He seems vaguely disappointed, the standard response Laughton gets whenever she has to explain what she does. "Still," he says, brightening up again, "sounds a lot more interesting than my work. I spend most of my days wading through paperwork."

He pulls his wallet from his pocket, slides out a business card, and hands it to her.

DEREK HILL

Deputy Assistant Planner
Gloucestershire County Council
www.gloucestershire.gov.uk Tel: 0788 489367

Laughton takes the card and starts tapping it in patterns of three against her leg, the hum of adrenaline still vibrating inside her.

"How are you feeling now?" Derek asks.

"Better, thank you." She forces herself to stop the stress tapping and looks back up the empty road, the sound of the car entirely gone now.

"Listen," he says, "if you're worried he might come back, I can follow you if you like, this road only goes in one direction for the next couple of miles anyway."

"Oh, no, really I'm fine, thank you."

"It's no problem, we're going in the same direction anyway. Where are you headed?"

"Cinderfield."

"Well, there you are then, that's where I'm going too, so I can follow you the whole way." He turns and heads back to his car in a way that suggests any discussion is now over.

44

THERE IS A PARTICULAR JUNCTION in the forest, a fork in the path like the viperous nock in an adder's tongue. He likes this spot for two reasons.

The first is because it presents the forest traveler with a choice: go right and continue following the wider path, or go left and take the narrower, more overgrown track, the one less traveled by.

The second reason is because this particular fork in the road is fringed by a natural laurel hedge growing thickly on either side of the path, blocking the way ahead until the unexpected dilemma of whether to go left or right is revealed. The same thick screen of laurel also allows him to stand at the point of the junction, hidden by the foliage and his own forest camouflage, so close he can observe the twitch and frown of the travelers' faces as they process their decision, close enough, even, that he could reach out and touch them if he wished to. Mostly he simply observes as they make their choice, like another species of tree in the forest watching the passing of people and time.

But not always.

Sometimes, when a solitary traveler comes his way at a certain time of day, when the forest is empty of people and the night creatures are beginning to stir, he might subtly make his presence known.

It might be a rustle of leaves or the crack of a twig, enough to let the traveler suspect they might not be alone here in this remote and private part of the forest.

But sometimes, when the traveler is of a certain type, and he feels the raw pull of the savage earth, he does much more than shake the leaves.

Much, much more.

For he is of the land and the land is of him. And the land will always protect him so long as he provides it with sacrifices.

45

LAUGHTON SPOTS ADELE BY THE memorial and pulls over into the same bus stop she'd pulled into earlier. Derek, her knight in shining armor, pulls up next to her and rolls down his window.

"You sure you're OK now?" he calls through his open window.

"Yes, thank you, I'm fine."

"Well, you have my number if you need anything."

"Yes, thanks again."

Derek smiles and drives on. Laughton watches him leave, thinking about what had happened in the forest. Just some joy-riding youth terrorizing tourists, Derek had said, but she wasn't entirely convinced. It had felt personal somehow, and she wonders whether she should tell Adele about it. She thinks not, not yet at least, and doesn't get the chance anyway, as Adele appears by her car fizzing with her own news. "I've found Maddie," she says.

"What?"

"On the CCTV. Look." She holds up her phone but the sun is too bright to see the screen and a blast on a horn makes Laughton jump. She jerks her head around, half expecting to see the black car with the faceless driver, but it's only a bus wanting, not unreasonably, to use the bus stop she's currently parked in.

Laughton waves an apology and turns back to Adele. "Is there a café somewhere that does good coffee and has Wi-Fi we can use?"

"Yes, there's a place called The Flour Pot, just along the High Street and next to the bookshop."

"OK, you go there and grab a table. I'll park and come find you."

———

Dog parks the black SUV in a garage on the edge of Cinderfield and pulls his backpack out from the backseat. He had spotted Adele sitting by the war memorial on his way through town and was pretty sure Goldilocks was on her way to meet her after their little encounter in the forest. He was keen to see how she reacted, and the High Street was busy enough now that he could probably get pretty close to them, maybe even overhear what their plans were.

He walks across the garage to where a trail bike leans against its stand, the helmet hooked over the end of one of the crossbars. He hangs his backpack next to it containing his field kit and broken-down crossbow. Hunting bows are illegal in the UK, so he has to keep it hidden, or he does in the town at least. In the forest it's less of a problem. No one will even see him in the forest.

He hurries out of the garage, locking it behind him, then heads back to the High Street, pulling a baseball cap low over his eyes.

46

THE FLOUR POT IS HEAVING with the morning crowd and smells deliciously of bacon and coffee. Adele and Laughton sit jammed together at a tiny table in the back corner, listening to the low burble of conversation and the chirpy chat and tunes of Forest Radio as Laughton copies the Wi-Fi code from the menu. She navigates to the Cinderfield webcam and clicks on the "Midsummer Parade" link. A wide shot of the High Street loads up on her screen, jammed with people wearing costumes and flowing away from the camera.

"It's about an hour in," Adele says. "I can find it."

Laughton slides her laptop over as a smiling waitress arrives with two cappuccinos and two bacon and egg rolls. Adele starts shuttling through the archived footage and Laughton takes a large bite out of her roll: crisped bacon, the yolk still runny enough to drip onto her plate, along with blood-red drops of ketchup—utterly delicious. She takes another bite, feeling instantly better after her strange encounter on the road. She hasn't mentioned it to Adele and probably won't. Adele has enough on her plate already, and her savior Derek was probably right, it was just some local youth playing at highwayman for the buzz.

"There," Adele says, hitting the space bar to pause the footage and pointing at a figure in a pale summer dress at the bottom edge of the screen. "That's Maddie. Now watch her as I play it through."

She hits the space bar again and the crowd comes back to life, a slow-moving, colorful river of people drifting in the same direction, up the High Street and away from the camera.

Laughton leans in, her eyes fixed on Maddie as the flow of the procession carries her along. At one point, for a brief moment, she glances over her shoulder and looks almost directly into the distant camera, and Laughton is struck by how similar she is to Adele, same face shape, same coloring, same body type, same way of moving. Maddie looks away again, back up the High Street to where a group of Morris men dance in formation, weaving in and out of each other while waving colored streamers above their heads.

"Now look there." Adele points at the left of the crowd, where a figure dressed in a hood drifts through the crowd and falls in step next to Maddie, a tall figure of darkness in among all the colors.

"Do you know who it is?" Laughton asks.

"No, but I know what it is. It's a Cinderman. Lots of people dress as Cindermen for the parade. Green Men are like the good spirits of the forest and are covered in leaves and vines. Cindermen are the evil spirits, the ones who will drag you away into the forest if you've been bad."

The dark figure continues to walk alongside Maddie, close enough that it looks like they're together though they never turn and look at each other. The only indication that they might be more than strangers is when Maddie leans her head to one side, just for a fraction of a second, and rests it on his shoulder.

"She knows him," Laughton murmurs, watching them walk on, together but separate after their blink-and-you'll-miss-it moment of intimacy.

"Watch now." Adele points at a small group of people cutting through the crowd toward Maddie. They reach her and she breaks off to hug a skinny guy with long, dark hair and a straggly beard.

"That's Ronan," Adele says, "one of Maddie's exes. I spoke to him yesterday after Maddie went missing and he said he'd seen her at the parade, but look there"—she points at the Cinderman, who has turned away from Maddie and is now heading deeper into the crowd— "she doesn't introduce him, doesn't even acknowledge him, and he moves away, like he's not even with her."

"Or like he doesn't want to be seen with her," Laughton says.

The hooded figure of the Cinderman reaches the heart of the parade then stops and glances back in Maddie's direction before facing forward and letting the parade flow around him, like a river around a gray rock.

"Looks like he's waiting for her," Laughton says.

"Yes, keep watching though."

The Cinderman's head continues to turn as he idly surveys the parade, then he raises a hand and moves away with purpose, pushing his way through the crowd.

"He's seen someone he knows," Laughton says, watching him until he disappears from view behind a row of shops on the left of the frame. She points at the spot. "Are there any cameras here?"

"Yes, there's one on a kind of country crafts shop, though the owner wasn't particularly helpful, said she couldn't show me the footage because of data protection laws."

Laughton shakes her head and takes a sip of coffee. "Everyone's an expert."

Adele points back at the screen. "Watch Maddie now." Maddie waves goodbye to her friends, who then drift away from her, carried along by the flow of the parade. Maddie starts walking too, slower than her friends and further from the camera, her head turning slowly left and right as she goes.

"She's looking for him," Laughton says.

"Yes. Watch."

Maddie continues to search, moving a little more slowly than the rest of the crowd until her eyes fix on the spot where the Cinderman disappeared.

"She's spotted him," Adele says. "But she's not going to him. She's keeping her distance. Why would she do that?"

Laughton thinks for a second. "Because he's talking to his friends now. She doesn't want to be seen by his friends any more than he wanted to be seen by hers. They're keeping each other secret. Maybe our mystery Cinderman is married."

"Possibly. It wouldn't be the first time Maddie got involved with someone she shouldn't. And everyone comes to the Midsummer Parade, so if they weren't really supposed to be together, it would explain why they're being so careful."

On-screen, Maddie starts moving again, following the crowd but drifting left slightly as it carries her down the High Street. After a few seconds the Cinderman reappears from the blind spot behind the shops. He doesn't look in Maddie's direction or raise an arm in greeting, he just drifts through the crowd until he's back by her side and they're walking shoulder to shoulder, together but not together, both facing forward as they follow the parade down the street toward the edge of town until they vanish from sight.

Laughton points at the blind spot. "We need to look at the footage from the camera here to see if we can find out who he is and who he was talking to. Eat up, we've got a lot to do."

Adele takes a bite of her breakfast roll and stares at the frozen image of the parade. She swallows her food and turns to Laughton. "Can I ask you something?"

"Of course."

"Do you think, now that you've seen this footage, that Maddie is probably OK? I mean, before this I was increasingly leaning toward the idea that something terrible must have happened to her, you know, some lunatic had grabbed her and thrown her in the back of a van or something. But now I've seen this, where she is clearly with someone she knows and feels safe with, I'm thinking that it's more likely she just took off and couldn't face telling me. That seems the most likely explanation now, right?"

Laughton takes a sip of coffee then turns to her. "It's possible," she says, "maybe even likely. She was evidently with someone we would categorize as 'friendly' in the hours leading up to her disappearance, but until we know more about who this person is, I think it's best that we reserve judgment. There have been an unusual and disturbing number of women going missing around here, so I'm not going to tell you I think Maddie's fine until we find her. We should definitely hope for the best, of course, but until we find out more we should continue to look for Maddie as if her life depended on it, just in case it does."

The laptop pings with an email alert and Laughton smiles when she sees it's from Tannahill.

I think I may have something on your historic missing persons. Just need to double-check a few things and I'll be in a lecture for the next hour but will call when I can. In the meantime, try not to annoy the locals, especially anyone with a shotgun.

T xx

"Who's that?" Adele asks, her mouth full of bacon and egg. "Colleague? Boyfriend?"

Laughton flushes and closes her laptop.

"Sorry," Adele says. "I couldn't help reading it, we're a bit jammed in in here. You don't have to answer, it's absolutely none of my business."

"No, it's fine," Laughton says, "I'm just not used to fielding those kinds of questions. He's kind of both really, a colleague and a . . . boyfriend. Jesus, that sounds like such a weird thing to call him. Maybe he is a boyfriend, I don't know yet. It's early days. He's a DCI in the Met, we met on a case."

Adele nods. "Sounds romantic."

"Ha! Yes, our eyes met over a bloody crime scene. Actually, that is pretty much what happened. It's complicated because, well, I'm not great at relationships. Also I have a daughter."

"Oh, right. How old?"

"Sixteen."

"No way! You barely look older than that yourself."

Laughton smiles. "Well, thank you! I was pretty young when I had her. In fact, I was her age now, which . . . seems incomprehensible to me. If Gracie fell pregnant I would hit the roof. She's just a kid."

"Is that how your parents reacted?"

Laughton takes a bite of her roll and chews it thoughtfully before answering. "My mum was already dead, and my dad . . . well, I wasn't really talking to him at the time." She smiles. "It's a long story. What about you? Anyone special?"

"Oh God no. I've been far too busy trying to sort my own life out to let anyone else into it. And I haven't even got a kid to look after, unless you count Maddie."

"Well, you're doing a pretty good job of that."

"Am I?"

"Yes, of course. You wouldn't be doing all this if you didn't care. Come on," Laughton says, finishing her coffee and picking up the remainder of her breakfast bap to go. "Let's go and have a little chat about data protection laws with your friendly neighborhood shopkeeper."

47

DEAN AND DALE COUNTRY CRAFT Shop is one of the newer additions
to Cinderfield High Street, with a newly varnished, modern feel that
is slightly at odds with the lo-fi nature of what it is selling. Next to
traditional hand-knitted, handwoven items and objects carved from
wood sourced locally in the forest sits an iPad and card reader on a
glass-topped counter where an old-fashioned cash register would have
seemed far more appropriate. The woman behind the counter looks up
from a tray of polished rocks and crystals as the bell tinkles above the
door, her welcoming smile for Laughton faltering a little when she sees
who follows in behind her.

"Morning," Laughton says, deliberately cheerful, "I wonder if you can
help."

The woman puts both her hands up like she's about to physically push
them away. "I already told your friend, we don't put flyers or circulars up
in our windows, and the security camera footage is private property. I'm
very sorry, but there it is."

"Of course." Laughton pulls her Met ID card out from her pocket,
places it on the counter, and glances at the name badge pinned to the
woman's blouse. "But as I'm sure you're aware, Margaret, the General
Data Protection Regulation and the Data Protection Act define video
footage of individuals as personal data. Therefore, refusing an individual's request to see footage you have captured of them is actually
illegal, and failure to comply to such a request could result in a fine
of up to five hundred thousand pounds and, in some cases, criminal
charges."

She lets that sink in for a second then turns to Adele. "Now, my client
was with her sister on the evening of the Cinderfield Parade and her
sister has now gone missing, possibly with someone she may have met

outside your shop, in which case your cameras would have captured his face. So, as your footage may feature my client, it is, legally speaking, her personal data, so you therefore have no legal right to refuse her access to it. Of course we need to follow proper protocols here, so could you tell me the name of the registered data controller for this shop, please?"

Margaret stares at Laughton for a few moments, her eyes wide behind her glasses. "Well, I suppose I could show you the security camera footage if you like."

"So you are the registered data controller?"

"Well, no, it's whoever's in the shop really."

Laughton frowns. "Oh, dear, Margaret, that's not how it's supposed to work. Personal data protection is a very serious business and only one specifically designated person is supposed to have access to it in a small business like this, with their name and position formerly registered with the ICO."

Margaret looks blank.

"The Information Commissioner's Office," Laughton explains. "Is your name registered with the ICO, Margaret?"

Margaret shakes her head.

"Oh, dear, looks like you're in breach of the regulations."

She lets this sink in too until Margaret looks like she's about to throw up.

"I'll tell you what I'll do," Laughton says, leaning in like she's about to share a secret. "If you let my client look at the footage of the parade from Midsummer's Eve right now without any more fuss, I'm prepared to turn a blind eye to your multiple breaches of GDPR and promise not to report you yet, which will give you plenty of time to get yourself up to code before the ICO sends an inspector round, OK?"

Margaret nods. "Thank you, that would be . . . thank you." She turns and starts heading toward a door next to a wall full of dreamcatchers. "It's in the office at the back."

"Actually, there is another thing you could do for us first."

Margaret stops and turns round, her eyes wide with worry.

Laughton takes a couple of flyers from Adele and lays them on the counter. "Would you mind putting these in your window for us?"

48

DOG WATCHES THE SHOP ASSISTANT stick some flyers in the window then disappear into the back of the shop.

He is standing across the street, using the passing traffic as cover and the phone in his hand as an excuse to be standing still. His face is angled down at the phone but behind the shades his eyes are looking up and fixed on the shop across the road, where he can just about see inside through the reflection on the front window. He waits for them to reappear, but they don't.

He glances up at the security camera fixed above the front of the shop, pointing directly down at the entrance. He can't be sure how wide the angle of the camera is so he's not going to take any chances.

He takes a step forward toward a lamppost and taps the screen on his phone like he's checking a map or something, though his eyes stay fixed on the shop. Whatever they're doing in the back room is taking a while and he starts to think maybe there is a back entrance. But then, why would the shop assistant have gone with them? Ducking out of a back exit was what you did to shake a tail, but he'd been careful, and they'd given no indication that they suspected they were being followed. He leans against the lamppost and a flyer wrapped in clear plastic crinkles against his shoulder. He looks at it. Studies the photograph of the missing girl and the headline above it.

MISSING
Maddie Friar.
Not seen since Midsummer's Eve.

Any information please call this number.

He raises his phone, takes a picture of the flyer, then copies the phone number into Google and does a quick search. It comes back as unlisted with no information about who owns it. He thinks about calling to see who answers. Maybe it would be the sister and he could tell her he has some information, use it to lure her somewhere private, though Goldi-locks would probably come along too. She wasn't showing any signs that he'd managed to scare her off in any way. Maybe if that do-gooder hadn't happened to come along he might have been more successful.

He looks back over at the shop.

Still no sign of them coming out.

He starts walking back up the High Street, instinctively feeling like he's been standing there too long. He crosses the road, heading past the war memorial and further up, to where he'd seen Goldilocks park earlier, thinking he needs to try something else. He slows his pace as he draws closer to her car and side-eyes it as he walks past. It's clean and tidy in the way only new cars and rentals are. He walks on and stops at the ticket machine. It's a one-hour maximum stay, which means she'll have to come back to move her car fairly soon. He heads back to the lockup to fetch his backpack and the trail bike before she returns.

Scaring her off might not be enough, and he wants to be ready if things escalate.

49

"CAN I GET YOU A cup of tea?"

Margaret, all smiles now and wringing of hands, stands in the doorway of the small office at the back of the shop.

Laughton glances up from the flatscreen monitor. "No, we're all good now, thank you, Margaret."

The bell tinkles in the shop behind her and Margaret looks over her shoulder. "I should probably go and . . ."

"Of course," Laughton says. "You go and serve your customers, we promise not to look at anything we're not meant to."

Margaret laughs nervously then hurries away. The moment the door closes Adele starts silent clapping. "That was amazing. She didn't stand a chance, are you sure you're not a lawyer?"

"I'm definitely not a lawyer." Laughton opens her laptop and places it on the desk next to the monitor showing a split-screen feed from the shop's three cameras. "I just know the law better than most. There's no way, for instance, Margaret should be leaving us alone with all this data. Legally she only needs to show us anything that has you in it from the day of the parade."

"But there isn't any footage of me at the parade."

"I know, fortunately Margaret doesn't. Come on, let's do this quickly in case she happens to call someone who actually knows the data privacy regs." She slides the laptop over to Adele. "Find the bit on the webcam where Maddie starts talking to her friends and the Cinderman wanders off."

Adele starts shuttling through the webcam footage at speed while Laughton clicks on the feed from the shopfront camera to make it fill the screen. It shows a wide-angle view of the front of the shop as well as a large section of pavement, which is currently occupied by a large woman holding a tiny dog.

"Here it is," Adele says, pausing the webcam at the point where the Cinderman is about to leave the frame and enter the blind spot covered by the shop camera.

"What's the time stamp?"

"It's, er—eight thirty-four p.m."

Laughton types "20:34" into the search field and hits Return.

The woman with the dog vanishes and the empty pavement is filled with the dense crowd of people that had been recorded two evenings earlier. Laughton hits Play and the people start moving right to left as they are swept along by the parade; all except two men in conversation, standing directly below the camera.

Laughton leans forward and stares hard at the man on the left. The high angle of the camera makes it hard to see his face, but the camera is new so the image is sharp and clear enough for her to see the color of his hair and skin.

"I think . . ." She studies the way he is standing, his legs planted wide apart and his hands resting across his belly as he talks to the other man. "I think that's Chief Constable Beech."

"Really?"

"Yes, he has that whole Henry the Eighth vibe about him."

"I forgot to ask how your meeting went."

"It was frosty. He wasn't particularly helpful with anything. Maybe this is why. Look—" She points at the top right of the screen where the Cinderman has appeared and is now moving directly toward the two men.

"Nooooo!" Adele says as she watches the hooded figure weave through the crowd and come to a halt directly in front of them. "He knows them."

Laughton and Adele watch in silence as Beech, the Cinderman, and the third person engage in what looks like friendly conversation as the parade flows around them. The high angle of the camera keeps the Cinderman's face hidden beneath his hood, with only an ash-smeared chin occasionally coming into view. The three continue their conversation, the Cinderman glancing in Maddie's direction from time to time as the third man appears to do most of the talking. At one point he puts his hand on the Cinderman's shoulder, resting it there for a moment in a gesture of easy intimacy.

"Do you recognize him?" Laughton asks.

Adele stares hard, equally frustrated by the unhelpful camera angle. "Not really. If I could just get a decent look at his face."

Laughton and Adele lean in, staring unblinkingly at the screen as the three men continue to talk, the Cinderman keeping his head down, the other two looking up occasionally to give tantalizing flashes of their faces and profiles.

"That's definitely Beech," Laughton says, holding up her phone and snapping a few pictures directly from the screen as it plays. "I could try asking him who he's talking to here, but after the chilly reception I got this morning I bet he wouldn't tell me. Have you got any more of an idea who the other guy is?"

Adele leans in closer to the screen, willing the third man to look up just for a second, the vague itch of recognition floating at the edge of her brain. The Cinderman glances over his shoulder, nods to both men then heads away, back into crowd, until he disappears from sight.

"He's rejoining Maddie," Laughton says. "Did you find any other cameras further along the route that might have picked him up?"

Adele shakes her head. "There's one outside the bank and another outside the Sainsbury's Local, but they're both the wrong way up the High Street."

Laughton frowns. "They might have caught him earlier, but unfortunately a bank and a national supermarket chain are not going to be as easy to talk into letting us look at their footage. We could go through the proper channels, but that's going to take time and is not going to help us much right now."

They continue to watch the two men talk, Adele staring so hard at the unidentified third man that her eyes start watering. It looks like neither man is going to look up until a vendor walks past carrying a fistful of colorful balloons and the third man finally glances up to look at them. Laughton pauses the footage and she and Adele both stare for a moment at the man's upturned face. They both recognize the Earl of Dean from their googling of Cinderfield Abbey the night before.

Laughton holds her phone up to snap a couple of photos of his face. "Maddie's phone data showed that she was heading in the direction of the Abbey on the night she disappeared," she says. "Which means . . ." She clicks on the main screen and rewinds the parade footage until the

Cinderman reappears, walking backward through the crowd. She stops it at the moment the Earl rests his hand on the Cinderman's shoulder. "Could he be the Earl's son?"

Adele stares at him. "Maybe. Has he replied to your email?"

Laughton starts the clip playing again and flips to her email and checks her inbox. "Not yet." She opens the website for Cinderfield Abbey and scrolls to the top, looking for a contact number.

"Let's see if we can talk to the Earl, see what he has to say for himself. At the very least we can show him these screen grabs and get him to confirm whether the Cinderman is his son or not. Maybe he hasn't heard from him for a couple of days either because he's eloped with your sister."

She looks up as she realizes Adele is not really listening. Instead she is staring intently at the screen where a big bear of a man is now talking to Beech and the Earl. He throws his head back as he laughs too hard at something one of the others has just said and Laughton hits the space bar to pause it.

"Who's that?"

"Bill," Adele murmurs. "His name is Bill Downham, he's my boss at the campsite, at least he used to be. I spoke to him this morning about . . ." She frowns as she remembers the conversation then turns to Laughton. "The day after Maddie disappeared, all her stuff vanished from my cabin. At first I thought it must have been Maddie, but Bill was at the campsite too when her stuff went missing, and when I spoke to him earlier I asked him if he'd seen anyone hanging around and he got, like, really weird about it. So I asked him straight up if he had taken her stuff for some reason and he basically hung up on me. Actually, he fired me first, then he hung up on me."

"Really!" Laughton lifts her phone and snaps a photograph of Bill frozen in his exaggerated laughter. "Was there anything of value among Maddie's things?"

"Not really, except . . . There was a letter from the council replying to a request Maddie had made for information about our fostering records when we were still . . . before we became Maddie and Adele."

"What did it say?"

"I didn't get a chance to read it, I only saw who it was from and what it was about before Bill burst in and made me go and empty the bins. But then when I got back, all her stuff had gone, including the letter."

Laughton nods. "So maybe Maddie's disappearance is somehow connected to her digging back into your past. She might have made contact with your old foster parents, or accidentally alerted them to her inquiries somehow and—"

"No!" Adele's reply is as strong and sudden as the night before when Laughton had mentioned her foster parents. Adele blinks a few times, almost as if she has surprised herself by her reaction, then softens a little. "Sorry, it's just . . . Maddie was not taken by our foster parents."

"How can you be so sure?"

"Because . . . they're both dead." Adele looks away and down at the desk. "After we got away from them there was a fire. News travels in the forest, especially when it's about a fire. They both died." She looks back at Laughton. "So they couldn't have taken Maddie."

"You're sure they both died in this fire?"

"Yes."

Laughton nods. She has sat across from hundreds of people in hundreds of interviews during the course of her career, some honest, some innocent, some guilty. And through the course of this she has learned to tell when someone was holding something back. Adele was hiding something. But she had also learned when to push and when to back off, and Adele clearly did not want to talk about her foster parents. This only made Laughton want to know more, but Adele was not going to tell her.

"I'm sorry if I was snappy," Adele says. "I'm still pretty stressed out about all of this, and on top of everything I just got fired, so I'm not having the best few days."

She looks back at the screen where Bill is still frozen in laughter and shakes her head.

"I don't know why Bill would take Maddie's stuff, maybe he was just being spiteful, it wouldn't be the first time he behaved like a child. Maybe Bill didn't take her things at all and she did sneak back to grab them before she eloped with the Earl's son, in which case, good luck to her."

Laughton nods and files away the subject of the foster parents and the fire as something to look into later on her own. If there were deaths there will be records, so it should be easy enough to check without forcing

Adele to go down the painful path of remembering. She pulls her laptop over and googles Cinderfield Abbey, looking for a contact number.

"Let's see if we can get hold of the Earl," she says, searching the menu for a Contacts page.

"Ask him what he was up to on the night of the Midsummer Parade and whether his son is missing too."

50

THE EARL'S PHONE STARTS BUZZING just as he steps through the security gate with the Keep Out signs on it. He closes it behind him, rattles it to make sure it is locked, then steps out of the shadow of the trees and into the blinding red wastelands of the old quarry. He fumbles his phone from his pocket, shielding his eyes against the glare to peer at the screen, hoping it's Sebastian and disappointed that it's only Cleo, his assistant.

"Hello, Clee," he says, squinting against the bright sun to see if anyone else is already here.

"Hi, Mal, where are you?"

"Oh, I had to pop off for a quick meeting, I'll be back in half an hour or so. What's up?" He heads across the quarry, past building materials arranged in neat rows and an earthmover with its long arm stretched out and resting on the ground.

"Well, I just got a call from someone who's something to do with an investigation into a missing person."

The Earl's step falters and he feels like the air has been sucked from his lungs. "Did this person say what they wanted?" he replies, his voice coming out in a strangled squeak.

"No, they said they wanted to talk directly to you."

The Earl nods and wipes away a tickle of sweat on his neck that is caused by more than the building heat of the day. "And did you give this person my number?"

"Of course not, I said I would pass on their number to you and would leave it up to you to call them back if you had time."

The Earl nods and heads past the digger toward the entrance to one of the old mine tunnels that honeycomb the hill.

"Thanks, Clee," he says.

"Not a problem. I've popped her details down in an email and sent them over."

"*Her* details?"

"Yes, though she has a funny name—LAW—ton. Odd name for a woman. Pretty odd name for a chap too, come to think of it. Anyway, the wedding planner wants to go over a few things with you about the event today when you have a moment. I'll tell them you'll be back mid-morning, shall I, and get her to meet you at the refectory?"

"Yes, perfect—thanks, Clee."

He hangs up and heads across the dusty red expanse of the quarry, gouged from the side of an ancient hill by his great-great-grandfather to mine stone to extend the Abbey. The same stone had built half the houses in Cinderfield and would hopefully soon be building more. He enters the blissful shade of one of the mine tunnels that chases the red-stone seams into the hillside and mops sweat from the back of his neck with his handkerchief. He reads the email Cleo has forwarded then reads the name of the sender aloud, trying to get a sense of the person through the sound.

"Laughton Rees."

He scrolls through the rest of his messages and emails, hoping to see something from his son, but there's nothing. He thinks about calling him again, to check he's OK and reassure him that everything will be fine, but decides against it. He's not sure he can trust himself to convey the calm reassurance his son needed right now.

The breeze shifts and brings the sound of an engine coming through the forest and drawing closer. He looks across the quarry, past the stacked pallets of building materials toward the service road that cuts through the trees. Beech will know what to do. He'll have some kind of plan that will make sense of things and show them all a clear way out. He can call Sebastian after the meeting, when he can hopefully tell him everything is going to be all right, and actually believe it himself.

Beech's Škoda appears from behind the trees, kicking up red dust as it bounces along the uneven track and comes to a stop in a rapidly dimin-ishing sliver of shade at the edge of the forest. Silence floods back into the quarry for a moment as the engine stops then the creak and slam of the car door echoes off the stone walls followed by the crunch of Beech's heavy footsteps as he makes his way over, holding a sheet of rolled-up paper in his hand.

"Not really built for off-roading, eh," the Earl says, nodding at Beech's car.

Beech glowers. "Unfortunately my Range Rover's in the garage getting polished." He looks over at the tree line on the far side of the clearing. "No sign of Her Majesty?"

"Not yet. She'll probably be late. She usually is. Listen, before she gets here, I wanted to ask your advice about something. I just got a call from this Laughton person asking to speak to me about a missing person."

Beech huffs into the shade and stares at him for a second, like he didn't quite catch what he'd said. "She called you?"

"Yes, or rather she called my assistant."

"So you haven't spoken to her?"

"No."

Beech blows out a long breath of relief. "Good! She's turning out to be a right pain in the arse, that woman."

"Well, quite. In fact that was rather what I wanted to talk to you about. She's hassling you and now she's contacting me. We need to nip all this in the bud. How did your little chat with her go?"

"Not well. I also found these papered all over Cinderfield as I was driving through." He hands the Earl a flyer with the smiling face of Maddie Friar below the banner headline: MISSING.

"Jesus! This is getting completely out of hand. It'll be all over the news next and then how are we going to control it?"

"That's not going to happen," Beech says, looking over at the trees again to check they are still alone. "But I do think we need to impress on Grizz the seriousness of the situation to make sure it gets dealt with swiftly."

"What do you have in mind?"

"I think we need to tell Grizz what happened so she knows what's at stake."

The Earl starts shaking his head. "No. Absolutely not. I think we tell her what she needs to hear in order to get her fully onside but there's no reason to tell her every detail of this . . . unpleasant business."

Beech looks at him with barely concealed disgust. "Let's be very clear about this, it's you and your family's unpleasant business we're dealing with here, and the only reason we're involved at all is because we can't allow your family's fuckups to ruin everything for the rest of us."

The Earl's face flushes as red as the quarry stone. "Listen, I do not appreciate your tone, and you should remember who you're talking to. We all have our family secrets and things we regret and do our best to bear, and you have only helped me and my family over the years for personal gain and professional advancement, so don't you dare try and lecture me. Don't forget who whispered your name to the kingmakers when they were looking for a new chief constable. We scratch each other's backs and we all benefit, that's how things have always been. You could have chosen to take the moral high ground years ago but you didn't, you chose the path of pragmatism and reward. There's no going back now. Just because you have your nice young wife and your new family doesn't mean you are somehow different. You don't get to wipe the slate clean any more than the rest of us do. So get that look off your face and earn your keep."

Movement over by the trees catches the Earl's eye and he looks up as Grizz emerges stiffly from the shadows, her gray dreadlocks and her rounded bulk beneath her smock making her look like the ghost of some ancient fertility symbol. She limps toward them, leaning on her staff for support. The Earl moves closer to Beech and lowers his voice.

"And just so we are perfectly clear on this, if any of my family suffer for any of the things you have been involved with over the years, then you are going down too. I can't imagine it's much fun for ex-policemen in prison. Think about your lovely young wife bringing your children to see you on visiting days. How long do you think she'll keep that up do you wonder? How long before she starts getting lonely and your kids don't want to come and see Daddy anymore because it makes them too sad? Don't fool yourself that you're protecting me or my family by doing any of this. You're protecting yourself and you'd be wise to remember that. So, we tell Grizz only what she needs to hear and no more, understand?"

He steps away from Beech and out of the shade ready to greet Grizz, a smile now spread across his face. "Dear lady, so lovely to see you, so sorry to make you trudge all the way through the forest, but at least it's a lovely day for a stroll."

Grizz nods at him as she walks past to join Beech in the oasis of the shade. "I'm way too old for this," she says, leaning against the wall to soak up the deep cold of the earth.

"We're all too old for this," Beech murmurs. "So, the sooner we can sort it all out the better."

Grizz looks up at him. "What are we sorting out exactly?"

Beech hands her the flyer. "This."

Grizz holds the flyer at arm's length so she can read it. "Adele will never stop looking for Maddie," she says.

Beech nods. "Well, we need to make her. The last thing we need right now is any unwanted scrutiny or scandal. Maddie's disappearance is an untimely distraction and threatens to open a can of worms we need to keep closed. We have to keep the past in the past because the plans are going to be a hard enough sell as it is with the conservation lobby watching any new developments in the forest like a hawk. Any excuse to object, any whiff of scandal, and they will use it to close us down, so we need to close it down before it gets to that and stop Adele looking for her sister."

Grizz hands the flyer back to him. "And why is this my problem? I thought closing down investigations was your department."

Beech nods. "Usually, yes, but there's been a complication."

Grizz nods. "The woman who picked her up from the police station last night?"

"Yes. She's affiliated with the Met but she's not police, she's an academic, a professional busybody. She's already contacted both me and the Earl, so we need to be careful. But she doesn't know about you or our partnership. She's also a city type who's well out of her comfort zone."

Grizz looks at Beech, both weary and annoyed that yet again she is going to have to do the dirty work for all of them. "So, what are you suggesting?"

Beech shrugs. "For now, get your man to continue keeping a close eye on her, see where she goes and who she talks to. If we stay close and act clever there's no reason to believe she'll find anything at all, so maybe she goes away without us needing to do a thing. But, if she does start getting too close, well . . . people from the city get injured in the forest all the time, don't they? Weekenders who wander off the beaten path. It's hunting season all year-round for wild boar and the forest is full of them." He smiles and opens his hands like he's being the most reasonable person you ever met. "And the great thing about busybodies is —they're always sticking their noses in places they shouldn't."

51

LAUGHTON PULLS TO A HALT in front of The Charcoal Burner Inn and looks up at the classic, country-pub frontage of dark beams and hanging baskets.

"Looks nice," she says. "What's the food like?"

"It's OK. Not sure I'd be very welcome here after my last visit though."

"No, probably not. Do you want me to hang around for a minute to make sure you're OK?"

"No, I'll be fine." Adele opens the passenger door and steps out. "Martin the landlord might spot me and tell me to clear off, but that's what I intend to do anyway." She closes the car door and points down the road. "If you drive back down this road then take a left at the first crossroads, you'll see signs for the Abbey after a mile or so. You can't miss it."

"Thanks." Laughton taps the screen of her satnav, which again has no signal. "I'll give you a call as soon as I've finished and come and pick you up at the campsite, if I get a signal on my phone, that is."

"Ah, you'll be fine at the Abbey. You're out of the trees there and pretty high up. See you later."

Laughton watches her walk away and head down the side of the pub, her hair swaying long and loose across her back and reminding her again of her daughter. It will probably take a couple of weeks to detangle her great mane once Gracie got back from spending a few days soaking it in the Cornish Sea.

Adele glances up at the barred upper windows of the pub like she's expecting someone to lean out and start shouting at her, then disappears behind a row of bins for a moment and reemerges wheeling a bike. She waves at Laughton then hops on the bike and cycles away down the road, hair flying behind her in the sunlight. If it weren't for the context she would look like something from an advert for summer holidays, or youth, or freedom.

Laughton watches her until the undulating road hides her from view then she turns her car around and heads back down the narrow country lane to the crossroads, enjoying the natural sounds of the countryside streaming in through her open window, marred only by the distant buzz of a motorbike.

52

SHE WAKES FROM A DREAM of sunshine and light and finds herself anchored back in the heavy dark.

She blinks a few times and stares into the dark, feeling the trapped weight of her situation settling back on her. She takes a deep breath to steady herself but some ancient alarm sounds in her mind as she catches the taint of something new in the earthy air. Woodsmoke. Woodsmoke means fire, and in a forest, fire means danger.

Her heart quickens but then she remembers.

She had left the candle burning when she slipped into slumber.

She had dripped wax onto the wooden tabletop, fixed the candle in the puddle, then fallen asleep bathed in its wavering golden light. She must have been asleep for a while, long enough for the candle to burn all the way down and singe the wooden tabletop before the flame snuffed out.

That's what must have happened. That's why she can smell burning. And if something else was burning down here, there would be light from the flames and there isn't, so the solid blackness is actually a comfort for once.

She lies there for a moment in the aftermath of her panic, taking deep, calming breaths of smoke-tinged air, studying the dark and trying to figure out which way she is facing. She had fallen asleep so quickly after eating the apple that she still feels disoriented. There must have been something in it to cause her such sudden and powerful drowsiness.

She stares ahead, fear sidling in at the edge of her consciousness as she thinks about who might have drugged the apple and why. She recalls her childhood nightmare of the figure rising up from below the bed and closes her eyes tight against the dark. She knows there's nothing here, she explored every inch of the room before falling asleep. It's all in her mind. There's nothing there. There's no one there.

Then something shifts in the room, something barely measurable, like a change in pressure or a tiny displacement of air, and she screws her eyes tighter, terrified now that there is something there, something in the darkness with her and just inches from her face.

Her breathing becomes rapid and the smell of woodsmoke grows stronger, dislodging another childhood memory, something almost forgotten, a warning wrapped in a fairy story.

You can smell smoke whenever the Cinderman is near.

Their foster mother told them those stories to keep them out of the forest.

She feels the subtle shift in the room again and the smell of wood-smoke grows stronger.

It's behind her. Whatever is displacing the dark and filling it with the smell of ash is standing in the room behind her, which means she must be facing the wall.

She doesn't move. Tries not to breathe in the hope that the dark might hide her. But the air shifts again, and the mattress she is lying on sinks a little, the springs creaking as whoever, or whatever, is in the room with her sits down gently on the edge of the bed.

53

LAUGHTON CATCHES GLIMPSES OF THE Abbey as she drives up the private, tree-lined drive to the visitors' car park. She recognizes it from the photos on the website, though none of them remotely did it justice. It is huge; part stately home, part cathedral, and the closer she gets, the bigger it seems to grow. She imagines what it must have looked like to ordinary farmworkers or foresters a few hundred years earlier, living in one-room hovels while their lords and masters lived in this monumental palace.

She parks in the visitors' car park, hauls her bag containing her laptop and a few other essentials out of the backseat, then follows signs for Reception up a broad flight of stone steps. Through an entrance door roughly the size of a modern house lies a hallway big enough to house a tennis court. A woman in a crisp white shirt and black pinafore dress is standing by a long table over to one side, loading it up with champagne glasses from a plastic storage container.

"Hi." Laughton smiles. "I've got an appointment to see the Earl, any idea where I might find him?"

"Just a sec." The woman picks up a bulky old walkie-talkie from the table. "Visitor in main reception for the Earl."

The radio crackles as she releases the transmit button. "Someone'll be along in a minute," the woman says as she resumes filling the table with champagne glasses. "You can wait in the chapel if you like." She nods over at a stone arch with two enormous, studded oak doors, one of which is standing slightly open.

Laughton smiles her thanks and drifts over to the chapel. In truth she does not have an appointment but wanted to see what would happen if she turned up unannounced. The Abbey is open to the public so she isn't trespassing.

She passes through the open door into an enormous space with soaring, vaulted ceilings that remind her of the dining room in the Harry Potter films. Large stone urns filled with flowers stand at either side of the aisle in readiness for a wedding, and sunlight streams in through huge, stained-glass windows depicting various saints in forest settings that look like scenes from fairy stories. She drifts through the shafts of colored light, drawn to a wall on the far side of the chapel where an elaborate painted tree spreads across the wall and twists its way up to the ceiling like a beanstalk. She stops in front of it and peers through the gloom to study the details. It is exquisitely painted, everything from the mossy bark to the curling leaves rendered in such detail they could almost be real. On every spreading branch hangs a painted banner bearing the names and dates of all the earls with their wives and children listed below, hundreds of names stretching back for centuries. She takes a step back to seek out Mallory Kingston, the current Earl, among the higher branches. She spots his name near the vaulted ceiling, his wife listed next to him along with her date of death and their son's name painted beneath, ready for his own branch when the time comes. Laughton traces the line back along the branches and stops one generation back. Mallory's name is there again beneath the name of his own father, but his is not the first name recorded. Above his name is another, Greville Stoker Hawthorn, b. 1968, two years before Mallory was born. Laughton recalls the Wikipedia entry she read the night before noting that Mallory had inherited the earldom after his elder brother had been deemed unsuitable to run the family estates and wondered what the story was there. In-breeding probably, leading to congenital idiocy. It was the curse of these old aristocratic families who had sought to keep their bloodlines pure by intermarrying and ended up doing the exact opposite.

"It was initially painted in fifteen thirty-seven." The voice makes her jump and she turns to see a dreadnought of a woman in a twinset and heels bearing down on her. "That's when the monastery was dissolved and the Abbey was gifted to the Kingston family." She extends a taloned hand and Laughton shakes it. "Cleo Mortimer," she says. "I'm the Earl's personal assistant."

"Laughton Rees." She pulls out her Met ID card and hands it over. "I was hoping I might have a few minutes of his time. I understand he's very busy but . . ."

"I did speak to the Earl this morning and passed on your details," Cleo says, handing back Laughton's ID card. "I'm sure if he has the time to talk to you he will contact you directly."

Cleo is in her early fifties and has the bearing and breeding of someone who probably married young and now has a bunch of grown-up kids of her own, possibly even grandchildren. Laughton checks her hand for a wedding ring and there it is.

"A girl is missing," Laughton says, pulling a flyer from her bag and handing it over, hoping to appeal to her emotions and bypass her business-like efficiency. "Her name is Madeleine Friar and she's twenty-two years old. The Earl is not in trouble, I would just like to talk to him in case he knows her and can help us find her."

Cleo takes the flyer and looks at Maddie's smiling face. "Well, as I say, I did pass on your details, so I'm sure the Earl will call you once he has a moment. As you may have gathered, we have a wedding today, so it's all a bit hectic. In fact, the Earl is scheduled to have a meeting with the wedding planner in about ten minutes to go through all the final details." She looks at her watch. "Those meetings tend to happen in the café at the Heritage Center." Laughton smiles as she realizes what she is doing. "I hope you find this missing girl," Cleo says, looking back at Maddie's smiling face on the flyer. "Too many women go missing around here. It's a mother's biggest worry."

54

SHE LIES PERFECTLY STILL, HEART hammering, eyes wide and staring into the darkness. Every nerve in her body is stretched piano-wire tight as she waits for whoever is sitting behind her on the bed to move.

Nothing stirs.

Nothing moves, and the only sound is the high-pitched whine of tension inside her head.

She wonders if maybe she imagined it and is actually having one of those terrifying dreams where she only thinks she has woken up but is actually still sleeping. She can still smell the smoke and wonders if it's even possible to smell things in dreams.

But this is not a dream.

She knows this for sure now because the thing behind her shifts its weight again and the springs of the bed creak beneath the thin mattress. She feels the bed sag then settle as the thing behind her lies down.

The smell of smoke is so strong now but she doesn't move. She feels if she can stay perfectly still, hold her breath, and make no sound, maybe it won't know she's even there.

A single tear escapes from the corner of her eye, runs across the bridge of her nose, then drops onto the cotton pillowcase with a soft noise that sounds deafening to her.

Maybe it hadn't heard. Maybe she is still safe.

Then an arm reaches out in the dark, and the moment it touches her she loses it completely in an explosion of fear and panic.

She twists and leaps from the bed, jabbing at the darkness with her elbows to drive the thing away. Her right elbow connects hard with something and pain shoots up her arm but she keeps on hitting out and kicking as she leaps forward, pushing off from the wall to propel herself into the room. She lands awkwardly on the ground, twisting her ankle and sending fresh pain lancing through her body as she stumbles forward. She bangs into the chair and grabs it, sweeping her spare arm ahead of her until she finds the far wall.

She spins around. Presses her back against the wooden paneling and holds the chair like a shield between herself and the darkness as she slides along the wall, looking for the open door. She bangs into the corner instead and stares ahead, her skin drenched in sweat, her breathing a series of rapid pants, the darkness swimming with points of light.

"You can't get out," a voice rumbles from the dark, low and soft and matter-of-fact.

All the strength drains from her body the moment she hears it. Her knees buckle. She slides to the floor.

Because she recognizes it.

She recognizes the voice, and so she knows who has her.

55

LAUGHTON SHIELDS HER EYES AGAINST the sun as she steps out of the Abbey and follows the signs to the Heritage Center past the huge wedding marquee. Movement over by the tree line catches her eye and she looks over to where a couple of groundsmen are shoveling ash into a wheelbarrow from the remains of what looks like a large bonfire.

She stops on the gravel path and watches them for a moment then pulls her phone from her pocket and scrolls through her emails until she finds the one containing Maddie's phone scan results. She opens the attached map and matches it up with her current position, figuring out where she is in relation to the Abbey and the buildings of the heritage center. The remains of the fire lie in a direct line with Maddie's last two recorded positions. She imagines her walking through the forest on Midsummer's Eve, drawn by the flames flickering through the trees. Did she ever reach the fire, she wonders; did she ever make it out of the forest at all?

She heads over to the groundsmen for a closer look and they look up as she approaches, their shovels suspended in air and ash blowing off them in the hot morning breeze like wisps of smoke. Both men look like a child's idea of what gardeners should look like—wild hair, weathered skin, faded green clothes, scuffed work boots.

"Hi," Laughton says, smiling at the older of the two men, assuming if anyone's in charge it will be him. "Was this fire from the other night?" The older man resumes shoveling ash, leaving the younger one to answer. Laughton studies the man who appears to be in charge, his full beard seeming to owe its existence more to laziness than fashion. He twists it now between dirty fingers, lines of black beneath bitten nails, and looks down at the circle of ash as if it's the first time he's noticed it.

"From Midsummer's Eve," Laughton adds. "Was it a beacon fire?"

"No," he says, then turns to the other man. "That'll do, Phil."

The older man lays his shovel on top of the wheelbarrow, lifts it by the handles, and starts pushing it away toward the Heritage Center. The younger man also turns and starts heading away, toward the forest, limping heavily as he goes. Laughton follows. "Are you sure?"

"Yep."

"Were you here on Midsummer's Eve?"

The man shakes his head.

"Where were you?"

"Cinderfield Parade, same as everyone."

"And there wasn't a beacon party here?"

"No," the man says, his face fixed firmly forward. "Just been burning some garden rubbish is all."

Laughton stops following and watches him limp away into the greenery, down a narrow path toward a glade with a collection of small cabins tucked away in the trees.

She looks back at the circle of ash, clearly visible from the Abbey—a strange place to burn garden rubbish on an estate as vast as this. Why build a fire on the lawn and burn the grass, unless it was for a party? Laughton turns back, but the groundsman has disappeared in the trees. She walks along the edge of the forest, trying to get her bearings and work out which angle Maddie might have been coming from. She spots a gap in the trees that opens up to reveal a straight, narrow pathway, meandering away into the distance. This must have been the one Maddie was walking down when the signal from her phone cut out.

Laughton steps into the forest and the temperature drops as she walks down the path until she feels she is far enough. She stops and looks back at the Abbey. She can still see it, hidden behind the screen of trees, and she can still see the spot where the fire was, which means anyone walking along this path would have been able to see it too.

She heads back, studying the ground as she goes, looking for footprints or any other evidence, and is almost out of the trees when she spots something, a flash of red in among the brown and green. She stops and leans over, squinting at the empty bottle of Red Stripe buried in the ferns a few feet off the path. It looks too clean to have been there for long. She holds up her phone, snaps a few photos to record where she found it and where it is in relation to the path, then pulls out an evidence bag and uses it to pick up the bottle without touching it herself. She holds it up to the light and spots some greasy smears around the body of the bottle that might yield prints, glass being about as good as it gets for latents. She sniffs the neck and catches the sour vinegar smell of stale beer. There's also still some wet residue inside, which suggests the summer heat has not yet had time to dry it out. She looks back at the white circle of ash and imagines someone standing by the fire, draining the bottle then tossing it into the woods.

"No party, you say?" She glances over at the section of forest where the groundsman had disappeared, then folds the sides of the evidence bag up around the bottle, seals it, drops it into her bag, and steps out of the forest, back into the sun.

56

SHE COWERS IN THE CORNER, trying to make herself as small as she can, like she did when she was little and he had come into her room.

"You can't get away," he says.

That voice. So familiar and horrifying. Her foster father's voice!

But it can't be him. It can't be. She had watched the cabin burn. Heard the coughing and the screams. No one had gotten out, she'd made sure of that. There were bars on every window and she'd locked the doors from the outside using the key they kept hidden under the rock by the kitchen window.

She had gone on her own, leaving her sister behind in case it went wrong. She had stolen a can of paraffin from the stores and carried it through the night, back the way they had come when they escaped, until she smelled woodsmoke coming from the cabin.

It had been a practical decision to return, a way of drawing a line under their past to ensure their future was safe. But there was another reason. She also wanted to hurt her foster parents like they had hurt her and her sister. She wanted them to feel helpless and afraid. She wanted revenge.

She had crept up to the dark cabin as dawn was beginning to break, her heart beating so loud in her chest she'd felt sure it would wake the people inside. She had found the key, locked the doors, then poured paraffin on the ground and under the doors so the fire would spread inside.

The match had flared like a comet in the predawn darkness, a bright, singular spot, the light at the end of her tunnel. It had fallen almost in slow motion, tumbling down toward the dark puddle of paraffin, which ignited suddenly and explosively with a soft *whump*.

She had scurried away from the purple and orange flames racing up the door, her eyes transfixed by the burning building, shocked and excited by how quickly the flames took hold of the dry wood of the cabin.

She remembers the tinkle of glass. The sound of fists hammering on the locked door. Screams and coughing, then nothing but the hungry roar of the fire and the gunshot crack of splintering wood as the flames consumed it.

And no one had got out.

No one.

"I can see you." The voice comes again from the dark and something shrivels inside her. "You can't see me, but I can see you."

It is him. It can't be, but it is.

"Why are you hiding behind that chair? You don't have to be afraid. I'm not angry at you for what you did."

The voice is moving. He is moving. Getting closer.

"All you have to do . . . is be nice."

She launches the chair at the voice, kicking it hard with both feet and a cry of surprise and pain erupts from where the voice had been.

"That wasn't nice." The voice comes again, from a different place now, and she hears the sound of a lock opening. She rushes forward, all instinct and fear, and her head connects with the edge of the door in a flash of white. She staggers back and hits the wall, knocking the breath from her lungs as she slides to the ground.

The voice comes again. "You will be nice to me. They're always nice in the end."

A loud bang echoes in the darkness as the door shuts, and she is left alone in the dark with pain in her head, fear in her heart, and the smell of smoke in the air.

57

LAUGHTON HEADS PAST A ROW of traditional foresters' dwellings with smoking heaps of turf in front of them and enters the refectory, a long building of wood and glass housing a café and gift shop. Two slightly overdressed women are spread out on the largest table, phones clamped to their ears and numerous printouts spilling from ring binders the size of old Bibles. These must be the wedding planners the Earl is due to meet, though there's no sign of him yet. Laughton orders a coffee then settles on a sofa by one of the picture windows to wait, and copies the Wi-Fi code from the blackboard into her laptop.

She looks back, out past the huge marquee to the remains of the fire, and sees that the younger of the two groundsmen is back and shoveling the rest of the ash into a wheelbarrow. The waitress brings her coffee and places it on the table.

"Who's that?" Laughton points at the distant figure.

"Oh, that's the head groundsman, MacGregor."

"MacGregor, like the farmer in *Peter Rabbit*?"

The waitress looks blank and Laughton realizes that Beatrix is probably not the most famous Potter anymore. "Do you know his first name?" she asks. "It's just he reminds me of someone my mum used to work with."

The waitress stares at the distant figure and shrugs. "Everyone just calls him MacGregor. He pops in for a pot of tea and a slice of cake every now and then, but I don't know what his first name is, sorry."

"Do you know how long he's worked here?"

The waitress shrugs. "Longer than me, so three years at least."

Laughton smiles. "Thanks."

The waitress scurries off and collects some empty mugs and plates from the wedding planners' table.

Laughton sips her coffee and looks back at the distant groundsman: MacGregor, no first name, said there'd been no party when clearly there had. He also said he'd been at the Cinderfield Parade on Midsummer's Eve. Maybe he'd lied about that too.

She opens her laptop, loads the Cinderfield webcam, then sets it playing, scrubbing through it at double speed, hitting the space bar to stop it whenever she spots someone who might be MacGregor. Her phone buzzes and she feels a weight lift when she sees who it is.

"Hey," she says.

"Hey, yourself, I just sent you an email." Tannahill sounds distracted and there's some kind of loud announcement going on behind him.

"You OK?"

"Not really, I just got a heads-up that a key witness in one of my main cases has been arrested and is currently being held in Kilburn nick."

"That's good, isn't it?"

"Not when I need to be the one interviewing him and am currently in a different country."

"OK, yeah, I suppose that's not ideal."

"It's fine, I managed to book a last-minute flight, which I'm now running to catch. Listen, the reason I'm calling is that I may have found something useful about your Cinderman cases."

"You found someone with some dirt on Beech?" She leans forward and clicks on Mail.

"Better than that. You know those nerds I was telling you about, the ones doing the presentation on the latest face-recognition software?"

"Yes?"

"They've developed a system where you can upload any photo and it will instantly compare it to an archive of about a hundred million existing case files using some kind of advanced AI and quantum computers, they lost me on the details, but the bottom line is, if the person in your photo has a record, the system will find it for you and do it in seconds." Laughton's email launches and she opens the one from Tannahill. "It's still in the beta-testing stage, but after the presentation I asked if I could run your missing persons through it to see if I got a match. The email I just sent contains the results."

The email opens and pdf attachments start downloading. Laughton scrolls down them to see how many there are, but there are too many to count.

"Whoa! How many did you run through this thing?"

"All fifty-seven. I told you it was quick. We didn't get a hit on all of them, but we got forty or so matches. The interesting thing is they came in from all over the place, some in Europe via Interpol, but all for the same thing."

Laughton clicks open the first attachment, an arrest sheet for a woman whose mug shot she recognizes but not her name. She scrolls down to the box recording the charge. "Soliciting."

"Yep, every single one of your vanished women ended up in the sex trade. Quite a few ended up dead, but some were interviewed in detail. I managed to skim a couple and they both talk about being trafficked from the South after volunteering for black-market seasonal work but being groomed for sex work instead. It's the usual story, enforced drug dependency, unpayable debts they knew nothing about, violence, coercion."

Laughton opens another attachment and skim-reads the report of another woman, this time arrested in a raid on a brothel in Liverpool who claimed to have been snatched somewhere down south, Wales, she thinks, or maybe Gloucestershire, somewhere with lots of trees.

"Why didn't Merseyside police flag any of this up with their Welsh or Gloucestershire counterparts?"

"They probably did, but if someone was keeping an eye out for these kinds of reports and was actively trying to head off any investigation into these missing women, they could easily make sure nothing happened."

"Beech."

"Most likely."

"So, these women disappear, have their identities taken away, and if they pop up in other jurisdictions they're either not listened to because they're unreliable, drugged-up sex workers, or their complaints don't get anywhere because they hit a brick wall as soon as they arrive here."

"Yep. Looks like you got yourself a trafficking ring with a senior-ranking police officer overseeing it. If I were you I would get the hell out of there, build the case remotely, then hand it over to the Independent Police Complaints Commission and let them handle it."

Laughton shakes her head. "I can't do that."

"'Course you can. It's way too dangerous for you to carry on conducting an independent investigation given what you've already found out."

Laughton thinks back to her encounter on the road earlier and wonders now if the timing of it, immediately after her meeting with Beech, was entirely coincidental.

"I need to make sure this latest missing person is OK first. I can't just abandon her sister, she's had enough of that already in her life."

There's a pause where Laughton hears a last flight announcement. "OK," Tannahill says, "but—"

"Be careful, I know," Laughton cuts in.

"OK, just make sure you come home. I've got to catch my flight now. If you leave as well, we could have dinner tonight, imagine that!"

Laughton smiles. "That would be nice."

"Think about it. I'll call you when I get back to London."

"OK, safe flight."

He hangs up and Laughton looks out of the window again. MacGregor has gone and there's still no sign of the Earl. She sips her coffee and clicks through the attachments on Tannahill's email one at a time, reading each report then saving it to the relevant folder in her Cinderman file. She thinks about Adele and imagines the look on her face if she announced she was packing up and heading off. She can't do that to her. If it's dangerous here for her, it's doubly so for Adele.

She finishes reading the last report, copies it to her folder, then counts the number of missing people who have now been located. Forty-three, which leaves fourteen still unaccounted for. It's possible some of these are dead, though in all likelihood they're probably still alive and just wishing they were dead. She thinks of Maddie, the smiling girl in the flyers, locked up in some bleak room now. It's sickening. Anger inducing. So many women over so many years who had just been looking for a way to make a living.

A thought strikes her and her skin runs cold as she picks up her phone, half-remembering something Adele had said the night before when she'd been talking about The Clearing. She finds her number and calls it, trapping the phone under her chin so her hands are free to forward Tannahill's email.

It was tougher on the women, she had said. *Younger women like us often only stayed a few days—then they left.*

58

HER HEAD STILL THROBS FROM banging it against the door edge and she feels dizzy when she moves, though that might be from whatever he had put in the apple that had zonked her out.

She licks her dry lips, already feeling thirsty after the frenzied panic of his visit. Was that how he got them to be nice to him, all those girls who had been in this room before her, marking the time by scratching marks on the walls? Would he starve her into weakness and compliance?

She finds her way to the table and fumbles a candle from the box.

Maybe he'd give her another apple or some water laced with sedative and wait until she was hungry or thirsty enough to swallow them.

She closes her eyes tight against the flare of the striking match then peers through narrowed eyelids to light the candle. She holds it up and surveys the room afresh. Apart from the chair lying on its side on the floor and the twisted blankets on the bed, there is no evidence that anything happened here at all.

She carefully touches the place on her forehead where the pain throbs and feels a large lump forming beneath the skin. Had it just been bad luck that she had collided with the edge of the door, or had it been deliberate?

I can see you, he had taunted from the dark. *You can't see me, but I can see you.*

She had seen a film once where some freak had kept women captive in a dark basement. He'd been able to see them using some kind of night-vision goggles that allowed him to move about without needing light.

She looks back at the corners of the room. He had built this room, built it for a specific purpose. Which means he would have designed it to suit those specific needs.

She picks up the chair, checks it isn't broken, then drags it over to the far corner of the room. She had already checked the room for cameras but had been looking for big ones, the kind you saw in shops and on the sides of houses. But you could get smaller ones too, like the tiny ones they had in cabs now. Keyhole cameras.

She stands on the chair, cupping her hand round the flame of the candle to steady the flame then studies the corner where the boards meet, poking her finger into the screw-holes, feeling for screwheads. On the fifth try, her fingertip touches something cold and glassy instead. She holds the candle up and peers into the hole. A tiny black marble stares back at her.

I can see you.

She drips wax onto her finger, then smears it over the hole, pushing it in as deep as she can.

"Not anymore, you fucking freak, not anymore."

59

YOU ONLY FAIL IF YOU quit.

Adele is unpinning the last of her handwritten quotes from the wall of the shack when her phone rings. She checks the number before answering.

"Hey," Laughton says. "I just sent you an email. I want you to look at the attachments and see if you recognize any of the people in the photographs."

"OK, hang on." Adele puts the phone on speaker then opens the new message from Laughton. She scrolls down to the attachments, clicks on the first one, and it starts slowly downloading.

"Have you talked to the Earl yet?"

"Not yet, I'm lying in wait in the café ready to pounce on him the moment he shows up for a meeting. There was definitely a beacon party here on Midsummer's Eve, though the groundsman claims there wasn't. I'm going to ask the Earl about it as soon as he shows up."

Adele's phone flashes in the gloom of the room when the file attachment opens, and she zooms in on the photo, a mug shot taken of an unsmiling woman with a hard face and dead eyes.

"I know this woman," Adele murmurs, studying the photo.

"Which one?"

"The file says Stella Finch, but she was called Sarah when she stayed at The Clearing. She wasn't with us for long, only a couple of days. She was nice, though. Friendly. I remember being sad when she left without saying goodbye."

"Do you recognize any of the others?"

Adele opens another file and a photo of an unsmiling woman stares out at her. She has sores around her mouth and a nose that looks like it's been broken. Adele is about to move on when she suddenly realizes who it is.

"Oh my God."

"What?"

She checks the name on the file. "The one called Jade Smith. I know her too."

"From The Clearing?"

"Yes, she was with us for longer, maybe a couple of weeks. Her name is Julie."

"Did she leave suddenly too?"

"Yes. She left on a work detail and didn't come back." She studies the photo of the broken woman, remembering the sunny, happy person she used to be. "I can't believe how she looks. What happened to her?"

"She was trafficked and forced into sex work. All these women were."

Adele scrolls through the rest of the attachments. "What are these?"

"They're my Cinderman files. All the women who have disappeared in the area over the last twenty years. The good news is that now we've found them, it means there's a very good chance we'll find Maddie too."

Adele stares at the mug shot of the girl she'd known as Julie, barely recognizable as the same girl she remembered. "Whatever these girls went through, I don't want it to happen to Maddie. I don't think she would . . . I mean, she's already been through so much."

"I know, of course. Listen, I think now we have this evidence, we are a big step closer to getting Maddie back." She lowers her voice. "There's definitely a link between Beech and whatever's been going on at The Clearing. Maybe he's in on it, maybe he gets a cut in exchange for turning a blind eye and closing down any missing persons reports. We've got enough evidence now to start an internal investigation but we still don't know exactly how or even if the Earl is involved. I'm going to try and talk to him now and feel him out, see how he reacts when I ask him about Beech and who the Cinderman was we saw him speaking to at the Cinderfield Parade."

She looks up as a sudden volley of parrot-like squawks pierces the calm tranquility of the café.

"He's here," Laughton murmurs. "Gotta go. I'll call you again after I've spoken to him."

60

LAUGHTON HANGS UP AS THE two women from the long table stand and totter over to a pink-faced man in an oversized white linen shirt she recognizes from the webcam of the Cinderfield Parade.

"There he is!" one of the women shrieks, giving him a look like he's a naughty boy or a mischievous puppy. "There's our gracious host."

"Ladies," he says, beaming, "you're both far too glamorous for this rustic little tearoom."

The women both titter and twitter like they're in some period drama and usher him to their table to order more coffee and start going through the order of service for the wedding.

Laughton grabs her laptop, strides across to the table, and sits down before any of them have even realized she's joined them.

"Hi!" Laughton says directly to the Earl, friendly but firm. "Sorry to bother you, I know you're very busy but I sent a request earlier through your assistant about a missing persons case I'm investigating and wondered if I could just grab two minutes of your time to ask a couple of questions?"

The two women on either side of the Earl glare at Laughton like they want to batter her to death with their oversize folders, but she ignores them and lays a flyer down on top of their map of the seating arrangements. "This is the missing woman," Laughton says, looking up at the Earl to catch his reaction. "She's called Maddie Friar and she went missing on the night of the Cinderfield Parade. Midsummer's Eve. Do you recognize her at all?"

The Earl stares at the flyer for a beat then looks away. "No, I'm afraid I don't."

She opens her laptop and spins it round so he can see the screen. "This is her too." She shuttles through the footage from the Cinderfield Parade until she finds her, walking away from the camera with the Cinderman by her side.

"What about this person she's walking with?" She points at the Cinderman. "Any idea who he might be?"

"No!" the Earl replies without even looking back at the screen. He seems to realize his reply was too hasty and looks down at the screen, making a show of taking his time to study the image. "I mean, I can't see his face because of the costume, so, no I couldn't say who it is."

"You're sure?"

"Yes."

"It's just that . . ." Laughton takes her phone, selects one of the images she took earlier from the CCTV in the craft shop, and holds it up for the Earl to see. "You seem to be pretty friendly with whoever it is."

The Earl stares at the picture, the color draining from his face. The wedding planners notice the change in his expression and some of the wind of indignation spills from their sails. The Earl opens his mouth as if he's about to say something, then a decision is made and the shutters come thundering down.

"I'm not prepared to say any more unless I have a lawyer present. This is . . . what you're doing here is . . . well, it's harassment and I will not . . . you cannot just come here and ambush me like this. I mean, do you even have a warrant?"

"I'm just trying to find a girl who's gone missing," Laughton says, swiping to another photograph showing a wider image with the Earl, the Cinderman, and Beech all standing in their little group. "I also assumed you'd be happy to cooperate with a police investigation, seeing as the other person you're talking to here is the Chief Constable. Is this third person your son perhaps?" She points again at the Cinderman.

The Earl looks from the phone to Laughton then back again, his mouth working as his brain scrambles for the right thing to say.

"I'm not prepared to say another word without a lawyer present," he says, "now, if you wouldn't mind, I have work to do."

Laughton holds his gaze and sees fear in his eyes behind all the pomp and bluster. She slides the flyer across the table until it is directly in front of him. "This woman is missing," she says, still looking him in the eye. She holds up her phone. "And this is the last person she was seen with, which makes him the number one person of interest. So, if you do know who this Cinderman is, you should tell me now, for her sake and for the sake of all the people who are worried about her. And we will find out who he is, sooner rather than later."

The Earl looks at the picture on Laughton's phone but says nothing.

"Think about it," Laughton says, closing her laptop and rising from her chair. "That's my number on there if you do remember anything."

She turns to the two women and smiles. "Sorry to interrupt your meeting," she says. "You picked a lovely day for a wedding."

61

ADELE SITS ON THE EDGE of her bed in the dusty heat of her old room, working her way through the files Laughton sent her, feeling something between anger and fear. She knows most of the women, though it often takes her a few moments to recognize the scarecrows in the photographs. They are all so changed, worn into shadows of themselves by whatever they had been through. She tries not to think about the hellish journey each of these broken women must have been on, because if she does, she imagines Maddie starting one now.

She reaches the end of the attachments and goes back through them again, counting the number of people she recognizes. Out of the forty-three women, she knew eighteen of them.

Eighteen women had vanished in front of her and it had never even occurred to her to question it. It was just how things were at The Clearing, that's what Grizz always said, people came, people went. But Grizz had known, hadn't she? And maybe she knows what happened to Maddie too.

Adele suddenly finds it hard to breathe and stands up, feeling crushed by the heavy gloom of the room and desperate to be free of it. She grabs her small backpack and her bundle of inspirational notes and stumbles from the office, bursting out of the dark cabin and into the light like a swimmer breaking the surface. She takes her phone, finds the entry for Grizz, and stares at the green icon to dial it. Grizz is never going to admit anything. She probably won't even answer the call when she sees who it is. Better to confront her in person; take her by surprise and ask her directly. But that would mean walking to The Clearing. It would mean going into the forest again.

She looks up at the gap in the distant trees where the footpath starts. At the end of that path is The Clearing, and answers she needs, maybe even the key to finding Maddie.

She starts walking, shouldering her bag and murmuring from memory some of the positive thoughts clutched in her hand as she gets closer to the gap.

Strength doesn't come from what you can do, it comes from overcoming the things you once thought you couldn't.

She reaches the gap and steps into the forest without hesitation, her eyes fixed on the way ahead, her hand clutching all the pieces of paper with her collected positive thoughts written on them, a bundle of spells to protect her against whatever evil awaits.

62

SHE STANDS IN THE MIDDLE of the room, the candle in her hand now little more than a stub. She has swept the room three times and found three cameras—two in the corners and one directly over the bed. She looks up at the plug of wax now covering it, wondering how long it will take him to realize he is now blind, and how long after that he will come back to do something about it.

Let him come.

This time she will not be drugged by a poisoned apple.

This time she will be ready.

63

LAUGHTON STRIDES PAST THE MARQUEE on her way back to the Abbey, her mind humming after her meeting with the Earl. He had been rattled when she'd shown him the images from the CCTV, which strongly suggested that it was his son walking with Maddie, just a few hours before she vanished.

She pulls out her phone as she steps back into the stone-cooled interior of the Abbey and checks her emails in case the Earl's son has finally replied, but he hasn't. She calls Tannahill and it goes straight to voicemail, which means he's probably still airborne. Glasgow to London is barely more than an hour's flight and he only has hand luggage, so he'll be heading into London in maybe an hour and a half, no more than two. She waits for the beep then covers her mouth with her hand as she leaves a message, speaking quietly as if the building might be listening.

"Hey, it's me. I have another favor to ask. I was wondering if you could take a tiny diversion on your way to interview your suspect and pay a quick visit to someone. He's an artist, the son of the Earl, who lives in a studio in Kew, so it's on your way. I just want you to look him in the eye and ask him if he knows Maddie Friar. I'll send you a picture of what I'm pretty sure is him. Show him the picture, ask him about Maddie and see how he reacts. I just asked his dad the same questions and he wanted to lawyer up so fast it was as good as a confession. I've tried emailing him and I could try calling but I think the drawbridge is already up, so a surprise knock on the door may be the best tactic. My feeling is he might cave if confronted. I'd do it myself but I'm still here. Probably going to head back to London this afternoon and set things in motion for a big internal investigation. You're right. This thing is too big now and there are too many high-profile players involved. Just need to do a couple more things but dinner tonight is definitely on the cards. Especially if you do this little favor for me. Give me a call when you land. Love you. Bye!"

She hangs up then instantly panics.

Love you!

Why the hell had she said that? She stares at her phone, thinking how she might recall the message and leave another, one where she doesn't drop the L-bomb at the end. She couldn't rerecord the message because she'd already hung up. Jesus! Why did she say that?

She passes through a set of doors and reenters the hallway where the long table is now filled with champagne glasses and the waitress is nowhere in sight. Maybe it's all this wedding stuff everywhere, corrupting her mind with romance.

Laughton sticks her head through the door of the chapel, hoping the Earl's assistant might still be there so she can thank her for her help, but the vast room contains nothing but stained-glass sunlight. She heads to the huge front door and is about to step through it when the shrill ring of an old phone starts up somewhere in the cavernous house. Laughton listens for a moment then follows the sound, down a dark-paneled hallway to a yellow door. Behind it the phone continues to ring, the sharp sound of the bells like something from the past. She knocks on the door, though if there was someone in the room they would surely have answered the phone by now. The phone rings again in reply, shrill and sharp, and she looks back down the corridor, then twists the handle and opens the door.

The room beyond is a glorious shambles of books and old, worn furniture. It feels more like a library than an office, but the modern printer and flatscreen computer perched on the cluttered leather-topped desk suggest otherwise. The phone stands next to it, still ringing and so much louder now she is in the room.

Laughton steps through the door and closes it behind her, leaving it slightly ajar as an excuse in case anyone comes along. She moves across to the desk, the thrill of being somewhere she shouldn't mixing with the residue of anger from her meeting with the Earl. She wants to prick at his conscience, rattle him a little and see if anything shakes loose.

She pulls another flyer from her bag just as the phone falls silent, the final ring of the bell swallowed by the wood paneling and all the books on the shelves. She pushes aside some of the mess of paperwork on the desk to create a space for the flyer, because she wants to make sure he will see it when he returns to his office, wants Maddie's face to be smiling up at him, reminding him that she is still missing and that he can potentially do something about it. Beneath the mess of papers is a large drawing that covers most of the desk. It appears to be architectural drawings showing a detailed plan of the grounds with the Abbey at the center and the forest all around. She clears more letters away revealing new details, a quarry and a campsite, which she assumes must be the one Adele works at. And the owner of that campsite had also chatted to Beech and the Earl at the Cinderfield Parade. They were neighbors. She smooths the drawing down and spots another settlement to the north, deep in the forest and labeled "The Clearing." Laughton looks at the three areas and is struck by how relatively close together everything is, each place neighboring the other, but also isolated and separated by what could be miles of forest.

Another scroll of paper is fixed to the edge of the main drawing and she clears more letters away then rolls out a semitransparent sheet of drafting paper that overlays the main drawing. The drawing has a network of squares on it, radiating out from the outlines of new roads that look like arteries or the branches of a huge tree. Each square is numbered, six hundred and eighty plots in total that cover ground currently occupied by the campsite and The Clearing. She smooths the paper down and reads the writing on the edge:

"Proposed Housing Development for Abbey Trust Land Holdings."

Laughton pulls out her phone and snaps a series of pictures of the map, wondering how much an average new house goes for in this area. Even if they were worth a relatively modest amount, the development would still be worth hundreds of millions. She lets the top sheet roll back and is about to lay the flyer down in the center of the desk when a noise behind her makes her turn round to find the Earl's assistant framed in the doorway with a severe look on her face.

"Oh, hi," Laughton says. "I was looking for you, actually. I wanted to say thanks for the tip about where to find the Earl. I spoke to him and he asked me to leave one of these behind for him." She holds up the flyer. "I was just going to put it on his desk but I can give it to you now you're here."

The stern assistant looks past her to the cluttered desk. "You shouldn't really be in here, this is the Earl's private study."

"Oh, sorry, I did knock, and the door was open so I didn't think it was . . . listen, thanks again, I'll just leave this here and be on my way."

She places the flyer in the center of the desk, covering the section of map outlining the Abbey, then heads to the door and into the corridor.

"Thanks again," she calls back. "You really have been very helpful."

64

SHE DRIPS CANDLE WAX ONTO the surface of the table then fixes the stub of the candle into it. Next, she drags the mattress off the bed and props it against the side of the bedframe, draping the blanket over the whole thing to create a kind of fort.

The candle flame gutters from the displaced air and she catches movement behind her. She spins around, heart hammering, ready to fight and claw and kick. But it's not him, not yet—it's only her shadow. It wavers and settles as the candle settles too, and she moves the chair back to the table and sits down, her shadow swallowing half of the room behind her.

She slides the box of candles over and looks inside.

There are eight left, maybe eight hours of light, probably less.

She looks up at the blob of wax covering the camera above the bed. Can he still see the candlelight, she wonders, a dull orange glow behind the wax? Maybe he will wait until all the candles are gone and he knows she will be in darkness. Or maybe he will come sooner, pissed off and wanting to clear the wax away so he can watch her again. When he does come, will it be with threats, or with offers of food in exchange for good behavior; good cop or bad cop?

She picks a candle up, turns it over in her hand, then holds it against her forehead, rolling the cool, waxy surface back and forth across the swelling.

She stares at the candle flame, perfectly still now the air has settled, then leans forward and blows it out.

In the darkness she can still see the image of the flame and smell the smoke from the cooling wick. It reminds her of him. When she was little she thought the fact that he always smelled of smoke was because he came from hell. It was one of the things that terrified her about him. One of the many things.

But she's not a kid anymore.

And he's not from hell, he's just a man.

So let him come.

Let him come.

65

LAUGHTON GETS INTO HER CAR and opens all the windows to relieve the ovenlike heat that has built up in the short time it's been parked. She turns on the engine and sets the fans blowing, wishing now that she'd stumped up the extra for air con as she rummages through her bag, looking for the card her roadside savior had given her earlier along with the packet of Polos. She finds it buried in a pile of receipts and holds it up to the light so she can copy the number into her phone:

DEREK HILL

Deputy Assistant Planner
Gloucestershire County Council
www.gloucestershire.gov.uk Tel: 0788 489367

She puts it on speaker, backs out of her space, and is already driving away from the Abbey when he answers.

"Hello. Derek Hill speaking."

"Hi, this is Laughton Rees, you very kindly came to my rescue on the road earlier."

"Ah, indeed, how are you?"

"I'm fine thanks. Listen, bit of a strange question, are you aware of plans for a very large housing development called Abbey Trust Land Holdings?"

"No, where is it?"

"It's in a large section of forest stretching eastward from Cinderfield

Abbey, starting at an old quarry and spreading north to a place known as The Clearing and south to a campsite."

"Oh, right, well then, that is in this area and that is actually a very interesting piece of land. The quarry belongs to the Abbey and could easily be developed because it's already been granted change of use status and so lies outside the usual forestry conservation orders. However, I know for a fact that historically the Earl's family has been reluctant to develop anything there because it's so close to the Abbey."

Laughton pictures the plans on the earl's desk. "On the plans I've seen the quarry looks more like it's being used as the access road for the main development."

"Well, that would make sense, as there'll already be a service road through the woods to get to the quarry, so it wouldn't require any additional planning permission. The forest beyond the quarry is a different matter, it's a funny one, because although it is covered by the conservation laws, it's also in a section which is classed as common land. Historically that means whoever lives there has the right to construct dwellings, although those laws have been gradually eroded over the years to the point where only existing tenants still retain those rights."

"So, in theory things could be built there, but only by people already living on the land?"

"Exactly. Again, historically there's been a blanket ban on any commercial development of forest land, even common land, but that's changing. There's a huge housing crisis in this area, especially now second-homers have started moving in and driving prices up. The simple fact is there are not enough houses to go around, so to try and address this problem, planning restrictions are being relaxed to allow areas that were previously off-limits to be developed. We've already got quite a number of new housing estates under construction on sites that if you'd asked me five years ago I would have said would never be developed in my lifetime, including sites in and around the forest, which is a huge shame in my opinion. I have to say though, I'm not familiar with this one, what did you say its name was again?"

"It's called Abbey Trust Land Holdings." Laughton turns left onto the main road and starts heading toward the campsite. "Is it possible someone else in your department might know about it?"

"No. There's only two of us in the office and I'd definitely know about a proposed development of this size. How many plots are we talking about, do you know?"

"Er, yes, there were six hundred and eighty marked on the plans."

"Crikey. That's huge. The biggest planning application I've ever dealt with was only for a hundred and sixteen plots, and I've been doing this job for over twenty years."

"Could they be bypassing the planning laws somehow?"

"Not really, not for something of this size. I mean, we get the odd illegal extension or garage, but something this big would have to go through the proper channels. They'd have to submit their plans then go through the consultation procedure, where the plans would be made public and people given twenty-one days to consider them and lodge any objections. Also, because it's a development covering both forest and common land, the various landlords would have to be in agreement."

"And who would they be?"

"Well, in this case it would be the Earl plus any legal tenants of the common lands, by which I mean anyone who has been in continuous residence there since before the rights in common laws changed fifteen or so years ago."

Laughton thinks back to the conversation she and Adele had in the middle of the night, when Adele told her about The Clearing and Grizz, the woman in charge. She must have been living in the forest for that long. "So, if the landlords agree, the land can be developed?"

"Not quite. Any legal matters relating to the common lands were traditionally presided over by the high sheriff of Gloucestershire, who was the principal law enforcement officer in the county."

"And who's that?"

"Well, the high sheriff is now a ceremonial role, opening village fetes and garden parties, that kind of thing, and their legal duties now fall under various administrative arms of the county council. Any legal duties, therefore, such as ratifying planning agreements and suchlike, would be the purview of the police."

"And would the person in charge of such duties be the Chief Constable, by any chance?"

"Well, actually, yes, it would. And the name of the current holder of that position is . . ."

"Beech!" Laughton says, easing her foot off the accelerator as she sees the sign for the campsite up ahead. "Chief Constable Russell Beech."

66

HE RUBS THE SHIN OF his right leg, which still hurts from where the chair had hit it.

Stupid bitch!

She had always been a stupid, annoying bitch.

They all were. That's why they needed to be taught. And now she's gone and done this.

He stares at the screen showing a three-way feed from the three cameras in the cell, each a perfect rectangle of black. He switches to night mode and the three rectangles turn a phosphorescent green, but he can still see nothing.

Annoying. Bitch!

He is looking forward to breaking her. Making her suffer for what she did, for what she tried to do. She was the reason he'd had to spend the last ten years hiding away, pretending he was dead, because it was easier than being alive. Safer. She had ruined his life and he was so going to enjoy ruining what was left of hers.

He walks over to his workbench and opens a drawer. Inside is a mess of tools and cables as well as a black, rectangular piece of heavy-duty plastic with two short, silver electrodes jutting out from one end. He takes it out and plugs it in next to the headset that is already charging.

Once they're both juiced up, he'll go back in the tunnels and give her a lesson in manners.

They all needed to be taught.

This one more than most.

67

MALLORY STOKER HAWTHORN KINGSTON, EIGHTEENTH Earl of Dean, stands again in the dusty privacy of his study staring down at the photo on his desk. He is vaguely aware of Cleo coming into the room and waiting for him to look up and acknowledge her, but he can't, he can't take his eyes off the girl, smiling up from the flyer. He feels frozen in the moment, frozen in the nightmare of his situation. He swallows and forces himself to look up at Cleo, who has an expression of concern on her face.

"Are you OK, Mal?" she asks. "You look a little pale."

No, he wants to say. *I am not OK. I am about as far from OK as it's possible to be.*

"I'm just . . ." He looks down at the flyer again. "Terrible business," he says, because it is, it really is.

"Yes, isn't it? Poor girl. I hope she turns up safe and sound."

The Earl looks up at her and forces a smile. "Could you give me a minute, please, Clee? I just need to make a call."

"Of course, I was just checking to see if you needed anything."

He sits down at his desk, not trusting his legs to support him for much longer. "A cup of tea would be lovely if you're making one. But don't worry if you're not."

Cleo smiles. "I'll go and pop the kettle on."

She leaves the room and closes the door behind her.

The Earl pulls his phone from his pocket and dials his son's number. He sits back in his chair and stares up at the stern portrait of his father hanging above the fireplace with his permanent look of disapproval. The phone connects and he hears Sebastian's voice but it's just his answering machine.

"Seb, it's me again. Listen, that person who emailed you, she just came to the Abbey and started asking me lots of questions and . . . I'm doing everything I can to try and sort things out this end, but in the meantime it's probably best if you keep your head down, all right? If you could call me when you get this message so I know you've got it that would be . . . Please call me back, Seb. You know how I worry."

He hangs up and rises from his chair, scooping the flyer from his desk before walking over to the window. Outside on the lawn the first wedding guests have started arriving, about an hour before they should, which always happens. Everyone wants to have a snoop around the house and the grounds. Everyone is so bloody nosy and impertinent these days, taking selfies in his house, pretending they live here.

He looks out beyond the marquee to the edge of the forest, ancient and unchanged since before the Abbey was built. The forest has always provided for his family in different ways—timber and stone for the house, wood to heat it, income from the tenants and food from the fields and orchards. And now it is going to provide in another way and allow him to restore the Abbey to its former status, where gawping wedding guests and their selfie-sticks will be nothing more than an unpleasant memory. He has to remember that. Keep his mind on the prize and not be rattled by bumps in the road.

He opens WhatsApp and starts a new audio call.

"What's happened?" Beech answers, sounding tetchy.

"She came here," he says, "the woman with the funny name practically jumped on me and started waving photos in my face."

"Photos of what?"

"Photos from security cameras showing you and me talking to each other at the parade, also talking to Seb."

"Seb?"

"Yes. I mean, you couldn't see it was him because he had his costume on and his hood up, thank God." He flips the flyer over and stares at the photo again. "There are pictures of him with the girl too."

"What did you tell her?"

"Nothing. I didn't tell her anything."

"Good!"

"I said I wasn't prepared to say anything to her without my lawyer present."

He hears a deep sigh come whistling down the line. "Why did you say that?"

"Well, because I wanted to make it abundantly clear that I wasn't prepared to talk to her informally. What's wrong with asking for legal counsel?"

"People who hide behind lawyers generally only do so because they have something to hide. Listen, don't worry. I think all this just proves that we need to stop pussyfooting around and start acting more decisively. We can't afford to keep crossing our fingers and hoping it all blows over. We need to make it go away and we need to do it fast. Leave it with me. And don't talk to anyone."

The call cuts off.

In his cluttered office Beech yanks open his desk drawer and looks around inside for a packet of Mentos but all he finds are empty wrappers. Jesus, if he were still smoking, today would probably have killed him. He bangs the drawer shut and launches himself out of his chair then stalks over to the window and stares out across the car park to the hills and the forest beyond.

He pulls his phone from his pocket and types the number Grizz gave him into WhatsApp with its peer-to-peer encryption. God bless Mark Zuckerberg and his morality-free, gangster-capitalism instincts.

"No more surveillance," he types. "Get your man to finish the job. Both targets. Let me know when it's done."

68

SHE LIFTS HER HEAD, TILTS it to the side. Listens.

In the hiss of silence she thinks she hears something, a soft crunch just outside the door, like a careful footstep.

She holds her breath, trying to make no sound of her own as she listens hard to the solid sound of the dark.

Outside the door he listens too, the tunnel glowing green in his night-vision goggles. He can see the door, flat and featureless and right in front of him, the key in his hand ready to fit into the lock. He can hear nothing beyond it, and since she disabled his cameras, he cannot see inside the cell either, which means opening the door will carry a risk.

He takes another soft step forward and presses his ear to the door, listening through the solid wood for any sound on the other side.

Nothing.

Maybe she is asleep, though he doubts it. He slides the key slowly and soundlessly into the lock, listens for a few more seconds, then twists it.

The door swings open and into the room. In bright vivid green he sees the child's fort she has made from the bed and smiles. A fort made from sheets and the thinnest of mattresses, like that's going to protect anyone from anything. Still. It's always more fun when they want to play. He raises the pipe and points it at the mattress, holding it close to his mouth, ready.

"Little pig," he says, keeping his voice low and feeling a thrill of power as he imagines her cowering behind the mattress at the sound of it. "Little pig, let me come in."

He takes a step into the room, pulling the fully charged Taser from his pocket in case she tries to rush him. The green phosphorescence makes the darkness dance.

"Little pig," he says again, quieter this time, his voice barely more than a hiss. He takes another step, a smile spreading across his face at what fun this is turning out to be. "Little pig."

He hears the soft whistle too late, the sound of something moving fast through the air.

Then pain explodes in his legs.

She feels the impact shudder through the metal frame of the chair, hears him cry in surprise and pain. She stumbles forward with the momentum of her swing, recovers, and swings again, bringing the chair down hard on the spot where she imagines he is standing. The chair bangs hard against the ground and bounces up again, glancing off him but not hurting him, not like the first blow, and she feels a surge of panic.

She can't see. She doesn't know where he is. He could be backing away and closing the door right now.

She leaps forward, swinging the chair wildly.

It connects with something and blue sparks crackle in the darkness, making her hands tingle with a hot, burning pain where they grip the metal frame of the chair. In the white light of that fraction of a second she sees him, a nightmare in rags with a hood and a blackened face, and some kind of goggles that make him look inhuman. He is crouched, spiderlike, in the open doorway, holding something long and thin in one hand and a small, black object in the other that sparks where it touches the chair.

Her hands burn and she wants to let go but she can't. Then the sparking stops and she is in darkness again, the image of him seared into her eyes. She throws the chair at the place where he was and hears another cry of pain.

She leaps forward, aiming for the gap she had glimpsed between him and the door.

He grabs her in the dark, pulling at her arm and yanking her down, and for a second she is on top of him. She feels his arm reach around her and knows it's the one holding the Taser. If he touches her with it she will feel the burning pain again and it will all be over, and she will never get out of this darkness.

She bucks and squirms, fighting him off.

She reaches behind her back and grabs a candle from the waistband of her jeans, stabs it down hard into the hand that holds her, the point of it sharpened in the darkness while she waited for him to come, and it draws another scream of angry pain. She feels the arm slacken for a second and she squirms free, clawing at his face, her fingernails hooking under the strap of the goggles and gouging skin as she yanks them free and holds them tight.

She feels a sudden hot sting on the back of her legs as something hits her and she grabs at the source of the pain. It's long and thin, like a pipe or the barrel of a gun.

She grabs and twists it, turning her body to lever it from his grasp and stop him from striking her again. Then she brings her knee up hard, striking wildly in the dark and connecting with something that makes a wet crunching sound and brings another wail of pain.

He lets go of her and she twists away and is out of the door and free, stumbling through the dark, her hands in front of her, searching the way ahead, putting as much distance between her and him as she can, the darkness finally her friend.

69

LAUGHTON TURNS OFF THE MAIN road and follows the track through the field of tents and parked camper vans to the shack on the far side of the field. She pulls up behind the ramshackle electric vehicle and looks over to where the door of the shack stands open. She assumes Adele must be inside and will have heard her car, so she quickly sends Tannahill a new email with the photographs from the CCTV cameras and a short message:

I'm 99% certain the hooded figure in these pics is the Earl's son. See how he reacts when you show them to him. His name is Sebastian Kingston. Here's a link to his studio in Kew with the address. XXX

She pastes in the link then stares at the three kisses at the end of her message. Was three too many, especially after accidentally dropping the "L" bomb in her voice message? She deletes two of them then sends it and looks across at the shack. Still no sign of Adele.

Laughton gets out of the car and walks up to the open door. She knocks loudly on the doorframe then steps through into the stifling interior, expecting to find Adele in her room, AirPods in her ears and oblivious to Laughton's presence as she clears out her stuff, but the door to her room is also open and there's no one inside.

Laughton checks the wall where Adele's hand-drawn notes of positivity had been pinned, and when she sees it is bare, heads back outside and pulls her phone from her pocket. She finds Adele's number and dials it, shielding her eyes against the bright sunlight as she scans the campsite for any sign of her. The phone connects.

Hey, this is Adele, leave a message.

"Hi, it's Laughton, I'm back at the campsite, where are you? Got lots to tell."

She hangs up and steps away from the shack to give her a wider view of the campsite, which is now humming with morning activities. An energetic game of five-a-side is under way on a clear stretch of lawn, a couple of tetherballs are being batted back and forth like it's the Wimbledon final, and people doze on blankets or read books in the shade of the trees. It's a picture-postcard vision of a British summer's day, but Adele is nowhere to be seen in it.

Laughton checks her phone to make sure she still has a signal and thinks about calling again but realizes there's no point. She must be here. Has to be, she only dropped her off about an hour earlier and knows she has no transport. She has an idea and walks back to her car, opens the boot, and fishes her water bottle out from the running bag she packed in the somewhat optimistic hope of maybe squeezing in some morning runs along leafy country lanes while she was here. The water is warm from being in the car but she drinks it anyway then pulls a couple of the flyers out of her bag. She closes the windows, locks the doors, then heads into the campsite, smiling as she approaches the nearest set of campers, sitting in their camping chairs under a shade sail, both doing Wordle on their phones.

"Hi," Laughton says. "I wonder if you can help. I'm supposed to be meeting my friend here but she's not answering her phone." She holds up the flyer. "She looks a bit like this. You haven't seen her by any chance, have you?"

Dog watches from the shade of a tree by the entrance to the campsite. The bike had been a sound move, not least because it is much smaller and therefore harder to spot than the car. He'd been able to buzz around behind her all morning, observing from a distance, reporting back on where she went and who she spoke to. Only now the message has changed.

At the far side of the campsite, Goldilocks walks away from the two campers in their chairs and heads to a camper van, holding up the piece of paper in her hand as she approaches a group of people sitting on a blanket in front of it. She's looking for the other one, which suits him fine. Let her find her and save him the bother. Then he can wait until dark and do what the message had told him to do.

Finish the job. Both targets. No witnesses.

70

ADELE MOVES THROUGH THE FOREST with steady purpose, not quite believing she'd had a panic attack here just the day before. She keeps her breathing steady and focused while in her head she repeats the phrase that spurred her on her journey and is now scrunched in her bag along with all her other talismans against failure:

Strength doesn't come from what you can do, it comes from overcoming the things you once thought you couldn't.

Everything is about fear and the way you react to it, that is what she has come to learn through a lifetime of being almost perpetually afraid. Fear defines you, one way or another, you either hide from it or you face it, the choice is yours and you have to own it. But something else she has learned is that the opposite of being afraid is not necessarily being brave. More often it's a question of choosing the lesser of two fears. And as she had stood at the edge of the forest, she had asked herself a simple question: Was she more scared of going in the forest or of not finding Maddie? The answer had been easy, and so here she is.

She follows the path now as it curves through a thick patch of laurel bushes that crowd in on her from both sides. Up ahead the path splits, right leading on toward The Clearing and left taking her down a narrower track and away toward the Abbey. She reaches the junction and stops, remembering the map showing Maddie's last recorded movements. The left fork must have been the track she had taken. She looks down it as far as she can before the path curves away and the forest swallows it up, like it had swallowed up Maddie. She feels suddenly uneasy, all her newfound confidence draining away as quickly as it had filled her. It feels almost like the forest is watching her, waiting to see which direction she chooses.

He stares at her through the veil of leaves, so close he could touch her, feeling the usual rush of power that he is right there and she does not know it. This feeling of invisibility is always intoxicating, but being invisible to her is almost too much to bear. He can feel himself trembling, like a leaf in a breeze, and wonders if she might sense his presence on some instinctive level.

She switches her attention from one side of the path to the other, and in the briefest of moments their eyes meet before her gaze sweeps on to stare down the wider pathway. She looks so much like her sister that it's almost unnerving. She looks down at the crumpled pages in her hand, the ink blotted with sweat, and he drops his eyes down but keeps his head perfectly still as he reads the words on the top page:

Things do not happen, they are made to happen.

He feels a new thrill shudder through him at the clear message the forest is giving him. It has brought her to him. It is giving him this offering.

She starts to move, away down the wider pathway, the path most traveled, and he swiftly raises the blowpipe to his lips. He aims at her back then coughs silently. The dart, dipped in a nerve agent brewed from henbane, hemlock, and belladonna, flies out of the laurel like an insect and strikes her on the back.

She reaches behind her and slaps at the spot, like she's batting away a hornet, and marches on, away down the path, her eyes fixed ahead, but her movements are already starting to waver as the drug takes hold and begins to drag her down into a sleepy summer slumber.

71

SHE RUNS FOR WHAT SEEMS like minutes—bumping along the dark tunnel, the glow from the headset in her hand casting a weak, green light on the ground—until her panicked brain calms enough for her to realize it would be better to wear the headset than to use it as a torch.

She slips it over her head, the smoky smell of him still clinging to the straps, and the tunnel comes alive in a buzzing flare of phosphorescent green. After so long in the dark she has to half-close her eyes against so much brightness.

The tunnel is smaller than she thought, the ceiling lower and the walls more even and straight, like they were cut by hand rather than formed naturally by underground streams.

She looks back the way she came, bracing herself in case he is there, but the floor of the tunnel curves upward and the low ceiling means she cannot see very far. She realizes now that she's moving deeper underground and considers going back the way she came to head upward again. Only he is back there too, somewhere in the dark.

She looks down at herself to check if she's injured or bleeding and sees the pipe in her hand, forgotten since she had grabbed it from him during her escape. She holds it up to examine it, turning it in her hand. It is short and thin, a mouthpiece at one end, not the barrel of a gun as she had first feared but a blowpipe, which is just as disturbing.

She looks ahead and sees the main tunnel split into three smaller tunnels, each curving away into darkness. She stares at the junction and remembers standing in the forest, at another junction. She remembers feeling the sting on her back, like a hornet's bite, then she had woken up here in the dark, her memory clouded by panic and fear and whatever drugs he had used to drag her here.

But now she remembers.

She looks at the blowpipe, useless without darts, but also useless to him because she has it. She drops it on the ground and stamps on the end of it to break it and it splinters along its length. She picks up one half and turns it in her hand, studying the splintered point. Better than a candle. Longer too.

She looks back up at the three-way junction, then takes the broken blowpipe and uses the point to draw a cross in the dirt on the ground by one of the passages so she will know which way she went if she ends up back here.

She takes a last look behind her, checking again he isn't there, then heads down the tunnel, now glowing green in her eyes.

72

LAUGHTON TRIES ADELE'S NUMBER AGAIN but again it goes straight to voicemail.

She scans the campsite, in case by some miracle she has been there all along and she's missed her, but she hasn't. There's no sign of her, no one has seen her, and Laughton is becoming increasingly worried.

She drifts over to the edge of the forest and stops where the track enters the woods, peering into the shadows at the path winding through the trees until it disappears from sight. She pulls her phone from her pocket, opens one of the pictures she snapped of the plans she'd found on the Earl's desk, and zooms in on the section where the outline of The Site is marked. She traces the edge of the campsite where it borders the forest and follows the line of a track through the forest as it meanders and splits, all the way up to The Clearing.

Maybe that's where Adele has gone. She thinks back to her reaction when she thought they were driving into the woods the night before. She'd been terrified. Would someone that frightened of the forest, someone properly psychologically scarred by what had happened to her there, go willingly into a place that triggering? Unlikely.

She turns and heads back across the campsite, thinking about everything Adele had told her in the dead of night—about her childhood, about her abusive foster father, fleeing the cabin she had been abused in. No wonder she never wanted to set foot in the forest again. Laughton carried her own psychological scars because of what happened in her childhood, and it had taken her years and another significant trauma to finally escape from under their shadow.

She gets back to her car and is almost knocked over by the wave of heat that assaults her when she opens the door. She pulls her laptop out of her bag, sits at one of the few unoccupied picnic tables, and clicks on the guest Wi-Fi to connect.

Adele said her foster parents had died when their cabin burned down, but Maddie had also been looking into their fostering record before she disappeared. Maybe the two things were connected; maybe the father had not died in that fire after all. She stares out at the chilled, summery scene, the fingers of her right hand tapping in patterns of three on the tabletop as she tries to figure out how she might quickly find out what she needs to know.

The local Coroner's Office would have records of all local deaths by fire, but getting access to them would require jumping through too many hoops and take way too long. Maybe there is an easier way. She taps some more. One-two-three. One-two-three. Watches a family playing cricket, the dad taking it *way* too seriously. She googles "Cinderfield Cabin Fire Death" and starts working through the results, domestic fires, vehicle fires, a fire in a disused building on a train line outside Cheltenham where two teenagers died, and one where a shed burned down on an allotment outside Stroud involving an eighty-six-year-old man who was believed to have had a heart attack that then led to the fire. There are no stories of anyone dying in a cabin fire. It's possible that it wasn't reported, but that's unlikely; any story involving a death by fire in a place surrounded by forest is always newsworthy.

She watches the cricket game again, tapping her fingers in threes. If she had a name it would help but Adele had not given one. She had said something about Maddie receiving a letter from the council fostering services, but getting any information from social services would be a nightmare. There would be Service Level Agreements, Information Sharing Agreements, and all kinds of other rules to comply with, and for good reason. Laughton would have to make a formal request just to get the ball rolling, the files would probably be hard copy only, so would then have to be copied, redacted, copied again, then collected in person and against signature, and after all that might not yield any useful information anyway. Laughton thinks about that for a moment then opens a file on her desktop labeled NEED, which stands for Nationwide Express Enquiry Directory and lists direct numbers for all social and law enforcement agencies in the country, enabling officers in a hurry to bypass all the slow and maddening automated switchboards. She finds a number for Gloucestershire Social Services and dials it, scanning the campsite again while she listens to it ring, hoping to see Adele heading her way.

"Social Services," a weary-sounding male voice answers.

"Hi, I wonder if you can help me. My name's Laughton Rees and I'm working with the Metropolitan Police investigating a missing person we believe was placed in foster care in your area. I was about to start drafting a formal request for information but thought, before I wasted everyone's time, I'd check first to see if there was anything on record worth requesting. I'm not expecting you to give me any details over the phone, of course, I just figured if you're as swamped as me with paperwork I would spare you a wild-goose chase if there's nothing there to chase."

There is a pause and Laughton imagines him surveying a desk buried beneath overstuffed folders and case files. "What are the names?"

"It's Donna and Helen Bailey." She hears the tapping of a keyboard then the clicking of a mouse wheel.

"I would advise that there's no point in making a formal request for the information we hold on those names."

"As in, there's not much useful information?"

"As in, there's no information at all."

"Right." Laughton smiles to hide the surprise in her voice. "Well, then, that's saved us both a bunch of paperwork. Thanks for your help."

She hangs up and frowns at the day. Another dead end and one that slams the door on Laughton's working theory that Maddie's inquiries might have brought the demons from her past back to her door. Except a pattern is starting to emerge, a trail of nothings where there should be something.

No record of any fire.

No record of anything relating to their fostering.

And there have to be records; councils don't just hand children over to strangers without carefully vetting them first and keeping detailed records. But there isn't anything and she has to wonder why. The absence of any information only leads her to believe that something is being hidden. She'd attended a lecture once where an eminent forensic accountant had talked about the absence of proof being a kind of proof in itself.

"If you see a white sheet thrown over something," he had said, "you don't need to see what's underneath it to know that something is there."

And the gaps in the record regarding Adele and Maddie's childhood are one massive white sheet.

She watches a group of kids chasing each other round the tents, enjoying their summer holiday, the sort Adele and Maddie had probably never had, the kind she had never had either.

Then it struck her.

Schools!

Adele had said it was their teacher who'd flagged concerns and called their mother to discuss it. That was what had set in motion their escape. And her Met credentials grant her access to the NSD, the National Schools Database. She opens a new window, logs into the NSD, and selects Gloucestershire from the drop-down menu. She types in "Donna Bailey and Helen Bailey" and gets an instant hit. Donna and Helen Bailey had been enrolled at Tutshill C of E Primary School. There is even a copy of their application form listing their names, dates of birth—and their home address.

Laughton feels the rush of the hunt as she copies the address into Google Maps and hits Return.

A map loads showing almost nothing but green with a single line of road running through it. She switches to satellite view and zooms in, looking on either side of the thin, dark ribbon of tarmac for a track or the telltale outline of a roof but can see nothing but the road and the soft green expanse of trees stretching away either side of it. Maybe whoever enrolled them at the school gave a false address and this is yet another dead end.

Then she sees something, only faint, but it stands out as a point of difference against the green. She zooms in until it starts to pixelate then studies the anomaly. It looks like what may have been a small glade, clearly overgrown and tucked well back from the road, but with something else in it that makes it stand out. A line. A straight line that could only be man-made. Part of a roof maybe, or a piece of old wall.

She switches to street view, grabs the icon of the yellow man, and drops it on the stretch of road closest to the glade. The image changes to a view of the road, crowded in on both sides by thick screens of established trees and saplings. There is no sign of a turnoff or a track. She clicks along the road, looking for a break in the verge, anything that might lead to the glade. There is nothing obvious, just a single lay-by that appears to be there to let cars pass each other on the narrow road. She zooms in as far as she can to try to peer beyond the green. There are a couple of large logs lying across the edge of the lay-by to create a kind of barrier, not fallen but placed. Placed there for what, though?

She copies the address into her Maps app on her phone and hits the icon for directions. It's over an hour's drive away, the road snaking around the edge of the wood, over a river, and then deep into the forest on the other side.

She tries calling Adele one last time and gets her voice message again.

She closes her laptop, heads back to the car, and puts the fans on full as she backs away from the shack and settles in for her long drive through the forest.

73

SHE FOLLOWS THE TUNNEL WALL round a curve then stops, her eyes fixed on the cross, glowing green on the ground in front of her.

Somehow, through all the dead ends and switchbacks, she has managed to end up right back where she started.

She looks left, back where the tunnel rises, listening for any sign he is there.

Nothing.

The other half of the broken blowpipe is still on the ground where she left it earlier.

Stupid!

Just because she has his night-vision goggles doesn't mean he won't be able to see her. He might have another set, or a torch he can use now that the darkness is no longer his ally. She needs to be smart if she wants to get out of here, and leaving clear tracks like this behind for him to follow is not smart.

She runs a dry tongue across her lips and realizes how thirsty she is getting. The air down here is dry and she has no idea when she last had a drink of water. Maybe he knows there's only one way out of here and is guarding the entrance now, like a cat by a mousehole, waiting for hunger or thirst to drive her his way.

She picks up the other half of the broken blowpipe and pulls away some of the splinters from the edge. She uses the point of it to draw another subtle cross in the dirt by the middle tunnel this time, easy to miss but useful for her. She needs to be smart and make sure she doesn't endlessly wander down the same dead ends if she's going to stand a chance of getting out of here.

She looks back one last time, double-checking he's not there, then heads down the middle tunnel, moving as quietly as she can, holding half of the broken pipe in each hand in case he is waiting for her, somewhere in the dark ahead.

74

LAUGHTON SLOWS AS SHE DRAWS close to the spot on the map where Adele and Maddie once lived. The trees here are tall and tower on either side of the road, creating the feeling that she is driving through a dark chasm rather than a forest.

She spots the lay-by over to the side and pulls into it, tucking the car in as tight as she can, mindful of scratching the paint on the large logs on one side or leaving it sticking out too far on the other where it might get clipped by passing cars on the incredibly narrow country lane.

She checks her phone, which is just about managing to keep one bar of signal in the midst of the dense forest, then gets out of the car and locks it behind her. She stands for a moment, listening to the whisper of the wind in the high tops of the trees and a chattering bird warning the forest that she is here. Moving over to the far side of the car, where the logs lie across the edge of the verge, she parts the screen of leaves with her hands then peers through the gap to where the remains of a track winds through the woods, overgrown and littered with fallen branches, but still identifiable as a pathway through the dense forest. She steps over the log, pushes through the veil of leaves, and enters the forest.

The track is long and curves gently through the trees as it goes deeper into them, keeping the way ahead hidden. She follows it for what seems like a long time, picking her way along the broken ground, pushing through saplings that have taken root and stepping over dead ones that have fallen across the path. The chattering bird continues its running commentary and startles her when it suddenly breaks cover and flaps noisily away down the track in a flurry of black and white feathers. With the bird now gone, the forest falls strangely silent, and it strikes Laughton how remote and foreboding this place must have seemed to two frightened and isolated young girls.

Ahead the track begins to straighten, gradually revealing the glade, or what's left of it. She can see remnants of a building poking out of the greenery, a rusted chain draped over a stone wall like a red snake, a square of rusted bars about the same size as a window, blackened timbers poking out of thick patches of blackberry bushes and ivy now growing in the ash-rich soil where the cabin had once stood.

Laughton scans the area like she is assessing a crime scene, which technically it is. She spots something over by the tangle of burnt timber and blackberries—a patch of nettles, dense and green—and makes her way to it, stepping over a low foundation wall and picking her way carefully through knots of ivy and rubble that would once have been a living room. She picks up a thick branch that has fallen in among the ivy and uses one end of it to part the nettles and poke at the ground beneath.

Laughton has never been to the Anthropology Research Center— better known as the "Body Farm"— in Tennessee but has read widely on their methods and research gleaned from leaving human corpses in various natural settings to see how the microbes and chemicals associated with decomposition, known as the necrobiome, affect the surrounding environment. One of the things they discovered was that plants could be an indicator of where a body might be buried. The average human corpse contains about two and a half kilos of nitrogen, one of the main ingredients in plant fertilizer. Therefore, a body decomposing underground not only promotes the growth of nitrogen-loving plants, these plants also tend to have more chlorophyll content in their leaves, making them greener. Nettles, for example, love nitrogen, and this particular patch is glowing like emeralds.

She pushes the stick into the soil as far as it will go then leans on it to lever up a section of ground. The earth beneath the nettle patch is dark and rich with white roots running through it like veins. She pushes the uprooted section of earth to one side then drives the stick into the hole again and continues to work the ground until her skin shines with sweat and a small mound of earth and stones and uprooted nettles lies on the ground beside her.

She stops for a second and leans on the stick, catching her breath and feeling the heat of the day closing in around her. Maybe she should go back into town and buy a pick and a shovel. She looks back down at the hole, the sides streaked with black charcoal from the fire and red and brown stones. She leans forward, shields her eyes, then reaches down and scoops up a handful of earth and stones from the bottom of the hole. She holds her hand up to the light, flicks away the stones one by one until just one remains. It is brown, about a centimeter long and oblong in shape. She gently blows away dirt from around it then tips her hand and studies it closely. The stone is cylindrical and slightly broader at one end, like a pawn in a game of chess. Only it's not a stone, it's a bone, a distal phalanx from a human hand, the tip of what used to be a finger.

She crouches down, carefully tips the bone and handful of dirt back into the hole, then pulls her phone from her pocket to call the Coroner's Office and turn this into a proper crime scene. Only she can't call anyone, because she has no phone signal.

She looks around and spots a place at the back of the glade where the ground is higher than the surrounding area and heads over, holding her phone high above her head and squinting at the screen to see if she can catch a signal. She climbs to the top of the mound, holding her phone as high as she can, and finally gets a single bar, which brings with it a message saying she has a missed call from Tannahill.

She dials her voicemail and puts it on speaker so she can hold her phone above her head while she listens to the message. Somewhere in the distance the buzz of a trail bike breaks through the softer sounds of the forest and she nudges the volume up as the phone connects and Tannahill's voice cuts in sounding serious.

"Hey, it's me. Listen, the Earl's son, Sebastian—he's dead. Apparent suicide. I found him when I came to his studio. Call me when you get this. He left a note."

Laughton stares wide-eyed at nothing for a few stunned seconds, then stabs 3 to call Tannahill back, pushing the volume to full as the buzz of the motorbike grows.

It starts ringing just as the motorbike tears round the corner of the track in a roar of noise and dirt then skids to a halt. Ice runs down Laughton's spine when she sees the rider. He has no face, just a long slit where the eyes should be, cut into a veil the same color as the forest. He holds her gaze for a second then pulls something round from where it is slung across his back and raises it up.

"Hey," Tannahill says, "listen, I'm just talking to the coroner on the other line, could you just . . ."

"*Trace my phone and send help*," Laughton says, already running down the slope, away from the rider and the crossbow he had pointed at her.

"Someone's here. I'm in trouble." She leaps over a fallen log, looking for a way through the woods that will be harder for the bike to follow.

"TRACE MY PHONE," she screams, holding her phone in front of her.

But Tannahill doesn't hear it.

She's already lost signal.

75

LAUGHTON RUNS.

Branches whip at her face and the ground tries to trip her with every step but she plows on through the forest as swiftly as she dares.

She can hear the bike behind her, the rattling buzz of its engine phasing in and out as she runs past trees and through bushes, her eyes fixed ahead because she knows one false step could turn her ankle, or break her leg, and leave her helpless and alone out here with him. The only time she looks away from the ground is to glance at her phone and check if she has a signal, but the dense and tangled forest shuts out everything but the sound of her pursuer. She needs to find higher ground, and she thinks about doubling back and finding her way to the road, but that would mean heading back toward him.

She listens through the gaps of her breathing to the angry buzz of the trail bike, trying to get a sense of where it is, but the forest moves the sound around, making it impossible to gauge accurately how close he might be. He's behind her somewhere, that's all she can gather, so the best move is to keep running forward, maintain the distance between them, and head upward as much as she can in the hope that sooner or later she'll catch a signal.

She settles into a rhythm, focusing only forward, maintaining a sustainable pace. In London she runs every day, three miles to Canary Wharf and back again along the Thames, six miles in all, so she knows she can cope with the distance, it's just the terrain she's not used to, especially as she is taking the most uneven and difficult route, to make it harder for the bike to follow.

She bursts out of a thicket and spots a low ridge to her right, the top of it almost as high as the trees. She sprints toward it, wary of the fact that this takes her over a section of more open ground, making her visible from further away. She focuses on the ridge, planning her way up it as she sprints closer, her boots feeling heavier as the strength begins to ebb from her legs, her jeans stiff and difficult to run in.

She makes it to the lower slope of the ridge, jams her phone in her back pocket, and starts scrambling upward, using her hands and feet to push her forward, keenly aware that the noise of the bike is growing louder behind her. The ground beneath her gives way as the slope gets steeper; dry, loose earth threatening to carry her down with the mini-landslide her climb is creating. She powers on, scrambling flat out, edging upward a few inches at a time. The sound of the angry bike is louder now, much louder, like it's right behind her. A low branch hits her on the back of the head, telling her she's near the top, and she reaches up and grabs it, using it to haul herself the last few feet before collapsing on the edge of the ridge.

She risks a look back and the rider is right there at the bottom of the slope looking up at her through the eye slits in the veil. He looks along the ridge for a way up and guns the bike's engine into a vicious snarl. Laughton rolls away from the edge and gets to her knees, keeping low so he can't see her.

She checks her phone.

Still no signal.

Shit!

She looks up, her elevated position giving her a view over vast acreage of forest. It's enormous. Someone could easily get lost in here and never be found.

The bike roars behind her, the sound of its engine growing quieter again as the rider moves along the bottom of the ridge looking for a way up. She looks out over the ocean of green, searching for the line of a road or a track, anything man-made that might mean other people. She spots something, maybe half a mile further down in the valley, a small cleared area with what looks like a flagpole sticking up from it.

She starts running toward it, down a slope and into thicker forest, sacrificing the high ground for the chance of finding someone else out here. If she can just make it to the glade and find someone else in this wilderness, someone who lives off the land and has a rifle or bow, she might have a chance.

She pushes on, battling through the half mile of wild, abandoned forest, the growl of the bike ever-present behind her, until she bursts out of the forest into the sunny clearing. She almost screams with frustration when she sees what it contains.

There are three shacks made from straw bales, scrap wood, and old tent canvas. All three roofs have caved in and whoever built them is long gone. Behind her the roar of the bike grows louder and she scans the ground, looking for something, anything she might use as a weapon. She spots the flagpole she'd seen on the ridge and feels a jolt of renewed hope, because it's not a flagpole, it's an aerial.

She runs toward it, figuring she can use it to boost her phone's signal but then the ground seems to dissolve beneath her. She falls forward, her foot sinking into a leaf-filled hole, jarring her ankle when it hits the bottom. Pain shoots up her right side and she bites down on the cry that rises in her throat. She pushes herself up and keeps on moving, scrambling out of the hole and limping over to the hut with the tall aerial, her ankle screaming in pain with every step.

She pulls her phone from her pocket and pushes through the gap in the half open door into a room ruined by rain and nature: a shredded sleeping bag on the floor, a car battery leaking acid onto the floor, a table sagging from water damage, and an old, rusted radio in the corner of it.

She grabs the radio and spins it around, yanking cables from the back then wrapping them round her phone, a dim memory telling her that this might boost her phone's built-in aerial.

Outside the snarl of the bike grows louder and she stares at her phone, willing it to work as she wraps the cable round it one more time. She glances back through the open door, expecting to see the bike burst out of the forest any second. Her phone buzzes in her hand.

Two bars of signal. Three missed calls, all from Tannahill.

Outside the bike engine screams as it jumps over something. He'll be here in seconds and she can't even run, not anymore, not on her twisted ankle.

She looks around the cabin for somewhere to hide then stares at her phone, finally with a signal but with no time to use it. She finds Tannahill's contact in the missed calls menu and calls him back anyway.

76

THE BIKE CRASHES THROUGH THE final screen of leaves and Dog enters the camp. He rides around the three abandoned buildings in a loud, wide circle, his rear wheel throwing up arcs of mulch and dirt as he looks for any movement inside.

She has to be here somewhere, it's the most logical place to come. It's where he would have run to if he'd been in her shoes and spotted it from up there on the ridge. He comes to a halt in front of the three tumbledown shacks. The one on the right looks the most solid, the one with the aerial towering above it. He pushes out the kickstand, kills the engine, and silence floods back into the glade.

Almost silence.

He can hear a voice, faint but distinct, coming from the shack with the aerial.

He slides off the bike, unslings the crossbow from his back, and flicks the safety from Safe to Fire. He points it at the door and moves forward in a crouch, his finger next to the trigger but not on it. The trigger pressure on his Ravin R29X Sniper is only three pounds and he doesn't want to trip and have an accidental misfire. You only get one shot with a crossbow before needing to recock it. It is part of the discipline and why he likes it.

The voice gets louder as he moves closer. It sounds frantic. Concerned.

He focuses on the gap in the partially opened door and curls his finger round the trigger, ready for her in case she rabbits and makes a break for it.

He stops just short of the door and listens to the voice inside. He frowns. It's a man's voice, distant sounding and compressed, like it's coming from a speaker.

He raises his foot and kicks hard, sending the door splintering off its hinges and crashing into the room. He quick scans the interior, ready to fire the moment he sees movement, zeroing in on any place she might be hiding—under the table, behind the door, beneath the filthy sleeping bag lying in tatters on the floor.

She's not here. The shack is empty.

He looks up to where the man's voice is coming from and sees the phone, wrapped in wires and propped up against an old radio.

"We have your location," the voice says. "A tactical response team is inbound right now. They will be with you in minutes. Just hang tight. We have your location, repeat, we have your location and a TAC team is on its way . . ."

He tunes out the voice and refocuses on the abandoned camp, looking for any sign of Goldilocks. The message is a bluff, there's no way they could scramble a response to this location that quickly. He still has time to get this done.

He moves on, leading with the bow, and pushes open the door of the next shack. It is filled with a tangle of rotting sticks and broken branches, like it was used as a woodshed. The final shack is full of rotting straw, suggesting that whoever had once lived here kept animals. He pokes at the mulch with the toe of his boot but it's clear no one has disturbed it for months, years even.

He hears a new sound, soft but getting louder and frowns when he realizes what it is. He looks up at the sky, scanning the blue for the helicopter and remembering something he'd overheard the night before, when he was pressed up against the window listening to the two women talk. Goldilocks had mentioned that her dad was someone high up in the Met. So maybe the TAC team is on its way, and it hadn't been a bluff after all.

He hurries back to his bike, scanning the edge of the camp in case she's watching from the shadows, waiting for the cavalry to arrive. Overhead the sound of the helicopter grows louder so he snicks the safety back on the crossbow and slings it over his shoulder. He kick-starts the bike and revs the engine so that the angry growl of it drowns out the sound of the inbound chopper.

He takes one last look at the abandoned camp then kicks the bike into gear and skids away, the rear wheel churning up leaves and dirt as he disappears back into the forest.

77

THE TUNNEL GLOWS GREEN IN the headset as she studies the floor ahead where scuffs in the dirt and marks that look like footprints suggest others may have been here recently.

Footprints might mean this is the way out, but they also might mean he is waiting for her, somewhere along this tunnel.

She moves as quietly as she can, listening ahead for the slightest sound that might be her only warning. Her hands are wet with sweat and almost cramping from gripping the two halves of the split blowpipe so tightly.

What if he has another?

What if he is waiting for her, as he had waited in the forest, like a spider in a web ready to strike?

She follows the curve of the tunnel around a corner then stops.

Ahead is a doorway that opens into what appears to be a much larger chamber. She raises the splintered halves of the blowpipe and takes another step, the night-vision goggles failing to penetrate the expanse of dark framed by the carved stone arch of the door.

She imagines him on the other side of that arch, tucked tight against the wall, waiting for her to slowly appear around the edge.

She stops just outside the archway. Listens again to the silence. The night-vision goggles are now just about able to see the far side of the chamber. The ceiling and walls are flat, cut with precision. She moves to one side, trying to see round the edge of the doorway, but the room beyond is too wide and the entrance too narrow to see very far. If there is another way out of this chamber, she can't see it from where she is standing.

She looks back down at the ground. The footprints and wheel ruts enter the room then head to the right. Something must be there. And she must enter the room to find out what it is.

She looks back up and grips the broken halves of the pipe in both hands. She takes a deep breath then leaps into the room.

She lands and twists round, the points of her two broken sticks raised against whoever might be hiding and waiting for her.

But there's no one there.

She spins again, scanning the room, looking for other places he might be hiding or, better still, a way out. The chamber seems unfinished, with neat, straight edges on one side where stone has been cut and removed, and piles of rocks and rubble on the other, like a tomb that had been abandoned half-built. And just like a tomb, there is only one entrance.

She moves further into the space, scanning the unfinished side of the room, searching the boulders and piles of rubble in case he is hidden there.

She reaches the far wall and takes a deep breath, relieved that he is not here but also feeling weary that this is another dead end. The air here tastes bitter, like it's too deep in the ground for the sweet breeze to reach it.

She looks back at the floor and follows the ruts of the tire marks to the far side of the room, the more complete side, then tenses again when she sees what looks like a ledge cut into the wall at waist height, deep enough that she can't see inside it from where she is standing.

She holds the sticks up in front of her again and moves to her right, the shadow of the niche glowing a noisy green as it gradually comes into view.

There is something there.

Something lying on the stone shelf.

She's too far away and the shadow in the niche too deep for the night-vision goggles to see enough detail so she takes another step, to the side and a little bit closer, eyes wide and fixed on the object. She takes another step and something else comes into view, another object the same size as the first, and a creeping sense of dread begins to form in her stomach.

She takes another step, then another, until she is standing directly in front of the deep stone shelf.

There are three objects lying upon it, each covered by a piece of material that looks like something her mind won't let her acknowledge.

She remembers the marks on the wooden walls of her cell, scratched by some unknown hand, marking the time. So much time. She takes another step closer to the ledge and her mind finally breaks and the word she has been holding back whispers through the cracks like a curse.

Shrouds.

The sheets draped over the three objects in this tomb of a place look like shrouds.

She takes another step forward. She is close enough now to reach out and touch the edge of the sheets but she doesn't want to. She doesn't want to remove them and reveal what lies beneath, because on some deep level of primal instinct she already knows. She reaches out anyway and takes hold of the edge of the one on the right that seems newer than the others.

She doesn't want to see what lies beneath it but she has to, because she also needs to know. So she pulls it and it slides toward her, making a dry sound in the somber silence as it slips across the stone to reveal a face.

Maddie's face.

78

LAUGHTON LISTENS TO THE ROAR of the motorbike fading away, ignoring the tickle from her own sweat and from insects crawling over her
skin. Only when the chop of helicopter rotors drowns out the bike does
she sit up, still not quite trusting that it isn't a trick and he's still there
waiting for her to reveal herself. But he's not there, the camp is empty.

She stands up from the leaf-filled depression that had almost sunk her
but ended up saving her. She shakes dry leaves from her hair and brushes
them off her clothes as she limps back to the shack with the aerial. As she
draws nearer she hears Tannahill's voice, still talking, still reassuring her
even as the helicopter he must have somehow sent starts to drown him
out. She pushes through the door, limps over to the phone, and listens to
him for a few more seconds—telling her help is coming, telling her he
knows where she is and to hold on. She could love this man, she really
could, and not even feel weird about telling him. She picks the phone
up, takes it off speaker, and presses it to one ear while covering the other
against the incoming noise of the helicopter.

"Hey," she says, "it's me."

"Jesus! I thought you were . . . are you OK?"

"Yeah, I'm fine. Also, there appears to be a helicopter overhead, how
the hell did you organize that so fast?"

"It's an air ambulance. I called them up and said you were critically
injured and needed airlifting to hospital urgently, so you might have some
explaining to do when they get there. Where are you, by the way? On my
map it looks like you're in the middle of a forest."

"I am in the middle of a forest. I was checking out the site of an old
burned-down cabin where my missing person used to live, when this
lunatic appeared on a bike and pointed a crossbow at me."

"Jesus. Sounds like *Deliverance* down there. I told you to be careful."

"It's fine. I'm fine. The helicopter scared him off so it was good thinking. Thank you, I don't know what I would have done if . . ."

"Hey, don't worry about it, what else was I supposed to do?"

Laughton smiles and looks up as the helicopter appears overhead, the downdraft nearly knocking the cabin flat.

"Listen," she says, having to shout against the noise. "Tell me about the Earl's son, you said he left a note. Was it a confession?"

"More like a smoking gun. He said he couldn't carry on living as part of a family that had killed the girl he loved."

"His family?"

"Yes, and get this, his studio was filled with photographs of your missing girl. They were everywhere, it looks like he had been up all night drinking, printing out photos, pinning them to the wall. He hanged himself in the middle of it all, surrounded by her image."

"Shit!" Laughton looks up to where a winchman is now hanging out of the side of the helicopter, preparing to drop down.

"So, who in his family is your main suspect?" Tannahill asks.

"There's only one person it can be," Laughton says, unwinding the cable from around the phone and getting ready to leave. "His father, the Earl."

79

ADELE STARES DOWN AT MADDIE, the night-vision goggles making her pale skin appear green and ghoulish. There is a gash on her forehead, deep and dark, but no blood leaks from it. Adele reaches across her sister's shrouded body and touches her face, as cold as the stone she lies upon, and her vision starts to fog as tears steam up the goggles from the inside.

She feels such unbearable sorrow and anger that it almost feels like nothing at all, as if it's too immense to express.

She brushes a stray strand of hair from her sister's cold, broken forehead.

"I'm sorry," she whispers.

Maddie had always been there for her, always protected her even if that meant putting herself in harm's way. And in the end, Adele had not been able to do the same for her.

She looks across at the other four figures, remembering all the photos of the missing women from Laughton's Cinderman file. Had he done the same to these women, caught them in the forest like some fairy-tale monster then dragged them down here to his personal hell?

She takes hold of the edge of the shroud covering the woman lying next to Maddie and gently pulls it down to reveal another face, and fresh tears mist the goggles again as she stares down at the sunken, shriveled skin, stretched over the sharp bones of a skull. She looks almost mummified, like the dry air down here has preserved her. Maybe that was why he brought them here. To preserve his collection.

Her head whips round at a sound. Out in the tunnel beyond the door. A sound like someone hitting the wall with something hard.

"I know where you are, little pig." His voice rumbles out of the darkness, making her shrink inside.

"I know where you are and there's no way out."

He's getting closer, too quickly to be feeling his way through the dark.

He must have another headset, which means he probably also has another blowpipe or maybe even a gun. She looks at Maddie, who had always been there for her, but now she's gone and Adele is on her own.

She looks back into the chamber for somewhere to hide and spots the boulders and piles of rubble on the other side. Too small for him to be able to hide behind, but maybe big enough for her.

80

IT HAD TAKEN ALL OF Laughton's powers of persuasion and a direct call from the helicopter captain to Tannahill to convince them not to take her to the nearest hospital but fly her to the Abbey instead. Fortunately, it was on their way back to base. She looks down at the Abbey now as the helicopter circles looking for a suitable place to land on the broad lawns surrounding it. From up here she can see the shape of the building's footprint, laid out like an enormous cross big enough for God to see.

She wanted to get here before the Earl found out about his son's suicide. A man of his means would be a flight risk if he knew the net was closing in. He could be in another country and out of their jurisdiction before the ink was dry on his arrest warrant. She wanted to surprise him with it and hopefully secure a confession before he could lawyer up. And Adele still isn't answering her phone. She wants to ask him about that too.

The helicopter banks to start its descent and Laughton spots a couple of squad cars driving up the tree-lined drive toward the Abbey. Tannahill had put in another call to his conference buddy and drafted them in from Herefordshire, the next county along because Laughton didn't trust Beech not to tip off the Earl about what was happening. She would deal with him next.

The helicopter touches down on the lawn and Laughton gives the thumbs-up to the crew, feeling vaguely bad that she has used them as a taxi service and making a mental note to look up their charity when she gets back to London so she can give them a hefty donation. She jumps out of the side door, keeping low as she runs clear of the rotors, then starts heading over to the Abbey.

Behind her the helicopter takes off and she braces herself against the downdraft and closes her eyes against the flying debris. When she opens them again she see the Earl bursting out of a large set of double doors, red-faced and furious and heading straight for her. Behind him, unseen by the Earl, the two squad cars pull to a halt in front of the Abbey and four uniformed officers spill out and start fitting their caps on, ready to assist in the arrest and start taking statements.

"What the hell do you think you're playing at!?" the Earl bellows, spit flying from his mouth as he continues his furious march toward her. "There's a wedding going on right this minute and you have absolutely no right to . . ."

"Sir!" Laughton shouts, the word so hard and firm that it cuts him off mid-sentence. "These gentlemen are here to place you under arrest." She nods at the uniformed officers now making their way toward them across the lawn.

The Earl turns and looks at them.

"On what charge?" he says, turning back to Laughton.

"Let's go inside, sir," Laughton says, gesturing back to the Abbey. "I also have some rather upsetting news to tell you."

81

HE SEES THE ARCHWAY AHEAD, blocks of smeary gray in his spare set of goggles. They are not as good as his others, but he plans on getting those back very soon.

He raises the shotgun, aiming it down slightly so he can catch her in the body and not in the head. After what she did earlier and the way she fought, he's not going to take any chances.

He stops short of the entrance and listens. He had heard movement in the chamber as he was approaching. Noise travels in these solid stone arteries of the forest. Now all is still. He imagines her in there somewhere, cowering, hiding. She may have been brave back in the cell, but now she is a weak coward again.

"Did you find your sister?" he says, his voice low and mocking.

He steps into the room, sweeping the shotgun quickly left then right in case she's waiting there ready to pull the same stunt she tried back in the cell.

But there's no one there.

82

THE EARL STARES AT THE worn carpet, his face and body slack.

Laughton sits across from him, studying his reaction, while two uniformed officers wait by the door. The distant sound of Vivaldi from a string quartet at the wedding floats in from outside, piercing the heavy silence that has settled in the Earl's study. Laughton has never delivered a death notice before and is surprised and confused by her own emotions. On the one hand she feels sadness, because any death is sad, and telling a parent their child has died is particularly tragic. But she also feels anger toward the man sitting opposite her, because his actions clearly played a part in that death, and she wants to know how.

"Did he . . . did he leave a note?" The Earl's voice sounds small. Fragile.

"Yes." Laughton places her phone on the desk between them, deliberately laying it next to the flyer she'd left earlier so the picture of Maddie is visible next to it. On the screen is a photo of the note Tannahill sent her on her short flight over. The Earl leans over and reads it without touching the phone then closes his eyes and turns his head away.

Laughton reaches back over to her phone, checks that the voice memo is still recording, then sits back in her seat.

"Could you tell me what you think your son meant when he wrote that he no longer wished to carry on living as part of a family that had killed the girl he loved?"

The Earl shakes his head slowly. Laughton can't tell whether this means he's not going to say anything at all or is preparing to tell her everything, so she lets the moment stretch, employing the most useful tool in any interviewer's bag of tricks to try to get a subject to talk—silence.

"It was an accident," the Earl says eventually, almost to himself. "It wasn't meant to happen. None of it was meant to happen."

"What wasn't meant to happen?"

He opens his eyes and looks down at Maddie's photo for a long time. Again, Laughton lets the silence stretch.

"I didn't even know Sebastian was seeing anyone until Midsummer's Eve. Then he suddenly announced that he wanted me to meet a girl, someone special, he said, someone he really liked and hoped I would like too. Well, I was delighted. He'd never really had any serious involvement with anyone and was always so secretive and private about anything like that. To be honest, I always feared Seb might be gay, so hearing he'd met a girl and was clearly seeking my approval was a relief."

He looks up as if realizing how this might sound. "It's a question of succession, you see. An heir must have an heir in order to continue the bloodline and family name."

He looks back down at the floor. "Anyway, we were planning on having a little beacon party, just a little family gathering, a few drinks round a fire, so I told him to bring her along. I actually saw Seb at the parade and he was already with her then but said he wanted to wait so I could meet her properly. So that's what happened.

"I drove back to the Abbey and made sure the fire was ready. Everyone else had gone by then because we always give the staff the evening off on Midsummer so they can enjoy the parade and the beacon parties too. Seb said he was going to come through the forest path so I got some drinks ready in a cool box, a few beers, a couple of bottles of champagne, then we lit the fire and waited."

"We?"

The Earl glances up, a guarded look on his face like he's realized he's showed his hand then seems to crumple again as he realizes there's no point in covering up anything anymore.

"Greville was there too," he says.

It takes Laughton a second to remember where she's heard this unusual name before. "Your brother," she says, recalling the Wikipedia entry she'd read on the Earl's family, "the one who should have inherited the earldom?"

"Yes. It was Greville who . . ." He glances at the photo of Maddie again then looks away. "It wasn't supposed to happen."

"Did Greville kill Maddie?" Laughton asks, trying to clarify what he meant.

The Earl closes his eyes and nods. "Yes."

"Why?"

He sighs and his head drops, like it's suddenly too heavy for him to hold.

"Every family has a black sheep," he says. "Greville is ours. He was always troubled, even as a boy. My father used to try to keep us apart because he played rough and I always seemed to get hurt.

"When I was about six or seven he took me into the woods one day and showed me this maze he'd dug into the forest floor. It was covered with chicken wire and had deeper sections with sharpened sticks at the bottom that Greville called traps. A rabbit was trapped in the middle of it. Greville gave me a stick and told me to poke it to make it move around the maze and fall into one of the traps but I didn't want to. I wanted to let it out but when I told him this he hit me hard enough to make my ear bleed and screamed at me to go away.

"That night I went back to the maze to let the rabbit out but it was too late, it was already dead. Greville had killed it, wrapped it in a piece of white cloth, then put it in a section of the maze I hadn't noticed before where other animals had been left too—birds, cats, all sorts, each wrapped in a square of white cloth.

"I told my father about it and things changed after that. The maze was filled in and Greville was taken away somewhere for tests. Ultimately he was diagnosed as a paranoid schizophrenic, and they attempted to treat him with various therapies. I didn't really see him much growing up. I was always away at boarding school and he was usually in some institute or other. In the end my father decided the earldom would be too much for him to cope with, so he named me as heir instead.

"Once my father died, however, and I became Earl, I felt sorry for my brother and brought Greville back to the estate. I didn't think it was right for my brother to be locked up in institutions his whole life, and he was now on a regimen of drugs that seemed to keep him on an even keel and had calmed him right down. He'd even met someone in his therapy sessions and wanted to get married, so it seemed like he'd turned a corner. It was something called 'nature therapy' that had done the trick. He loved being outdoors, you see, it really calmed him. Anyway, I set him up in a house in the forest, on a distant piece of the estate where he could be close, but not too close, and try to live a vaguely normal life. He and his partner even started a family, though they couldn't have children of their own, something to do with the medication they were both on, and fostering wasn't an option given their history. So I made some calls, pulled a few strings, and they ended up with two girls. Sisters."

Laughton feels an urge to leap forward and slam his head down on the desk for what he has just so casually revealed. She remembers what Adele told her the night before, about the horrors she and her sister had endured in that cabin for years as part of that "little family" and clenches her jaw so hard it hurts, forcing herself to remain silent so the Earl can continue talking.

"A few years back, there was a fire in the cabin. The whole place burned to the ground and Greville was very badly burned, almost died. His wife did die, unfortunately. Terrible thing. I wanted to keep it all quiet, avoid any scandal, so I brought him back here to recover and hired private nurses."

"What about the girls," Laughton asks through clenched teeth. "What happened to them?"

"Greville told me they'd run away a few weeks before the fire."

"And you didn't follow that up and check they were OK?"

"No. No, I didn't."

"Why? Did you not care what happened to them?"

"No, it wasn't that." A pained expression pinches the Earl's face. "It was more a question of . . . keeping things contained. Not drawing attention to any of it. I knew the girls were . . . off the record, so to speak, so wouldn't be missed by anyone. I didn't for one second imagine that any harm had befallen them. Truth be told, I thought they'd had a lucky escape and that wherever they'd gone to it was much better than being burned up in a cabin fire. My focus, naturally, was on my own family."

"Naturally," Laughton says.

"When Greville started to get back on his feet," the Earl continues, staring at the worn rug again, "I moved him to a new place in the woods, closer by, so I could keep my eye on him." He shakes his head. "He always seemed like a fairly harmless soul to me, pottering around the grounds and vanishing into the woods for days on end, doing whatever he did in there, communing with nature or whatever. Truth be told, I liked having him around." The Earl looks up at her. "You've met him actually."

"Really?"

"Yes. He helps out around the grounds."

"MacGregor?"

The Earl nods.

"Why the different name?"

"Oh, it's after the farmer in Beatrix Potter, he was obsessed with those stories as a boy. Maybe that's where the love of nature came from. After the fire it seemed like a good idea to start afresh, new home, new beginning, new name. All the old staff had left by then, so no one knew who he was. It felt useful to keep it that way, given his . . . difficult history. I didn't think he was dangerous. I never thought he might . . ." He looks out of the window toward the spot where the fire had been.

"Tell me, what happened on Midsummer's Eve?" Laughton says.

"We were sitting by the fire, drinking a few beers." He frowns and shakes his head as he remembers. "Seb arrived first, emerging from the forest with the girl behind him, and I stood up ready to welcome her and I remember Grev stood too, champagne bottle in hand, ready to open it. But when Seb stepped aside to introduce me, I saw her look across at Greville and her face switched from a smile to . . . I don't know, shock, terror. It all happened so fast."

He continues to stare at Maddie's photo on the desk.

"So what happened?" Laughton prompts.

"Greville, he . . . well, he hit her. He swung the champagne bottle around and smashed it on the side of her head. So hard. I'll never forget the sound it made. Horrible. Just horrible. She fell to the ground like a ragdoll. Seb screamed and tried to give her the kiss of life but she was . . . there was so much blood. It was too late, she was already. . . . When Seb realized she was dead he went for Grev. I had to pull him off, I thought he was going to kill him. Maybe I should have let him. I couldn't believe it either. Grev told us she was one of the girls he had fostered. One of the girls who had run away then come back one night, locked him in the shack with his wife, and set fire to it. She had tried to kill him, he said."

The Earl looks up at Laughton. "You have to understand, my brother is . . . well, he's not responsible for his actions, not like you or I would be. I said the same thing to Sebastian that night, told him we needed to calm down and think things through. Nothing could undo what had been done, and though it was awful we needed to think about what was best—for the family. I gave him a sedative and called a family friend to ask his advice."

"Beech," Laughton says.

The Earl looks up like he's been caught out again then slumps further down in his chair and nods. "What you don't appreciate is that my family name . . . well, it's . . . it's something old and precious that needs looking after. It's part of our history, all of our history, and needs protecting, just like the crown jewels, or a great palace."

Laughton shakes her head. "You're right," she says, "it is hard for me to appreciate. A woman died here, she was murdered, and you're talking about protecting your family name. You think your family name is worth more than a human life?"

A hard look creeps across the Earl's face. "A dynasty is worth more than one human life, yes, and I would include my own life in that equation."

"What about your son's life? Is that worth less than your family name?" The earl glares at her but says nothing. "You know Maddie has a sister."

"Yes."

"Do you know she's also missing?"

The Earl looks at her with genuine surprise. "No. I did not know that."

"And presumably if your brother blamed Maddie for the death of his wife, he would hold a similar grudge against her. Do you have any idea where he is now?"

The Earl pauses as if still considering how to pull up the drawbridge and protect his family. "In his cabin, I expect." He points out of the window to the right of the marquee. "It's out there in the forest. He might be there, he might not. He spends a lot of time in the forest. He's at his happiest there."

Laughton grabs her phone and turns to the two uniformed officers as she stands.

"You," she says, pointing at one. "Arrest him. You"—she points at the larger of the two— "come with me."

83

LAUGHTON SPRINTS ACROSS THE LAWN to where the fire had been, her ankle still hurting where she twisted it earlier, the uniformed officer beside her, breathing heavily and struggling to keep up.

She passes the circle of ash and heads into the woods where Greville had disappeared that morning, following the path through the trees to a small cleared area with the building she had spotted at the center. She stops at the tree line, listening for any sign of life inside before turning to the uniformed officer. "What's your name?"

"Morgan."

"Well get your baton out, Morgan, if he's in there he may resist arrest."

Morgan pulls the collapsible baton from his utility belt and snaps it out to its full length.

Laughton nods. "OK, let's do it."

She moves out of the forest and into the dappled sunlight, scanning the small clearing as she approaches the main cabin. Tangles of gardening equipment are piled up next to jumbled stacks of branches, logs, and root balls that seem to have been arranged in loose collections all over the make-shift yard. She reaches the cabin door and bangs on it twice with her fist.

She listens for movement inside then moves across to the window and peers through it. The inside of the cabin is a stark contrast to the mess outside, everything is neat and tidy, the cot bed, the table and chair, the potbelly stove with a neat stack of logs beside it, the metal sink on the far wall. It looks more like an exhibit from the Heritage Center of how people used to live than an actual home.

She turns to Morgan. "He's not here." She points at the smaller shed next to the cabin. "Let's check in there."

She moves over to it and pushes the door open to reveal a small workshop with tools hanging on every wall, a workbench filled with pieces of wood and assorted other junk and a selection of work boots and Wellingtons. Other than that, it's empty.

Laughton steps into the shed and does a slow circle, taking it all in and thinking. When she'd seen him earlier he had been walking stiffly with a limp, which suggested if he was on foot he couldn't have gone far. She pulls her phone from her pocket and opens up the photo she had taken earlier of the plans on the Earl's desk, zooming into the area around the Abbey, looking for anything that might be a likely point of destination, the Earl's words echoing in her head:

He spends a lot of time in the forest. He's at his happiest there.

Her eyes flit across to the boots lined up by the door on a patch of floor that has turned red with dust. She picks one of the boots up and turns it over. The underside has the same red earth packed into the treads of the heel and sole alongside darker earth and forest mulch.

"Do you know what this red stuff might be?" she asks Morgan, holding the boot up for him to see.

Morgan peers at it and shakes his head. "Looks to be the same color as the Cinderfield police station," he says.

Laughton pictures the old, stone building she had collected Adele from in the middle of the night.

Stone!!

She looks back at the photo on her phone and zooms out a little until she finds what she's looking for, just above the Abbey, buried in the woods but with a service road leading to it and walkable from where she is now standing.

"Radio for more backup units equipped for a search," she says, pushing past Morgan and looking around to get her bearings. "Get them to head to the quarry north of Cinderfield Abbey as fast as they can make it."

84

HE TAKES ANOTHER STEP INTO the room, sweeping the shotgun left to right, ready to shoot the moment he sees movement. He stops in the center of the room and looks back at the ledge in case she is hiding among the previous sacrifices, but they are undisturbed.

He turns back to the main chamber and focuses on the unfinished side, pointing the barrel of the shotgun at each mound of rubble and boulder in turn, moving slightly so he can see behind them for any hint that she is there.

And then he sees her.

She is crouched behind one of the larger boulders, tucked tight into a little ball.

He raises the shotgun. Takes a step to his left so he can see a little more of her behind the rock. His finger curls round the first of the double triggers. He holds the gun steady.

"One for sorrow," he murmurs, then squeezes the trigger.

85

LAUGHTON HEARS THE BLAST AS she passes through the gate into the quarry, low and muffled like distant thunder. She turns to Morgan and sees from his face that he heard it too.

"When's the backup getting here?" she says, moving into the quarry and looking around for any sign of life.

"Ten minutes," Morgan replies.

Laughton shakes her head. "You should probably get an ambulance here too." She spots the entrance to what looks like a mine tunnel and jogs over to it, the pain in her ankle throbbing with each step.

She reaches the entrance, activates the torch on her phone, and holds it up to light the way ahead. The tunnel stretches away into darkness. She angles her phone down and sees tracks in the red, rock dust on the floor. She spots a clear footprint that looks like a match for the boots in the cabin then looks back up at the tunnel.

"Have you got a better torch than this?" she asks Morgan as he appears next to her.

Morgan unclips a small, black Maglight from his belt and hands it to her. Laughton twists it on and the beam pushes away the darkness, showing that the tunnel ends about a hundred feet ahead of them at a plywood wall with a door set in the center.

"Come on," Laughton says, "and get your baton ready."

"Shouldn't we wait for backup?" Morgan says. "Some of the officers inbound will be armed."

"We haven't got time," Laughton says, heading down the tunnel toward the door. "We might be too late already."

86

THE FLASH FROM THE BLAST makes his headset flare out and he is blinded for a second. He blinks away the glare and waits for the headset to settle then shifts his finger to the second trigger, peering through the clearing smoke to where she is now lying on her side where the first blast had thrown her clear of the boulder she was hiding behind. She isn't moving but he doesn't trust her, not after what happened earlier. She could be playing dead, waiting for him to get close enough to kick him again and try and grab the gun and he's not going to let that happen.

He levels the shotgun at her and smiles.

"Two for joy," he says, and squeezes the trigger.

Fire and noise spits from the barrel a second time, tearing up the floor and making the girl's body jump from the impact as lead shot shreds her clothes and the flesh beneath.

The blast blinds him again and his ears ring from the noise but he knows she is dead. No one could get up from a point-blank blast like that. He lowers the gun and feels the usual emptiness in his stomach when it's over. The crash after the high. He looks down at the body of the girl and a glassy, sightless eye stares back at him through the messy veil of her hair. Then he frowns as he realizes something. She isn't wearing the headset.

He takes a step forward to look behind the boulder she'd been hiding behind. It's not there either. He is about to turn and search the chamber when something sharp bangs into the soft flesh of his neck. He spins around and stares in shocked surprise at the girl, not dead but standing in front of him, the missing goggles covering her eyes and a look of hard hatred on her face. Instinctively he raises the shotgun and pulls both triggers but the hammers fall with a dry click. He steps backward and reaches up to the painful spot on his neck and finds a thin piece of wood sticking out of it. He tries to grip it to pull it out but it is already slick with blood and slips beneath his grip. He takes another step backward, turning the useless shotgun over in his hands and gripping the still-warm barrel so he can swing it like a club.

The girl stares at him, and behind her he sees one of the shrouds lying on the floor and he growls as he realizes how she tricked him.

He lunges forward, swinging the shotgun hard and aiming for her head but she ducks, and he misses, and the momentum of the heavy gun pulls him forward, making him stumble and lose balance. He falls to one knee and twists round ready to get up and swing at her again but she is already on him, jabbing a second spike hard into his neck.

Pain lances through him and he clamps a hand on the source of it, his fingers touching the jagged edge of a fresh wound, blood pumping out around his fingers. He keeps his hand pressed to his neck and tries to get up. He takes the shotgun and tries to push himself back up with it but he has no strength in his arms.

He looks up at her, one hand on his neck, the other on the useless gun. She is standing just out of reach, looking down at him with a look on her face he wants to smash in with the butt of the gun.

"You can't kill me," he hisses. "You tried before, remember? It didn't work then and it won't work now."

She steps forward and kicks the shotgun out from under him so he falls flat on his face in the dirt, jarring the piece of wood in his neck and sending more pain lancing through him.

"I remember," she says.

He feels a hand on the back of his head and tries to reach up and grab her but she is too fast. She rips off the headset and steps away again.

He can see nothing now. Nothing but solid black.

"This is how they died," she says, her voice circling him close by. "Frightened and in the dark. And now this is how you die too."

87

LAUGHTON HEARS THE SECOND SHOTGUN blast while Morgan is kicking down the door that blocks the tunnel. The moment the door flies open she rushes through it, running down the tunnels as fast as her ankle will let her, shouting Adele's name, checking round every turn in the maze of tunnels in case a madman is there waiting with shotgun in hand.

She follows the tracks in the dirt, past the cell with the marks on the wall, following the smell of cordite mixed with the metallic smell of blood, until the beam of the torch lights up a scene almost like a painting, framed by a large stone doorway.

Adele looks away from the light and pulls the headset off. She looks up at Laughton as she approaches, her sister lying in her arms, her body wrapped in a shroud. Maddie looks serene despite the deep gash on the right side of her forehead that runs into her hairline.

"I couldn't save her," Adele says, her voice sounding detached and distant. "I couldn't save her, but she saved me. Just like she always did."

88

GRIZZ SEES THE UNIFORMED POLICE officers walking through the forest toward The Clearing and immediately calls Beech to find out what's going on.

It goes straight to voicemail so she tries again as she watches them draw closer. The Clearing was supposed to be off-limits, that was their deal, it had always been their deal. Beech turned a blind eye to what they did and got a cut of the profits in exchange. The phone connects and again goes to voicemail.

She finds another number and calls the Earl. After two rings it is picked up, but it is a woman's voice that answers.

"Hello?"

Grizz frowns. "Hi, who is this please?"

"This is Cleo Mortimer, the Earl's personal assistant."

"Could I speak to the Earl please?"

"Erm. I'm afraid that won't be possible. The Earl is currently . . . indisposed." The woman sounds posh and flustered and Grizz thinks she knows why. She looks back at the line of approaching police officers, their presence becoming known to everyone now.

"The Earl has been arrested, hasn't he?" Grizz says. There's a pause which gives her all the answer she needs.

"I'm afraid you'll have to call back," the woman says then the phone cuts off.

The line of police officers breaks through the trees and enters The Clearing. One of them starts talking to Merlin, who turns around and points directly at Grizz. She looks down at her phone, thinks of calling Beech one last time, but she knows it's a waste of time. If the Earl has been arrested, it's already too late. He'll do everything he can to save his own skin and Beech will do the same. At least the Earl knows nothing about the trafficking. He was never in on that part of things. But Beech knows everything.

She glances up and the police officer is walking toward her now. She quickly dials another number and listens to it ring as she watches the police officer draw closer.

"Yes?" a voice says.

"Change of plan," Grizz says, then she tells Dog what she needs him to do.

89

"JESUS, THANK GOD YOU'RE OK." Tannahill sounds about as stressed as Laughton has ever heard him when he answers her call.

"I'm fine, honestly." Laughton turns a corner and squints against the sun blasting through the windscreen of the borrowed squad car, which feels way too big for these narrow country lanes.

"Where are you now?" he asks.

"Driving back to the Airbnb to pick up Adele's stuff and take it to her in the hospital."

"Oh Christ, is she OK?"

"Yeah, she's fine, I think. Her sister didn't make it though."

"Oh shit, I'm so sorry. What happened?"

Laughton tells him as she drives back to her cabin, about the Earl's son, his brother, everything. It's only as she's pulling off the road and coming to a halt outside the wood cabin that she realizes her phone ran out of charge somewhere along the way and that Tannahill is no longer listening. No matter. She can call him again at the hospital.

She bursts into the cabin and starts disconnecting everything, packing up her office and scooping everything into her bag as fast as she can, figuring she won't need to come back here again. She'll stay with Adele in the hospital as long as she needs her to then she'll head back to London, even if it means driving through the night. She can write up all her notes remotely and let the Herefordshire Constabulary continue the investigation and carry out all the subsequent prosecutions. She's had enough of the forest and this whole damn place anyway. So much for leafy calm and woodland views. She actually can't wait to get back to the noise and chaos of London.

She zips up her bag, dumps it next to the door, then heads up the stairs and into the room Adele slept in. There's almost nothing to pack, just a few toiletries and clothes, and the tin on her bedside table containing her savings. Her "freedom money" she had called it, the money she had saved to buy her and Maddie a fresh start. Hopefully now she could use it. Laughton picks it up, grabs the rest of her stuff, then heads back down the stairs, picking up her main bag on her way out to the car and pulling the door closed behind her.

"Drop all that shit on the floor and turn around."

Laughton recognizes the voice immediately. She gently lowers everything to the ground then turns around slowly.

Beech is standing a few feet away in the shadow of the cabin, a standard-issue Glock-17 in his hand and pointed right at her.

"What are you doing?" Laughton says.

"Settling scores," Beech replies. "Start walking toward the forest."

Laughton stays where she is. "What's the point in this?" she says, keeping her voice calm. "What's your plan?"

"My plan is to shoot you in the leg if you don't start walking and drag you into the woods by your hair."

She looks at him, bloodshot eyes, large circles of sweat beneath his armpits and down his chest, his face pink and shining, his thinning hair sticking up in salt-and-pepper tufts. He's a mess. He looks desperate. And desperate people do stupid things. She turns around and starts walking.

"Try and run and I'll shoot you in the back," he says.

She believes him. She can hear him behind her, keeping step, maintaining distance between them. The edge of the forest is less than thirty feet away. At the moment they are just about visible from the road so any passing car might see them, though she can't hear the sound of an engine. Once she's in the forest, however, they'll be hidden from view. No passing car will see her then, so she needs to act now, before they get there. She focuses on keeping her pace regular but shortening it slightly with each step. If she can close the gap between them she might have a chance to do something.

"You've gone quiet," Beech says.

"What do you want me to say?"

"How about 'Sorry'?"

"For what?"

"For coming here and fucking up my life."

"I didn't help cover up Maddie Friar's murder. I didn't cover up all those other missing girls either. You created this mess yourself. You want someone to say sorry to you, go find a mirror."

The edge of the forest is close now. Too close. She can see the shadows beyond it. She can't tell if she's managed to close the gap between them enough, but she knows she's running out of time.

"Tell me one thing," she says as the edge of the forest draws closer.

"What's that?"

"How much money did you stand to make on the land deal?"

Beech snorts. "More than your life's worth."

Laughton spins around and lashes out with her foot, catching him on the side of his head, enough to knock him off balance but no more. He was still too far back and now she has lost the element of surprise. The momentum of her kick carries her around and pain explodes in her ankle as she lands. She cries out and rolls instead, trying to stay close to Beech because her only weapon is close combat, and the gun is already swinging round to point at her.

She forces herself up with her good leg, driving upward and catching hold of the arm holding the gun. She clings on and tries to wrench it around, hoping she can make him fall in a way that her weight will land on top of him and knock the gun loose. But he's too big and he manages to stay upright. He clubs her on the back of her head with his spare hand but Laughton clings on, knowing if she lets go she'll have lost the battle.

She can smell his sweat now, a rank odor of fear and anger. He hits her again and white light flashes in her skull, then he roars and twists around and her bad leg catches the ground. Pain lances through it, weakening her enough to let him twist free.

She falls heavily to the ground and is winded but rolls over and starts kicking to get away from him. She stops when she sees that it's pointless. He stands over her, utter hate on his purple face, too far away for her to attack him again.

"You are such a pain in the arse," he says, spit flying from his mouth. He smiles and raises the gun. "At least you were."

The arrow seems to spring from the side of his head like a magic trick, the feathered end sticking out from a spot just above his ear. Beech goes slack and crumples, like someone has just switched him off. He hits the ground face-first, so heavily it makes Laughton wince. Beech doesn't move at all. He just lies where he fell, blood leaking from around the shaft of the arrow.

Laughton looks up as a piece of the forest seems to tear itself away and start walking toward her. She stares at the slit where the man's eyes should be, the camouflaged veil covering his face, his clothes making him blend in almost perfectly with the background. In his hand he carries his lethal-looking crossbow and it occurs to Laughton that, as he has already fired the bolt, he is effectively unarmed. She looks down at the gun lying on the ground by Beech's hand and about six feet away from her.

"Don't," the man says, reading her mind.

She looks back up at him, registering the slow, confident way he walks, even though he has just shot a man through the head with an arrow. She has no doubt that if she tries to get to the gun he will get there first, and it won't end well for her.

"Why have you been following me? Who are you?" she asks, figuring if he's going to kill her, she might as well know his name.

"You don't need to know who I am," he says.

He drops down by Beech and presses his fingers into the side of his neck then reaches over and picks up the gun, racking the chamber repeatedly to eject the shells until all of them are lying on the ground. He stands and pockets the empty gun, looking down at Beech.

He shakes his head. Then he turns and walks away, vanishing into the forest the moment he steps into it.

90

BY THE TIME LAUGHTON FINALLY manages to get away from the crime scene at the Airbnb it is already evening and Adele has been sedated and hooked to a saline drip to reverse the dehydration and flush the toxins from her system.

She looks so young and small, lying in the hospital bed, and again Laughton thinks of Gracie. The thought of her daughter having to endure the things Adele has survived makes Laughton want to scream. She thinks of the men who ruined her childhood and how they had ended, Greville lying on the floor of the cave in a wide pool of his own blood, Beech on his face in the dirt. She feels nothing for either of them.

She creeps out of the room, and calls Gracie in the quiet of the corridor, the soft clinks and whispers of the evening wards murmuring all around her.

"Hey, Mum," Gracie says.

"Hey." Laughton leans against the wall and smiles at the sound of her voice, so light and untroubled that it seems to be beaming in from a parallel universe.

"How's Wales?"

"I'm not in Wales. How's Cornwall?"

"Cornwall is cool. We should come here, it's awesome. Hang on a sec." Laughton hears rustling as Gracie covers the phone and the muffled sound of excitable voices. "Hey, Mum, can I call you back later? A bunch of people are heading out for pizza."

"Yeah, sure, no worries. You have a good time, I'll talk to you tomorrow morning."

"OK, Mum, love you."

"Love you too, oh, and wait."

"What?"

"Don't go anywhere on your own."

"I won't. Love you."

She hangs up before Laughton can tell her she loves her again and Laughton stares at the phone for a few lonely moments, thinking she might call back on some pretext just to get another hit of her sunny voice when the phone rings in her hand anyway.

"Hey," she says. "Sounds like you're driving."

"I am driving," Tannahill says, his voice mingling with the background hiss of wheels on road. "I am just about to finish driving, though, so we can talk without me getting arrested for breaking the law. Listen, I've been talking to our friends at Herefordshire Constabulary and it turns out they've managed to identify the other victims they found in the quarry. One is called Amanda Rutherford, disappeared four years ago, and the other is Scarlett Banks, known locally as 'Star,' who vanished last year." Laughton nods, recognizing both names from her Cinderman files. She blows out a long breath and stares at the floor. "So, most of the women who disappeared got sold into sex slavery and the rest got snatched and locked up underground by a depraved lunatic."

"Yeah, pretty much, and the man supposed to be in charge of protecting them was actually covering it all up. Hang on a sec, just parking."

Through the phone she hears the engine cut out and the clunk of a door then footsteps instead of tire noise.

"Do you think Beech knew about the Earl's brother?" Laughton says.

"I don't know. I don't think so. I think he was just treating all missing persons the same because he didn't want anyone doing a proper investigation into any of them. But in covering his own tracks he ended up covering other tracks at the same time. Looking at the dates of the last trafficked woman it seems they stopped their operation a couple of years ago, probably when this land deal presented itself and they saw they could make much more money another way and didn't want to do anything that might draw unwanted attention. Except the Earl's degenerate brother didn't get the memo."

Laughton thinks of the Earl in his study trying to convince her, or maybe himself, that everything that had happened was somehow an inconvenience to his illustrious name that had to be kept quiet at all costs.

"What a fucked-up family," she says, and catches a raised eyebrow from a nurse hurrying by in the corridor.

"Yeah. Pretty good argument against inbreeding. Hold on a sec." She hears handling noise as Tannahill covers his phone then the muffled sound of a short conversation before he's back again with the sound of footsteps as a backdrop. "I don't quite understand why the Earl got involved with Beech and this forest witch though, surely he's already minted?"

Laughton thinks about the Abbey with its cracked windows and visitors' center. "I think he's actually pretty skint, another one of these cash-strapped old aristos who's having to let commoners get married in their back garden to pay the heating bill. Beech was an old contact who fixed things for the family from time to time who was also in a position to make this land deal happen. Grizz, the witch in the woods, was one of Beech's contacts who'd obviously figured out she could earn more from selling people than getting them to pick fruit. The fact that she was also a long-term sitting tenant on a large piece of common land meant she was the last piece of a potentially very lucrative puzzle. So much for her being some cuddly, hippie, earth-mother type."

Laughton looks back into the ward where Adele lies sleeping. "I can't believe how much this poor girl has had to go through at the hands of these scumbags, and for what? A bit of money. Just because your ancestor killed some people for a king and got a big house and a title as a reward doesn't make you any better than anyone else. It's all just so unfair. It makes me want to smash things and burn everything down."

"That's why you need someone like me to calm you down."

"Maybe. But you're in London and I'm in Gloucestershire."

"Actually, I'm not in London, I'm right behind you."

Laughton spins round and there he is, walking down the corridor, his phone still pressed to his ear. "I did tell you I was driving," Tannahill says. "I just didn't tell you where I was driving to."

Laughton hangs up, limps over, and practically falls onto him. "You didn't have to come all the way down here," she says.

"Yeah, I did. Look at you, you can hardly walk. Besides"—he holds her chin and turns her face up to his—"I sort of love you."

Laughton stares up at him, Irish blue eyes in his dark-skinned face. She has been avoiding this moment ever since they tentatively got together, this scary declaration, this terrifying intimacy, which requires a dangerous vulnerability. But now she is faced with it, it doesn't feel like any of those things. It feels, in fact, like the exact opposite.

"I know," she says, leaning her head against his chest and feeling like she never wants to take it away again. "I sort of love you too."

EPILOGUE

ADELE LOOKS AROUND THE SMALL studio flat she is paying for with the money from the tin she had been saving to buy her and Maddie's freedom.

So this is what freedom looks like.

It's nice actually. It feels safe. No one knows her in this city and she likes that. Work had been easy to find for someone who didn't mind doing anything and never complained and she is making much more than she ever had at the campsite. Laughton had sorted out her National Insurance number for her so she is also legit now, aboveboard, which is weird. Weird but nice. It's nice not hiding anymore. Nice to not have anyone to hide from.

She still misses Maddie though.

That is the worst part of it, not being able to share her freedom with her sister. Sometimes she misses her so much she doesn't think she'll ever get past it, thinks her sorrow and the weight of it will drag her back down into the dark earth.

Times like right now.

Adele stares down at the knife in her hand.

She turns the blade, following the light back and forth as it catches the sharpened edge.

Someone told her once that a knife was the most powerful tool there was, an ancient key to life and death: use it one way—to sharpen sticks, make traps—and it would keep you alive; use it the other way and life would end as quickly as the heart could pump.

Her eyes follow the point of light to the tip of the blade then back to the tang, then pause when she remembers who'd said it.

Grizz had always been handy with the homespun wisdom, delivered with that low, serious voice of hers, like she was sharing some higher knowledge. It's a trick all abusers use, make you feel included and special, like they're protecting you and looking after your best interests when in fact they only ever have eyes on their own.

She raises the knife, feeling the weight of it in her hand.

Grizz had been wrong. A knife is no ancient mystical key, it's just a knife, nothing more, nothing less, a tool that is only ever as useful or sinister as the hand that holds it.

She picks up her pencil and carefully slices through the wood to sharpen the point. A pencil, now there is a truly powerful tool. All of human knowledge had flowed through the end of a pencil, the deepest thoughts, the highest buildings, the darkest desires.

She puts the knife down on the table next to the small pile of curled shavings, tests the point of the pencil with her thumb, then opens the black notebook Laughton had given her.

When she had first suggested the idea of keeping a hope diary, Adele had been skeptical. What was she possibly going to write in it that would do any good?

Maddie still missing? Police still dicks?

But after Maddie had been found and the days had trudged relentlessly on, numb and empty, she had found herself opening the book often and staring at the blank pages. It struck her that these blank sheets of paper had once been part of a forest too, just as she had been, and if they could become something else, something unspoiled and unmarked then maybe she could too.

She stares at the blank page for a long time in the quiet of her cozy, anonymous room where she can lock the door and live without worry. Then she takes her freshly sharpened pencil, places the point on the page, and begins to write.

ACKNOWLEDGMENTS

My thanks again to my old school friend Peter Fairweather, formerly of the Cambridgeshire Police Force, who was invaluable in helping make the police aspect of the story as accurate as it could be. Any remaining mistakes are all down to me.

On the publishing side, huge thanks again to everyone at Harper-Collins on both sides of the Atlantic, Tessa James in the US and Julia Wisdom in the UK. Super-agent and even super-er (not a word) friend, Alice Saunders at the Soho Agency. Everyone at ILA who takes my books to readers all around the world.

To all the many brilliant and dedicated people behind the scenes who help turn a bunch of scribbled notes into an actual book. I owe a huge debt of thanks, so I have listed you separately and individually so everyone else can know your contribution (and you can also show it to your parents/aunts/grandparents). Your contribution is immense, and I thank you for it.

Finally, huge thanks to my family—Kathryn, Roxy, Stan, and Betsy—for all the love and support, and to Woody and Stevie for getting me out of the house at least once a day.

Simon Toyne
Brighton—December 2022

CREDITS

Tessa James—Editor

Mallory McCurdy—Marketing

Sharyn Rosenblum—Publicity

Marie Rossi—Production Supervisor

Leah Carlson-Stanisic—Interior Design

Kelsey Heiss-O'Brien—Composition

Mark Robinson—Cover Designer

Anne Cherry—Copy Editor

Andrea Molitor—Production Editor